AFTERLIFE IN HARLEM

A NOVEL OF REDEMPTION

TERRY BAKER MULLIGAN

Cover design by Kristina Blank Makansi

ISBN: 978-0-984692934

To: Mike

PROLOGUE

HARLEM

Overhead, a rare January mix of snow and thunder rolled the metropolitan area. Down below in fading light the old auntie trudged face first into icy crystals that stung like needles; still, she moved with a sense of purpose. Flexing first one then a second stiff finger, she winced as pain radiated through her hand. Her feet, brown, splayed and toughened from years of running barefoot, were stuck inside an ancient pair of men's boots.

For today's journey, she'd wrapped her toes in oilskin rags. Now the rags were bunched and knotted. Three blocks back, she'd tried shifting the rags away from a spot rubbed raw by the wet cloth. But it no longer mattered. The old woman hardly felt her toes.

She passed a vest-pocket park where dark-skinned children romped in the snow, all of them swaddled in heavy pants and padded coats. The sight and sound of squealing children born into freedom lifted her spirits and, pulling her wrap tighter, she adjusted the bundle.

Gaining another block, Auntie again patted her chest, secure in the knowledge that Sarafina's precious missive remained pinned to her thin bosom. Over countless weeks, the trusted wife of Reverend Huelett Brown, pastor of the New Africa Church, had painstakingly read and reread the missive's contents to Auntie until she grasped and memorized its magical words:

"Dear Auntie," Sarafina had started," even though I be older than the childrens, the white ladies at New York Manumission School received me kindly. Our little school room be filled with soft firelight thus allowing for lesson learning. They schooling me how to read and write. Oh, Auntie, you should see my writing stick that the mistress calls a quill. When I press it into the page it forms dark blue droplets like the color of larkspur. Is there any wonder, Auntie, that my quill once were the outer wing of an eagle, the mightiest beast to fly? Each symbol I makes feel like I soaring with birds above, and I beholds my words with wonder.

"Have you ever heard of verbs, Auntie? By the end of this year, Mistress Mary say my verbs be straighten up better. These verbs always be altering in shape, much as stages in butterfly life. Verbs, I learned, are the centerpieces of sentences, like cog pins that bind up wheel spokes.

"Teacher tell me I powerful smart. The mens say I pretty, but none be pestering me now for his enjoyment. That be a relief. The one exception, though he far-flung from local riffraff, be Mr. Alexander Hamilton, the gentleman with the rosy look who been around from before. At first, 'cause of the terror at Master Shields's house, I too bereft to be noticing Mr. Hamilton's requests for continued audiences. But the gentleman talk sweet, then gift me with two whalebone combs, each carved with a prettified 'S' the first symbol of my name. I confess to feeling stirrings for him.

"He a fighting captain now, in General Washington's army, but his head still be bursting with lawyerly bookishness. Though small of stature, he struts about in the manner of a peacock expanding its feathers. The edges of his eyes slope like weeping branches on the cherry tree. Didn't you say, Auntie, that the cherry's bittersweet fruit were the essence of man?

"Mr. Hamilton tell me pin my hair back so he can be studying my face. Beyond hair frillery, on occasion, the gentleman gifts me a silver coin and insists it not be spent like my meager earnings, but squirreled away into my money pouch.

"You should hear his fiery tone when defending our peoples who still be enslaved. He say, 'Slaves are men, human beings, and subject to the same governing laws as white mens and to the higher laws of God.' Ain't those words just grand, Auntie? The goodness of some white peoples ofttimes lifts melancholy that shrouds my heart and makes me pray God you found Judith. Nighttime now well-fallen and my tallow burns low, but I remain your obedient Sarafina."

Though Auntie was well beyond them now, the children's gleeful cries carried in the hard cold air. Her thoughts shifted from Sarafina to another day of long-ago laughter, when she and her sisters climbed a bluebush tree, gorging on its sweet fruit while stripping tender branches to repair Father's hut.

Despite the passing of ages, how Auntie still longed for Africa's sun-drenched soil, warm and soft between her toes. And though long accustomed to the cruelties of man, for a moment she felt her old face, rigid with cold and deeply scored by wrinkles, muster a faint smile. She remembered village monkeys chattering in protest as boys and girls chased the devilish apes from piles of picked fruit. And always, off in the distance, the rhythmic beat of drums from warriors—her warrior—broadcasting love messages over the treetops.

The momentary absentmindedness made her stumble, and the image of her village faded. In this new country, the first time Auntie witnessed snowfall, she hoped it was a sign from the great god Wuonoruo responding to her gift of crow's claws, finely ground with red cock feathers, that she buried under the sweet gum tree. In time she learned snow was just another misery in this miserable white man's land.

At 120th Street and Malcolm X Boulevard, Auntie found her path partly blocked by a great mound of icy snow. Stepping gingerly, the old woman skirted the slippery mass and didn't see a young black man, head bent against blinding snow, until they nearly collided.

"Oops, sorry, ma'am," he apologized, "my fault." Reaching out, he steadied the wisp of a woman, but instead of her arm, his gloved hand came away with flimsy cloth. "I guess we're both focusing on just getting out of this storm," he said, making sure she regained her footing.

When she didn't answer, he asked, "You okay, ma'am? If you don't mind my saying so, it's a little rough for a senior citizen to be out in these conditions." His muffler, striped sideways like red and white railroad tracks, was tied snugly and covered the lower half of his face. He tugged it loose and wiped frost off his lashes to get a better look at the stooped figure and to see what she was carrying.

"What the hell, lady?" He recoiled at the movement of tiny brown fingers inside her ragged shawl. "You crazy or something, out here in this weather with a baby? Are you looking to buy diapers? Milk?" he asked, scanning Malcolm X Boulevard for the nearest grocery store. Although this was his neighborhood, whiteout conditions made it hard to see more than thirty feet, much less recognize store signs. His breath billowed between them, and the chill cut through his down jacket.

"Look, we can't just stand here and freeze to death." He searched her face for a clue to why such an old woman would risk her health and a child's in this weather. Considering the circumstances, she was eerily serene, and he wondered if she might already be experiencing the first stages of exposure, when lethargy takes over. "Ma'am, the weathermen are saying this is New York's worst blizzard in years. You've heard, haven't you," he prodded, "that everyone's been asked to remain indoors?"

From the rags she wore, he realized she and the child must be homeless. The woman's mittens, improvised strips of gingham cloth, were tightly wrapped around both hands, the way a boxer pads his fists before the big fight. As a barrier against cold, her frail body was draped with mismatched layers of wool; a black shawl, soaked through, covered the mass of wooly gray atop her head.

"Please, won't you follow me to Abyssinian Baptist Church? It's not far," he urged. His heart lurched at the sight of spindly bare legs sticking out of beaten-down work boots. "They'll give you and the child shelter," he added, deciding problems with his wife prevented him from inviting them home.

Around them, he glimpsed other stragglers and an emergency four-wheel drive-vehicle crawling down the avenue. He remembered seeing a taxi, a few blocks earlier, sliding its way back to the garage on Broadway. Futilely, he searched for another.

"I be thanking you kindly," the old woman said, as though suddenly coming alive. He watched her carefully readjust the baby's thin covering. From what he glimpsed, the child's simple homespun blanket was ancient but clean and lovingly edged with thin strips of fraying lace. A deep rasping cough momentarily doubled the old crone over. When she recovered, she surprised him.

"Son, you best be gettin' on home to your woman; you got troubles yourn self. We jest headed up the road apiece. I done seen my share of stormy weather, and this ain't the worse of it," she said, momentarily thinking of another storm that had brought untold suffering as she and her countrymen crossed the big water.

For nine hours the hurricane had tossed their flimsy slave ship into twenty-foot swells. Late that night the seas calmed, but not the cries of half-dead captives in that stinking hole. For two days she'd prayed for death that refused to come. Instead, she lay pinned down and shackled to Utey, listening as the final swishing moan of air passed through his lungs.

Lifting her shawl slightly, the old woman reached out and gripped the stranger's arm; her bony hand, though crippled with cold, jolted him to the roots of his being.

"I best be gettin' dis child to safety, jest like her mama asted," she said, releasing him. "After that, my journeying be done."

"Where you headed?" he asked weakly and, suddenly feeling the presence of some dark primordial power, backed away. But the old hag was already making her way up Malcolm X and didn't hear him. He watched her back until she disappeared like a phantom.

CHAPTER 1

HAMILTON TAKES A SABBATICAL
five years later

Even though Cumulo-Nimbus Number 4, the designated area for America's founders and presidents, remained one of the firmament's most celebrated sections of heaven, its famous residents, much to their chagrin, no longer controlled affairs of government. However, that fall from power hadn't stopped Hamilton and Jefferson, longtime adversaries, from incessantly jockeying for political one-upmanship. Earlier, during a heated discussion, Jefferson had provoked Hamilton by renewing one of their two-hundred-year-old arguments about taxation.

"Alexander," he'd started in, "I still believe the 1791 Whiskey Tax you levied was a grave mistake. By compounding financial woes of farmers and upping the price of their favorite drink, it almost led to another war."

Hamilton rolled his eyes. "I could list fifty potential disasters, including the poverty of our fledgling nation that nearly led us back into war, so unless you have a new issue to raise, I consider the matter closed."

Savoring a morning mug of manna, Jefferson daintily wiped his thin lips before pressing home his point. "Sir, as a foreigner from that exotic Caribbean isle where you were born," he jabbed, "you failed to understand the mentality of America's agrarian men."

"Pure poppycock." Hamilton, red-faced, sputtered his frustration by stomping around. "Thomas," he shouted, puncturing the air with spittle, "had you actually participated in war, rather than simply pontificated from the pillared halls of Monticello, you might recall that we had no means to pay for our glorious Revolution. Our proud troops often went without salary, provisions, or weaponry to defend themselves, much less defend the country. We're damn lucky not to still be ruled by the British."

Despite the sting of his words, Hamilton knew Jefferson was not likely to lose his composure. Rather than respond immediately, Hamilton's old nemesis bought time by rising from his cushy seat and walking to the edge of their section. He pretended to find interest in the firmament's endless stretch of pristine white. This morning, at least, the sky had turned a milky blue, allowing occasional shards of sun to penetrate the mass of nimbus clouds like the one on which they stood.

At last Jefferson faced his companion. "My dear man, after three centuries, you still cleverly misconstrue my thoughts and deeds with pretty phrases. In truth, your damnable Whiskey Tax fell most grievously on the weakest members of society."

Weary of reminding him that federal taxes had saved the Republic from bankruptcy and collapse, Hamilton thought of another way to annoy the old goat.

"Tell me, sir, have you been following the news?"

"Not at all. You know my interest waned when projections showed the woman winning."

His trap set, Alexander tried not to gloat. "Exactly my point, Thomas. You remain hopelessly out of step with progress. The lady's already been elected."

Though genuinely surprised, Jefferson, always cool under pressure, simply dismissed the news with an elegant shake of his bewigged head. "If indeed so," he added, "then I shall make my own projection. Madame will last a month, if that."

Exhaling in exasperation, Hamilton said, "Then you're a fool and a chauvinist. The president's been in office four months now. The populace is quite taken with her."

Both founders took a moment to mull over America's new political climate. Then Jefferson peeked below at the still snow-packed streets of Washington, DC. "Does her election have anything to do with your planned visit to earth?" he asked.

As much as any pastime, Hamilton enjoyed a good argument with Thomas, as long as they avoided slavery, but this question was not unlike what he'd been asking himself. Less combatively, he answered, "I've been granted a sabbatical from heaven to observe a ceremony that the people of Harlem will hold in my honor."

"Isn't that where you once lived?"

"It is indeed, and I'm anxious to revisit the Grange, my old homestead. You know I didn't get to live there long. It's now a national memorial, like your place at Monticello, but on a less opulent scale." Before continuing, Hamilton paused and squinted into the distance, where the gilded outline of His office was barely discernible. "Since He requires us to combine good deeds with a leave of absence, I also intend to make contact with former president William Jefferson Clinton."

"Now you're talking sense, man." A beaming Jefferson whirled and slapped his favorite antagonist on the back, dislodging particles of dust. "Just don't scare the poor fellow to death. He has a history of heart trouble. I follow ex-presidents, and from observations of Mr. Clinton, a far-distant relative of mine, the gentleman is drifting again. He trots all over the world doing so-called good deeds, instead of retiring peacefully to his study with a fine wine and his pipe. Then, by letting that woman of his usurp his former role, he's not only sullying the Jefferson heritage, but also giving our Presidents Club, an organization you quite rightly never belonged to, a bad name."

Alexander ignored the provocation, as he had no appetite for further argument. Thomas knew well that he'd never aspired to the presidency. "Thomas, may I suggest that you reread my Essay 68, I believe it was, in the Federalist Papers. There, one necessarily interprets that I was strongly against foreign-born nationals, such as myself, ever becoming president."

Although weary of Jefferson's nasty biases, Hamilton was tempted to remind him of something else: someday, President Obama, the ex-president he sneeringly referred to as "that son of an African slave who slipped into the Oval Office," would be joining his hallowed Presidents and Founders Club.

Instead, Alexander carefully calculated what he wanted to say next. "Setting aside your damnable vanities, Thomas, may I say that if ever there were an ex-president who wandered among the people like a discontented ghost, it is you. Since you've been out of office, you act like a quarrelsome old woman who refuses to accept that the world has changed. You prefer to dwell on the past.

"As for former President Clinton, I agree that he might benefit from some advice, but there are two matters I have no intention of discussing with him. One is Madame Clinton's current tenure. And I will not suggest that he retire to his study with a pipe. In fact, my recollection is that he prefers a cigar to the pipe. No, what interests me about the man is his private life. We have much in common, and there are numerous matters I need to discuss with him."

CHAPTER 2

THE WHITE HOUSE

It was 8:45 a.m., and one cup of coffee was probably enough, but Bill helped himself to another. Caffeine was a tradeoff for whole wheat toast with a dab of jam, the closest he came to his old favorite, jelly donuts. He licked grape goo from the edge of the Times, folded it in half, then creased the column with sticky fingers. Watching Bill with distaste and balling her napkin, Hillary threw it down and pushed her plate away. "Oh, for heaven's sake, Bill, are you listening?"

He wasn't, but he said, "Uh, huh," anyway. Still focused on his article, he groped blindly for the coffee cup.

"I know Tom Friedman wrote a sterling op-ed piece about your foundation, but can't you read that later? And that reminds me," she added. "Last week Maureen Dowd paid me an outright compliment. I read Maureen's piece twice, and I couldn't detect one note of sarcasm. The woman actually called me 'charming.'"

"Hmm," Bill offered neutrally.

"Bill," she tried again, "can you please forget the news and talk to me about this house? We're back in the White House. We are the news, for God's sake."

When he looked up, he was grinning. "It's generous of you to use the royal 'we.'" Putting aside the paper, he said, "Face it, Hillary, right now, folks aren't interested in Bill Clinton. You're in charge, and I've never been more proud. Except maybe the day you delivered Chelsea."

His wife stopped jiggling her knee and unfurled her brow. "The old cliché is true. Giving birth is truly a labor of love. Once that baby cries, you're oblivious to anything but the indescribable joy of being a mother. Still," she said, smiling, "those long hours of labor were a piece of cake compared to the next... ."

An in-house line rang, and through lowered lids, Bill watched Hillary swivel her chair, remove a clip-on earring, and deftly grasp the receiver. Third button down, a flashing green light told Bill the secretary of state was on the line, probably to talk about the upcoming trip to Nigeria.

While his wife scribbled notes, he reflected on his 1998 goodwill swing through Africa. He'd stimulated international trade, improved relations, and had millions of Africans fall on their knees in reverence for him. "Damn," he muttered under his breath, "I could still do that job with my eyes closed."

Even though Bill felt he could still run the country, he had to admit Hillary knew her stuff. Decisive, pragmatic, cool under pressure, she handled stress well. Only half listening to Hillary's conversation with the secretary, Bill took note of her healthy, pink complexion against a snowy blouse and a string of pearls. A cardinal red jacket rested on the chair back. Despite a grueling campaign and a few more wrinkles, she looked great; he needed to tell her that.

When his wife clicked off, he spoke. "Hillary, you look lovely. I don't tell you that nearly enough."

Fluffing her hair, she beamed. "Thank you, darling. Do you like the auburn color?"

"I do." He peered at what looked to him like the same fringe of blond hair she'd had forever—well, maybe with a hint of auburn, whatever that was.

"The color's terrific."

"I think it's an improvement, but look," she changed the subject, "since you're free today except for your lunch date, please remember I need you at six p.m." She shrugged into her suit coat. "I better get downstairs. You do remember, don't you," she avoided looking him in the eye, "that you promised to attend the meeting with Helen Steigman?"

"Well, hell." He crossed his arms and glared. "That's unfair, and you know it. One reason I have so much time on my hands, as you remind me, is because my wings have been clipped 'to avoid all conflict.'" He sarcastically mimicked the words he'd heard a million times over the past few months.

"Bill, we've gone over and over this. If I get a second term, some of the scrutiny and pressure might be reduced, and you can operate more independently."

"In four years, after playing hostess to you, I'll be roadkill. Already, I've had to cut ties to organizations and people that matter to me."

"Yes, honey, I know, but that's the point. When the media raised issues about your associations or your past, you laid low and defused potential trouble. The public didn't want to hear all that stuff again. People want new red meat, but you refused to give it to them."

Skipping over Hillary's reference to his last turbulent year in office, he said, "And as for Audrey, I have zero interest in talking to that annoying woman. If you can't do it, just let her choose the damn fabrics and colors. She may have a good eye, or whatever it's called, but she's a grandstander; she likes prolonging the agony."

"Honey, I know," Hillary soothed, "but the White House made a real exception by letting her consult with the head decorator. Ever since she got sued by a client's husband who hated everything his wife selected, Audrey insists both spouses be present at her consultations. Once we give the okay, you can bow out and the White House coordinator will take over."

"I thought Chelsea was going to help you with some of this ridiculous social stuff."

"She will, but she's awfully busy now. She'll pitch in for me when she can, but she couldn't pop in down here for one meeting, so you and I need to be a team."

"You're the president, for Christ's sake. Any other decorator would just be glad to have you as a client."

Pulling two tissues from the box, Hillary pocketed them and closed her portfolio. "Audrey knows I'm pressed for time. The appointment won't take more than twenty minutes. Besides," she teased, "she said you're such a cute 'first gentleman.'"

"Don't even start with that stuff. I'm not in the mood, and it's not funny."

"Just kidding. Relax. But if we want to bring in our own decorator, we have to authorize her to do things like replace the wallpaper."

Knowing this was another argument he wasn't likely to win, Bill leaned back and studied the breakfast room for the first time since returning to the White House. Frowning, he stared at a ceiling fixture, straining to remember if it had been there before.

"Those bulbs could be brighter," he offered helpfully. "What's wrong with the wallpaper? You can hang some pictures, maybe a calendar or something."

"Oh, please," was the best Hillary could do to dignify the calendar comment. "I'm sick of paint and fabric too; been there, done that. But this house is a national treasure, so I need your support on this one. Gotta run."

That about summed it up, he thought grimly, watching her tear through the door. My new job is to pick paint.

Putting off a call to his publisher, Bill contemplated a forbidden third cup and retrieved the newspaper, just as an attendant appeared in the archway.

"Sir, excuse the interruption, but I have a message for you." Rosario de la Cruz, a White House usher, stood hesitantly at the door.

"Rosario, how are you, man?" Bill greeted the short attendant who handed him a pink slip of paper marked, "Important: From the Switchboard."

Glancing quickly at the sender's name, Bill saw that Mattie, the housekeeper at the Harlem townhouse, had left a long message. Slipping it into his bathrobe pocket, he said, "Come in, pull up a chair. I've hardly laid eyes on you in days. You're looking fit as ever and haven't aged a bit."

"Thank you, sir. Life has been good to me and my family."

"Glad to hear it. How's Florentina?" Talk about retaining fighting form. Bill brightened as the woman's name rolled off his tongue.

"It's kind of you to ask, Mr. President." Rosario bobbed his head in thanks but remained standing, arms clasped behind his white jacket. "Florentina is well."

Shifting the focus from himself, Rosario hurried on. "Mr. President, while we're discussing family, sir, may I add that senior staff, such as myself, remembers the gaiety of your administration and welcomes you back."

"I'm not sure if we're still up to our old partying level, but thank you just the same. We had some good times, didn't we?" He chuckled. "But there is one other thing. Hillary is president now, so it's best not to refer to me as Mr. President."

"Very good, sir. We were instructed on that point, but force of habit caused me to forget myself. Please excuse me. If there's nothing else," he said, eyeing crumbs and a stained table cloth, "I'll return momentarily to clear your dining area."

Back in his office, Bill picked up a dramatic aerial photo of the Clinton Presidential Library. The cantilevered building soared through the air like a hulking locomotive racing into the great unknown. He loved looking at this picture. When it came to original design for presidential libraries, he'd hit a home run.

The photograph was heavy, and after one last look, Bill put it down and glanced at his grandfather clock. "Yikes," he gulped, realizing he'd taken too long reading the newspapers. Now, if he hoped to shower, shave, and get to Georgetown by one, he could no longer put off calling his New York editor. Aware that the publisher was losing patience over his delay in getting them the next installment of his manuscript, Bill slowly punched in the eleven digits.

"Loddard here," the man barked in his usual harried manner.

"Hey, buddy, how're ya'll doing up there?" Bill hoped his editor was in a good mood. "Bob, hello? Are you there?" he asked, hearing no response. "It's me, Bill."

"Yeah. Like I said, I'm here."

Irked at the man's familiarity, he tried another approach "Why so friendly? Already having a bad day?"

"You could say that. You could also say I know why you're calling—to tell me what you've written. Nothing, right?"

A bit taken aback, Bill hedged. "Well, not exactly. I might be suffering a mild case of writer's block. The election was a big distraction, but why'd you think I hadn't been writing?"

"Because, first thing, you start with the good ol' boy talk. Hang on a sec, will ya," Bob added, before Bill could react. Irritated, he propped the phone on his shoulder and started doodling. Through the receiver he heard his editor's muffled voice talking to someone and pictured Bob in his plush corner office, high above bustling Broadway.

"Yeah, I'm back," the baritone came through again.

"What's wrong with good ol' boys?" Bill asked, filling the back of an envelope with linked triangles. "You make it sound like bullshit."

"No offense, but yeah. I'm your friend and your editor, remember. Sorry for the cliché, but I read you like a book. You get all 'down-on-the-farm' with me when you can't come clean about the writing not going well. Look, my friend, I'm pretty busy up here ..." Bill heard Bob's hand cover the speaker again.

"Talk about bullshit; this is bullshit," Bill sputtered into the void. Flipping the envelope across the room, he swung his feet off the desk and used the delay to survey his own digs, a space that still felt foreign: Hillary's former office. With its still empty walls and gutted shelves, it was far from plush and further from the Oval Office than he remembered.

"Okay, Bill, sorry about the interruptions, but you caught me in the middle of a meeting. I just kicked everybody the hell out of here. They can finish up in the conference room. You have my full attention." Then getting right to the point, he asked, "How many pages have you got for me?"

"None," Bill admitted, reaching for another envelope. "I'm stuck." He drew a Star of David and inked in one of the points.

"No surprise there. Listen, do you mind if I speak frankly?"

"You mean you weren't already?" Bill asked, although he knew the worst was yet to come. "But go ahead. What's up?"

"Has it occurred to you that you may have said it all the first time? There is only so much a man can write about his life, especially one as young as you."

Feeling the wind shift, Bill knew he was now being humored. He got up and walked to the window. "Bob, I'm standing in the White House looking out at the Mall." For a clearer view, Bill opened the plantation shutters. "It's a glorious day; the sun's bouncing off the Washington Monument. Need I remind you that I, like George Washington, am a former president of the United States? My wife's the current president. That's got to be worth something, don't you think?"

"Absolutely; it's worth another bestseller. Potentially. But, you can't just tell me about life, or envision it from a window. You gotta write the book." Bob articulated the last words slowly, and Bill resented his tone. He wasn't a two-year-old.

"While we're being frank, I gotta say, your early material ain't exactly lighting my fire. And you're right about Hillary; she's all the buzz. The shelf life of former presidents, including yours, quickly fizzles, especially when the wife becomes president. If you're going to write a book that sells, say something that's not already in the first 600-page version.

Turning his back on Washington, Bill thought bleakly: There it is, the other shoe. He moved a pile of books and slumped into one of two leather chairs meant for visitors. "Okay, you're the expert here. How do I fix this thing?"

"You let it breathe a little; give yourself space. Right now your words lack conviction, passion. Try looking at your writing through a fresh prism. You're a 'name,' but if you aren't saying anything, it doesn't matter who you are.

"Try to come up with new and unusual aspects to your life, not just the bureaucratic side of raising money for poor kids and good causes. Throw in human interest stories about the people and the kids you've helped. You're great with kids. Just last month, at Margie's party, you told that story about the little girl who wouldn't high five you. The Haitian interpreter explained it was because she didn't want you to catch her family's bad luck. You were very moved by that, and frankly, so was I. Throw in stuff like that."

Remembering the child, Bill smiled. "Okay, so that's a good example, but every time I sit down to write, I choke. You're the expert. How do I get beyond this writer's block?"

Now it was the editor's turn to laugh, and he unloosed a rousing guffaw. "That, my friend, is a question for the ages. If I had the answer, celebrity authors like you would have made me even richer than I am."

After finishing the call, Bill sat a minute before rising and heading down the hall. If he didn't want to be unreasonably late, he needed to refocus and get ready for his luncheon appointment with Mary Townsend, his former secretary. Hillary was right. He needed to avoid any whiff of impropriety with old friends, many of whom were lobbyists or executives in companies that had government contracts. Mary was a beloved former staff member "without connections."

Padding into the bathroom, he checked the mirror to see how badly he needed a shave. Nothing wrong in sharing a meal with a former staff person, he reassured himself, but in his heyday, he had dined with kings and prime ministers.

Before turning on the faucet, Bill remembered the message from Mattie. Retrieving it, he read: "Call me. I think somebody other than you, me, or Mrs. Clinton has been inside the house. Ray and the cop on beat came over, investigated—said break-in impossible. Said cameras and monitors constantly scan inside, and security team patrols the outside. Cop acted like I was losing my mind. I'm not."

There was more, but he didn't bother reading. Two days ago, Mattie claimed someone had rearranged something in her pantry. Reluctantly, he hit speed dial and waited. His housekeeper was always there on Wednesdays but never answered before five rings. She was also a straight shooter, not prone to exaggeration, and fiercely protective of both him and the community she loved.

"Clinton residence," she answered formally, knowing he was on the other end.

"Morning, Mattie. I'm in a bit of a hurry," he said, realizing it was no longer morning, "but I just got your message." Then, without preamble, he asked, "What's going on up there? Do you suspect something else out of order?"

"Only the den television, sir."

That got his attention. "Was it missing or something?"

"Not missing. It was on when I arrived this morning."

Bill didn't use the house that often, but he occasionally set the DVR to record a sporting event if he thought he might be in transit to New York. But football was over, baseball teams were just starting spring training, and MLB wasn't yet broadcasting games. Although he couldn't remember doing so, he said, "Mattie, I must have set it to record."

"That's what I thought too," she said, anticipating his response, "but the television was on channel 452, a station that doesn't come through, and the DVR was off."

Anything's possible, he thought, glancing at his watch. "Look, I'll be in New York tomorrow. If something else happens, don't touch and let the Service send over a fingerprint unit."

"They're just finishing up now."

"Really?" He tried not to sound incredulous that Ray, his main Secret Service guy in New York, had followed up with an investigation because a television was on. The townhouse was impenetrable.

"Ray made the fingerprint request," Mattie said, "after I told him if he and the people assigned to this house didn't stop ignoring me, Bill Clinton would have to find a new housekeeper."

Running forty minutes late, Bill hustled through the elaborate archway of Sophia, a new Greek restaurant Chelsea recommended. "Welcome, and right this way, Mr. President," greeted a man in tight black pants and a turtleneck who'd been anticipating his arrival. "I'm Nick, Sophia's maître d'." Ignoring Bill's security man, Nick waved toward the back and self-importantly hurried Bill through the darkened restaurant, past tables of diners engaged in quiet conversation.

Nick slid open a door to a private dining room. "I've seated your party in our special VIP section." He looked pleased with himself.

Bill would have preferred the main dining area and paused, looking back to see who of importance might be there. As his eyes adjusted to the dim lighting, he spotted the Russian ambassador tucked in the far corner. From the number of juiced-up bodyguards sitting at the bar, he figured Sergey's lunch companion must be a Russian oligarch. They were the only ones in Washington more paranoid about security than the Secret Service.

Inside the VIP room, a curly-haired grandmotherly figure was seated before an empty bread basket, draining a lemony-colored cocktail.

"Mr. President," Mary squealed. Struggling to get up, she threw her arms around his neck.

"Boy, is this a treat to see you, Mary." Bill hugged her tight, feeling soft rolls of flesh.

"Oh, get out of here," she replied, blushing like a school girl. "Talk about a treat. I'm lunching with Bill Clinton at this exciting new restaurant."

He held her chair, pushed it in. After drinks, they quickly ordered.

"Mary, retirement obviously agrees with you."

"Yes, and I hope it's been the same for you. It's been thrilling to watch Mrs. Clinton's presidency." She clinked her water glass onto his and sipped. "Should have toasted you sooner. Be sure to give Mrs.—or should I say, President—Clinton, my very best."

"I will, and likewise, Hillary sends regards," he said, although he couldn't recall his wife mentioning Mary by name.

Grinning mischievously, she asked, "Sir, how do you like your promotion to first gentleman?"

He searched for the right tone to respond to Mary's question. "Frankly, Hillary's assistants take care of everything."

"Of course, but you're a very social being. People just love that about you. Although," she added, "I can't picture you hosting tea parties. You wouldn't want to give me a little inside information on any plans for your position, now would you?" she asked coyly.

"No, Mary, I wouldn't," he replied more civilly than he felt. No longer feeling hungry, he pushed back from the table. It occurred to him that of the three women he'd spoken with today, Mattie was the only one who hadn't ticked him off.

"At the moment, there are no future plans," he improvised to be polite, but he definitely needed to find something else to do besides lunch with secretaries.

Hours later, after visiting a hospitalized college buddy, his driver deposited him back at 1600 Pennsylvania Avenue. Bill hoped the appointment with Audrey would be well underway so he could just sign off on whatever Hillary had decided. Inside he punched the button again, but true to form, the West Wing elevator took forever, and he began feeling guilty for making his wife wait.

Since his years as Arkansas governor, Hillary had been his loyal companion, rarely disappointing or running late. Although, he thought a bit uncharitably, sticking with him hadn't hurt her career one bit.

Other than learning that his buddy's tumor was benign, Bill realized his day hadn't gone well. Even his lunch salad was too oily. Now, walking into the drawing room, he realized things were not about to get any better.

"Audrey, where's Hillary?" he asked crossly.

"Come in. Come in, you dear man." After waving him over imperiously, the decorator continued studying cream-colored fabric swatches she'd artfully draped over the love seats. Oversized wallpaper books dominated other surfaces.

"The president has been briefly detained. I'm just laying out a few samples." Satisfied with her arrangement, Audrey turned to squint at his white shirt and green tie. "Have you ever had your colors done?" she asked. "It used to be all the rage, and now the concept is catching on again." Walking closer, she slipped a pair of trendy Pradas on her long nose and frankly appraised Bill.

An old school chum from his and Hillary's days at Yale, Audrey was once married to their classmate, Al Steigman. After the divorce, she built up a decorating business in which she had previously only dabbled. Give her credit, he thought;

the woman certainly landed on her feet and now earned more than the US president.

"Purple is the new blue," she prattled on. "You should wear it. Purple would bring out more violet in those lovely baby blues." Standing close but resisting the urge to touch, Audrey instead patted the surgically tightened skin beneath the sockets of her own brown eyes. "And," she added, "no disrespect intended, but you might consider doing a little something to those bags under your eyes."

"Don't be absurd," he sputtered. "No one's touching my damn face."

"And that thick mane," she cooed, hurrying ahead. "To die for is what that head of hair is. Every man should be so lucky, if I may say so."

To die for. Hmmm, he thought, pleased by the compliment, despite its source. He took the bait. "What does it mean to have your colors done?"

"Each of us is either a spring, summer, winter, or autumn—unless of course, we fall a bit in the middle. I'd say you're a spring."

Bill groaned. "Sorry I asked."

Just then, Hillary breezed through the French doors, tossed a "Hi, honey" in his direction, and honed in on the love seat nearest the fireplace. "Audrey, sorry to detain you, but it's been a day. What've we got here? Hmmm, this palette has appeal," she said, grabbing a handful of samples to study under the lamp on the gate leg table.

Bill retreated into the room's shadows, leaned against a pillar, and watched his wife work. From Hillary's look of determination he knew it wouldn't take long to zip through samples.

Twenty minutes later, Bill helped load heavy sample books onto a cart, while Hillary rang for an attendant who appeared and professionally hustled the decorator to a waiting elevator.

When Bill turned to ask his wife how her day went, he recognized the signs of fatigue. Already light years beyond the business with Audrey, her red suit was now wrinkled, and Hillary stood hunched in the middle of the vast room, carrying the world's weight on those thin shoulders.

"I just came from my sixth meeting," she said, reading his face. "I'm okay, but l could use a day off; I haven't had one in months. How about I meet you at the Harlem house on Saturday? I need to get out of Washington to clear my head."

CHAPTER 3

PLEASURES ON EARTH

The rapid motion and endless noise on earth bewildered Alexander, causing him to—at least temporarily—cease touring the city in his corporeal state. Sights and sounds of motorized vehicles, some with as many as eighteen wheels, terrified him. He feared sabotaging this visit with an embarrassing blunder that might bring undue attention. He had to be careful.

There were advantages, certainly, to remaining invisible to the populous. That point was driven home on a recent morning spent flitting through the Wall Street area. First he visited his grave and that of his wife, Eliza, at Trinity Cemetery. He also stopped at the plot of General William Alexander, one of the bravest men he'd ever had the pleasure of serving alongside.

While in lower Manhattan he also wanted to observe the modern day banking system he helped establish, and he had fortunately stumbled upon an in-progress financial meeting. Though he could not comprehend the newfangled gadgetry participants used, his wealth of banking knowledge allowed him to follow the presentation. The main speaker, a scoundrel he quickly discovered, had artfully obfuscated a portion of earning numbers being presented to the gathering. Alexander considered confronting the gentleman but decided to wait and, at some point, ask Mr. Clinton about relieving the fellow of his ill-gotten gains.

Earlier today, while exploring a nearby area just north of his home, Alexander happened upon a more pleasant discovery, the Morris-Jumel Mansion, General Washington's 1776 headquarters, where he and the general spent many tense hours planning the Battle of Harlem Heights.

But now, as the day waned, he was anxious to return to his former home, the Grange, currently a museum. That it was routinely locked each evening and conveniently emptied of caretakers well suited his and Sarafina's needs.

He slipped invisibly through the clapboard siding of the east wall into his octagonal dining room. A few days ago, when he first set eyes on the room, he was touched to see someone's attempt to preserve pieces of his past. Among the furnishings was a replica of Eliza's cherished dining set, now artfully staged as though she were giving a dinner party.

Taking the stairs quickly he entered the master suite, which closely resembled the chamber he long ago occupied. However, at present, Hamilton was most intrigued by the sight of Sarafina's coppery brown skin as she unwrapped a tiny piece of gossamer. He watched her finger the finery with care as though fearful of damaging its delicacy.

"Alexander," she sighed, "lo, those many years ago, ne'er did I touch such softness on my skin." Turning her scantily clad bottom away from him, she bent to retrieve another matching frill. As he watched her stand unselfconsciously, he realized that none of the other women in his past had ever been so comfortable displaying their natural glory.

Dreamily dangling the sheer, red nylon close for him to see, she asked, "Remember our first audience? Did you think my poor ragged self would ever be clad in such?"

His heart beat rapidly. "I don't believe so," he said thickly, watching her move the prettiness away.

"How best does one address this?" She held the item in question, a bra, by the straps. From his perch on the four-poster, Hamilton shifted his eyes from Sarafina's bushy triangle of hair up to her ripe breasts and finally to the piece of frippery.

Willing her to hurry, he reached forward to assist. "May I?" he asked.

"No, no." Like a child, she pulled away, determined to do it herself.

"Try latching it from the back," he suggested, flopping onto a pillow. She was thirsty to practice her new earthly independence, but he checked a lingerie model's picture in Elle, a reference they'd ostensibly obtained for Sarafina's wardrobe guidance. In truth, he was the one transfixed by the images. "The circles go in front; the book calls that a bra. But, my dear, why don these garments now?"

In a few moments he hoped to delight in every curvy inch of her tall brown beauty. By modern standards, she was not a tall woman, but in their day, this long-limbed girl who measured five-feet-eight had eclipsed him and much of the young country's populace.

Impatient with another correction, she said, "I know the bra piece, but this garment joins in front, just so." Connecting three tiny hooks, she glanced his way. "Have patience, Alexander. Don't you see, I have a ways to travel in this experiment." Having solved what puzzled her, he watched her satisfaction as she slipped first one then a second bountiful breast into soft lacy-edged, cone-shaped circles.

As she faced him, her movements were graceful and natural. "With this journey, I desire to be like a woman, not piece goods."

Right now his aching desire was for her to finish dressing and attend to him. But he also felt chastened for hurrying her small womanly triumph.

"Sarafina, your life, not your character, was stunted by racial injustice; you're a fine woman." Seeking to assure her, he said, "Please don't disparage yourself. But I am wondering: do you intend to wear this provocative frill beyond these walls?"

Her look left little doubt that she did. "Former mistresses, important ladies I dress, ne'er were beguiled by the likes of such garments. Their most lovely silk chemise or long pantaloon don't compare. Do you think God only intend you to enjoy this journey? I think not," she answered brightly, then seeing his ready desire surprised him by playfully tweaking him. "I know what troubling you, Alexander: other men's eyes." Electrified by her touch and uncharacteristic mischievousness, he nearly jumped out of his skin. In just the short time they'd been here on earth, she'd begun to change. For one, her adjustment to these new surroundings far exceeded his.

Eyes still wide, he asked, "My pretty one, when did you learn to do that?"

Instead of responding, Sarafina plucked the last item, an odd lacy snippet with suspended garters and not much else, from its tissue wrapping. Holding the mysterious piece aloft, she stretched the elastic, then closed a metal snap before looking at him. "The things women do, Alexander, they just do. Be not quick to parse a woman's actions, unless you disapprove," she added slyly.

The reality of being in a time warp weighed on Alexander, causing his ears to ring. Suddenly a one-time slave woman was making the rules, and he was happy to obey her orders.

"How right you are, my dear," he said.

When Sarafina returned the garter belt to its box and placed her bottom on the bed, Hamilton blinked and muttered, "Praise God," under his breath.

Her voluptuous body in its see-through material thrilled him. Both dark nipples showed through, their color matching the unruly tangle of fur below, much of it refusing to be contained by this skimpy garment that he had learned was called a thong.

Sarafina used her considerable assets to arouse his most base desires. Her smile alone, and he wished she displayed it more often, enticed him. By anyone's measure she was the perfect lover: loyal, pleasing, and capable, despite a lingering innocence and vulnerability. But she had blue periods and was often distant, leaving little doubt that she needed to fill an empty place in her heart.

"Just ravishing, my dear. Are you quite done?"

Before scooting her bronzed limbs closer to his pale body, Sarafina took another glance down at herself. "This is no mere dream. These togs belong to me." Preening, she asked, "How I appear to you?"

Hamilton drank in the nest of black ringlets framing her face and tried to see into the depths of eyes that were the color of amber. "Beautiful inside and out, and as much as I burn to touch you, before I do and words fail me, let me say that had we lived as moderns, ours would be a happier story."

"What's done been done," she said with a touch of yearning. "Might we not attempt happiness now, before it pass?"

"Indeed, but allow me a moment to speak. He took a deep breath. "I don't regret any of my life with my devoted Eliza and our children, but had I met you first, and had it been possible, I would have formally courted you, as I see modern men doing with ladies of another race. And who knows where fate would have led us."

"I hear you speak," she said, "from a place where passion overrules judgment. Had you always reasoned so, your creation, your democracy that now enthralls us, would not be."

"True, I am besotted, my dear, but my words ring sincere."

Sarafina looked at him for a long time before gently resting a hand on either side of his face. "Dear sir, permit me to drink in this memory." She placed two fingers over his lips, preventing interruption. "Always men desire me, but none so decent and delicate of manner as you. Being here with you lift my heart and give me reason to hope."

Though pleased by her sentiment, Sarafina's manner puzzled him. Frowning, he said, "I no longer understand you, my dear. Sometimes I wonder if you're that sunny girl from long ago who cheekily accosted me at Mr. Shields's gate. You've not been the same since that day at the auction block. Are those ancient memories the cause of your melancholy?"

"Alas, dear sir," she whispered, "on that day, the wind of change shifted mightily."

"That was indeed a grim experience. But since then you've made unparalleled strides." Suddenly fearing that her mood had darkened, he hastened to brighten his tone. "In fact," he blurted, "you've more than changed; you clearly sparkle in this environment."

Without seeming to do so, Hamilton shifted slightly to his left and reached out to touch a lacy length of strap supporting her pendulous breasts. "How splendidly you've taken to your new freedom as an earth being." Sensing no resistance he lowered his hand to her thigh, let it linger for a while, then urged her to lie back on the pillow next to him. He rested his hand on her leg and slowly caressed a spot behind her knee.

"Do you realize" he asked, as she relaxed, "that the body's most erogenous zones often lie within the unlikeliest parameters of skin, such as that behind the knee?"

"The what?" she asked quietly.

"Love zones, my dear." As he moved his hand further up the thigh, Sarafina tossed her hips to better accommodate his caress, allowing him to deftly slip a finger inside the scant material covering her sex. He probed until he located her clitoris, already alert and awaiting his touch. Gently then more insistently he stroked, searching for a rhythm, until her breath, like his, quickened and he heard a moan.

After they made love, Sarafina burrowed into the crook of Alexander's elbow. Thinking her asleep, he was surprised when she whispered, "Do you suppose I can find a heaven here on earth?"

"What an odd concept." Without dislodging her he twisted slightly, trying to scan her face, but it was turned. "Were you not content in the arms of Saint Peter?"

"For all its tranquility, a sadness lingers in heaven. And up there," she added, "I could not love you in a physical way."

"Well, yes, that is a glaring deficiency." Dreamily, he contemplated endlessly loving this alluring woman. "It's somewhat fortuitous, I believe, that the carnal urges are not part of the divine experience." Lazily raising an eyebrow heavenward, he added, "So they can't be missed. Yet when you ponder the alternative," he continued with a brittle laugh, "heaven works quite well. Until Saint Peter opened the gate, I wasn't sure he'd let me in, but praise God, he did. Are you not also inclined to be grateful?"

"Oh, yes, but heaven's plan falls short of expectation," she sighed, "for there be those from the past that I failed to meet."

Running his eye over the room's rose-patterned wallpaper, he said offhandedly, "If that be the case, I think you best face the truth of their likely descent into the netherworld."

"Never," she shot back, startling him. "You know not of what you speak. Never are innocents punished for the sins of others."

"Forgive me, my dear." He struggled to an upright position. "How callous of me to speak so. One must always harbor hope for the souls of our loved ones."

Though he and Sarafina remained mostly immune to temperature change, he felt her shiver. "There, there, my sweet. See, you're already so acclimatized to earth that the cold room troubles you. Shall I fetch a wrap?"

Sarafina shook her head. "No," she whispered, pointing toward a bank of windows across from the bed. Though the windows were dark and shuddered, his eyes followed where she indicated, checking for a breach in the closing. He saw none.

"Yonder," Sarafina whispered, clearly focusing on something beyond the room. "Someone walks over my grave."

Though he dismissed all reports of grave-walking sensations, from Sarafina's intensity, he realized this would not be a good time to explain the impossibility of her claim. So he politely muttered, "Well, perhaps at some point we can discuss that matter."

By his calculation, the Negro cemetery from their era lay seven miles south and east of their current location. Even from as far away as heaven, he'd been able to discern that those four acres of sacred ground were buried under massive modern structures, making it impossible for anyone to be treading directly on the Negros' graves. Now that he'd descended and gotten a firsthand perspective of that area, he'd been shocked to discover that these tall buildings literally scraped the sky.

"Certainly anything's possible," he said to please her. Then, seeking to forestall further melancholy and recapture the evening's balance, he offered a suggestion. "Perhaps we might now review our earth plan; that is, if you're not feeling too indisposed."

When Sarafina looked at him her eyes had cleared and refocused. "The shadow gone now," she said with a faint smile. "Tell me of our journey."

Nodding, he relaxed against the tall headboard and placed both arms behind his head. "While I await the festivities in my honor, I'd be wise to study the fruits of democracy. The new world is a confounding place, and, as I navigate, I will have good counsel beside me." Gently squeezing her knee, he said, "I couldn't have chosen a more apt companion."

Glancing over at the threadbare dusty blue suit he'd arrived in, which now lay neatly folded in the corner, she said, "Henceforth, your wardrobe be causing less perplexity among the people."

"Indeed, your instincts about proper attire are entirely correct. However, when I approach Mr. Clinton, I believe I'd do best to revert to my former appearance."

In a more serious tone, Sarafina asked, "When do you plan to make the gentleman's acquaintance?"

"Soon, but Mr. Clinton has a history of heart ailment, so I must proceed with care. In my observations of his leisure moments, which, of late, are numerous, I've come to believe early evening will be the best time to approach him."

As Sarafina drifted off to sleep, Alexander lay awake and thought of the event that brought Sarafina back into his life. It had occurred on a cold clear morning in 1777 when he was on a combined furlough and official assignment from the winter army at Valley Forge. Although accompanied by his longtime friend, John Laurens, the then Captain Hamilton's visit to New York City was far from recreational. The war was going badly; troops lay bivouacked, freezing and pinned down on a stretch of barren land south of the city.

Before releasing Hamilton to travel to New York, General Washington's instructions to him had been brief and to the point: "Short of stealing them, man, find blankets, boots, victuals—whatever citizens can spare. Our army has been reduced to skin and bone, and they're at their limit." Then, as the two of them tramped dispiritedly past a ragtag group of soldiers huddled by a bonfire, Washington had pointed his hickory walking stick at them. "Just observe the depleted state of our fighting force."

Many men were shoeless, their naked feet swollen with the beginnings of frostbite. "Captain Hamilton," Washington added, "we must offer these patriots a lifeline before they mutiny." After a pause, the general grimly added, "Or freeze to death."

Hamilton couldn't have agreed more. "General, I pray God gives me the power to someday support a standing army with financial resources we now lack." About three yards ahead, Hamilton spotted a wounded man reclining against a tree, eyes filled with hate, his ruined right knee bound in bloodied rags. Reaching into his pocket, Hamilton retrieved a limp piece of dried beef and, without missing a step, startled the wretched fellow by dropping it into his lap.

"Sir," he picked up his thought, "if our vision for a new world is to succeed, we need a reliable, well-financed army." Hamilton looked again at the human suffering surrounding them. "And, if I may be so bold, sir, I've been formulating a financial plan to do just that once we win this war."

After completing their field tour, Hamilton saluted smartly and said, "Sir, you can count on me for supplies. I have old contacts from my days at King's College who do not know the gravity of our situation. Trust me to inform them. They can help us."

Washington, aware of his young aide's persuasive powers, was counting on him to do that very thing. If anyone could persuade citizens to cough up a few precious coins for the cause of liberty, Alexander was the man. Everything he touched turned to gold.

Very well, then." The general returned Hamilton's salute.

"Go with God."

The need to bring along a supply wagon had added a day to Hamilton's journey into the city. After settling into a Water Street boarding house, he and Laurens were now scouring the docks for usable and affordable goods. Despite the dangers inherent in winter seafaring, the air was filled with a cacophony of foreign tongues and accented English, as passengers, sailors, and dockhands tended luggage and cargo, hoisted or unfurled sails, and tugged on clew and bunt lines.

At one point they stopped to watch in amusement as a gang of Spanish sailors pushed, prodded, and dragged a terrified stallion down the galleon's steeply angled gangway. "Mira los cascos," a sailor yelled, dodging the animal's powerful kick. The grayish-white Andalusian was on the lean side, and its once sleek coat was dirty and matted with manure and straw. Yet the horse had good lines and had survived the journey remarkably intact.

Observing the seamen's lack of experience with horses, Hamilton commented, "Someone might have thought to blindfold that big fellow. A handsome beast, though," he added. "Scrub him down, fatten him up, and he's fit as a fiddle."

Laurens gave Hamilton an inquiring look. "I didn't think horses were a current priority for troop supplies."

"They're not; I'm just admiring one of God's more perfect creatures." They resumed walking, leaving the frightened horse, now settled on firm footing, snorting and flinging its large head.

Soon they emerged into the main section of the quay, just

as a group of raucous Marines, in colorful stripes and boater hats, hurried by. When in town, Hamilton relished such lively waterfront scenes, but today he was on a mission. He hoped to add winter wear to his growing wagonload of supplies that waited, five streets over, in front of Fraunces Tavern. Two of Hamilton's foot soldiers were guarding the precious cargo that included yams and apples that he'd gotten off a ship from the islands, four chickens, one pig, and a dozen sacks of vermin-filled rice. For the rice, Hamilton had bargained with a captain from Charles Towne, after the intended recipient refused to accept tainted grain.

Over on the northernmost pier, just east of the graveyard, Hamilton spotted a lately arrived frigate. Its crewmen were unloading several battered ten-foot-tall crates that appeared to contain sodden, water-damaged textiles.

Alexander turned to his friend. "What do you say, John? If I can ascertain who's in charge here, might it be worth bargaining for these goods?"

"Most certainly." John was enjoying the resourceful Hamilton's shopping skills. "That ship," he said, pointing to the heavily laden Marie Noel, "arrives intermittently with dry goods from the best Parisian wholesalers. Take note of what's written on that damaged crate."

Hamilton turned his head sideways and read the name: Charles Forberges Compagnie, rue de St. Genelle. The name and address meant nothing to him.

"Your men," Laurens said, laughing, "should be quite content wearing haute couture clothing from Paris's top clothier."

Hamilton responded with a quip of his own. "Our troops

are brave men, John. They'd be content wearing these stinking fish scales," he said, pointing to the carcass of a rotting flounder lying in the melting snow, "if only the poor creature's skin offered protection from the elements. Now, if I can persuade the French captain that I'm the only one willing to buy this soggy mess …"

Hearing no further comment from Laurens, Hamilton focused on a craggy-faced, sun-darkened fellow wearing faded navy blue. Despite the man's scruffy attire and four-month growth of beard, his greatcoat and trousers were well-brushed, and he moved with authority. Hamilton approached him.

"*Bonjour, monsieur. Je vois que vous avez de la laine abimée. A quel prix me la céderiez-vous?* Receiving nothing more than a glare from the man, Hamilton switched to English. "I can take these badly damaged woolens off your hands cheaply. How much for the entire load?"

"Thief!" the captain yelled, then directed an obscene gesture Hamilton's way.

Undaunted, Hamilton ignored the smirk on Lauren's face and said, "It was worth a try. Come, let us press on."

While on his quest, Hamilton turned down nothing, and a few well-meaning citizens had given him unexpected items. He was about to ask his companion how to best utilize a fifteen-foot bolt of red calico cloth donated by Lauren's kindly former landlady, when he abruptly halted.

"What in God's name are those Negroes doing there, John? Are they shackled?"

The answer to his question became self-evident as the two men moved closer and an auctioneer wearing a black pilgrim suit yelled into the gathering crowd, "Do I hear a first bid of ten shillings for the young boy to my right? Who'll-give-me-ten-shillings?" he asked in rapid-fire cadence.

From the rear of the throng, Laurens and Hamilton picked up a high-pitched keening coming from one of the five slaves who stood upon a raised platform that reminded Hamilton of a gallows he'd once seen while growing up on the island of St. Croix.

Visibly distressed, Hamilton turned his back on the spectacle and asked, "Why in God's name are we fighting the yoke of England, when this type of travesty is still permitted? At the very least," he added disgustedly, "I thought public auctions of human beings had finally been moved indoors."

"I'm afraid not, my friend. And such travesties have been going on for weeks. Roaming bands of militia are wreaking havoc on wealthy English loyalists who've dared stay in the New World. These vandals confiscate property, steal food and drink, and, in some cases, even tar and feather the head of the household. Their slaves and what's not been stolen is then sold for the 'good' of the government."

Amazed, Hamilton asked, "What are the authorities doing to stem these atrocities?"

Laurens took a deep breath before answering. "Alexander, you've been out of town too long. At times the city teeters on the brink of lawlessness."

While stunned by the news, Hamilton's quick mind was already formulating a report for General Washington about localized violence when he detected shifting on the platform and a murmur among the crowd. Refocusing on the slaves, he watched helplessly as the auctioneer prepared to put a sobbing woman up for sale.

"Gentlemen," the man addressed the mostly male audience, "next we have this comely slave wench. Notice her skin tone, the unusual color of tan cowhide. They tell me she speaks good English and has sound teeth. Using his dirty hands to lift her bowed head, he roughly forced her mouth open.

Something about the woman's demeanor, that even her shame and despair could not hide, seemed familiar to Hamilton. He strode about ten paces forward and peered intently at the platform. As his friend caught up, Hamilton whispered, "God in heaven. Who would think it possible, but I once knew that woman before the war began."

As the two friends stared, the man in black winked lecherously and said, "With these lengthwise proportions, she'd make an excellent breeder." His remark drew ribald laughter from a sprinkling of observers; others, like John and Alexander, looked on appalled.

"Bah." Hamilton expressed his fury by spitting on the ground. "May he and his kind rot in hell." Then, through a clenched jaw, he asked, "Will the scoundrel next display her sound body by stripping her bare?"

Instead, the auctioneer lifted the woman's limp arm high above her bowed head. She began keening again, her audible grief piercing all but the hardest heart as she stood sobbing and shivering under a thin gray shawl.

Observing his friend's distress, Laurens ventured to ask, "How do you happen to know this woman?"

Without making eye contact, Alexander spoke out of the side of his mouth. "That is of no matter. What matters is that this must stop."

Nevertheless, the sale continued unabated. "For this beauty, who'll give me thirty shillings?" The crowd gasped. Using his verbal skills to sweeten the pot, the auctioneer did the math. "In time, you will double … triple … quadruple your investment. Do I hear an opening bid of thirty shillings?"

For what seemed like an eternity, the auctioneer silently scanned the assemblage. "Thirty shillings," a deep masculine voice offered.

"A bid of thirty shillings from the gentleman in back," the agent yelled out, pointing to a weather-beaten fellow in an expensive but mud-spattered leather jerkin and breeches.

"Do I hear thirty-five?"

Hamilton, increasingly beside himself, fiddled with a gold button on his uniform sleeve until it popped off in his hand. Absentmindedly pocketing it, he leaned over and whispered, "John, we must put a stop to this."

"How?" Laurens whispered back. "You know the law better than most. Our hands are tied."

Impulsively, Hamilton raised his hand and thundered, "Forty shillings," causing the throng of frock-coated men to turn in unison and appraise the new bidder, erroneously assuming him to be a wealthy officer who needed slave labor to run his farm while he was in the Army.

Standing stock still, Hamilton croaked, "What have I just done, John?"

Equally stunned, Laurens replied, "Sir, I believe you just bought a human being."

"I know that," he snapped. "It is not my intention to keep her, you ass, but what am I to do? Where can I house her?"

John had no answer for him. As the crowd stirred, waiting for the buyer to approach the platform, Hamilton remembered the name, John Simmons, an abolitionist he'd met the year before at a dinner party.

"Come ahead, man," Hamilton intoned, stumbling forth nervously to claim his merchandise. "Pray God I can find John Simmons."

CHAPTER 4

ONE OF HARLEM'S OWN

Bill and Ray went down the back stairs of the townhouse, cut through the security path, then walked the few steps to 141st Street. They waited to cross, as a slow-moving City College maintenance truck, gears grinding, crawled up the hill, belching smoke and forcing traffic to inch along behind it. It was early evening, and the streets were filled with students heading to or from the campus. Tonight there were also two beefy men in suits, their jackets unbuttoned, who walked behind or ahead of Bill and Ray.

To the casual observer, Raymond Hairston, Bill's special bodyguard, looked like any well-put-together guy wearing soft-sided boots, a leather jacket, and low-slung jeans. But despite his hip look, Ray was a seasoned agent who, at Bill's special request, had been allowed to leave a desk job at the Service and again work with the ex-president. Bill, in his Thinsulate parka, horn-rimmed glasses, and a newsboy cap mashed low on his head could easily be mistaken for one of the CCNY professors who were increasingly moving into Harlem Heights.

"I'm ashamed to admit it," Bill said, pointing across at Hamilton Grange, "but it wasn't until 1993 that I even knew this old house was here in Harlem. When Bruce Babbitt came on board as Secretary of the Interior, he briefed me on all our national memorials. Despite Hamilton's historical significance and the home's provenance, Bruce said the place was mostly ignored and one step above a neighborhood eyesore. Neighbors were just starting to petition the government to turn it into a national historic site."

When the traffic cleared, they crossed the street and stood a moment in front of the venerable old building, which sat solidly behind a wrought iron fence. Scattered landscape lighting and a variety of maturing trees and shrubs dotted the site.

"Chief, you should have been here the day movers and magicians—because that's really what those engineers were— eased this old beauty around the corner then halfway down this steep hill. I call it 'Miracle on 142nd St.'"

"Yeah, when we bought our townhouse, my buddy Gordon showed me some photos and the video of the move. Houses get relocated with some frequency, but that old gal was jammed so tight between the church and apartment house, it looked like a sausage stuck inside a cement bun."

"That about describes it."

The two men resumed walking, but halfway up the hill, Bill was slightly out of breath. Ray sometimes forgot that the chief, though fit, was not a young man, and he imperceptibly slowed the pace. After several female students gave Ray the once-over, his famous boss observed, "Am I right that you're getting all the attention tonight?"

Ray laughed and glanced back at a speedy jogger in a red hoodie whose momentum had already carried her halfway down the long hill. "That's good. It means your hat and glasses are doing the trick, and I'm just doing my job, Chief. No rule says you get to have all the fun on these walks."

"Speaking of rules, what made the Bureau loosen its dress code?"

"Frankly, you shook things up by insisting on more freedom to move around. Since they couldn't start gang-tackling you every time you walked outside your door, they agreed to make some accommodations. Truthfully, they're making more than a few accommodations for you. Take my new threads." Ray looked down at his jeans. "In these clothes, I attract less attention. Besides, no chicks would be looking my way if I still wore a military haircut and dressed like a square."

"Good point," Bill said, laughing. "So the ladies are looking, but are you ever going to let one of them win your heart? Have I mentioned that you spend too much time with old government hacks like me?"

"Chief, you sound like my mother. She tells me nobody gets old and gray wishing they'd clocked more hours on the job; says I need a woman in my life."

"Better listen to Mom."

"I'm working on it, but my moves with the ladies are a bit rusty." Ray again checked his pace. "If it's any consolation, they call this incline, 'Killer Hill.' In the old days, horse-drawn wagons with full loads couldn't get up this hill. They had to use 145th Street."

"No surprise there. This old horse is barely making it."

Ray had always been Bill's favorite agent. A homegrown, nut-brown package of brains and brawn, he once lived on 156th Street and Amsterdam Avenue and still had ties to this neighborhood. Like many agents, he was a former college athlete. Unlike others, Ray's sport was boxing, which left him with quick hands, catlike movements, and uncanny instincts for fighting his way out of tight corners.

"Chief," he said, "if you don't have a preference for tonight's walk, I want to show you one of my favorite spots in Harlem. It's behind the college. You game?"

Bill eyed a bank of fast-moving dark clouds, but answered, "Hell, just being on a public street makes me happy as a kid in a candy store. So yeah, I'm up for seeing something special. What'd you have in mind? I hope it's not the site of more luxury condos."

"You and me both. No, it's just a great view of Harlem and brings to mind so much of its history. You can also catch a different angle of where the big celebration for Hamilton will be held." As they walked, Ray explained that the neighborhood was preparing to celebrate the life of Alexander Hamilton, not only a significant founding father, but one of Harlem's most cherished past inhabitants.

Along the way, they bumped into Nathan Carmody and his young daughter, Taylor, who was attempting to make her frisky new puppy walk on a long retractable leash. Catching up to them, Bill said, "Nathan, ever think of starting him with a shorter leash? At least that worked with all our dogs."

"Oh, Bill, hi. Didn't recognize you. Hello, Ray." Turning to his daughter, Carmody asked, "Taylor, do you remember Mr. Clinton and his assistant, Mr. Hairston?"

Taylor waved, then stooped for the puppy and struggled to hold it up to Bill. "This is Lola. We got her last week. She's three months old."

Bill ruffled Lola's floppy ears. "Sorry. I bet Lola didn't like me calling her a boy."

"Oh, that's okay; she doesn't speak English," Taylor said, drawing smiles from the men. "But my mom's going to take her to dog school."

Rolling his eyes, Nathan sighed. "The sooner, the better. Come on, Taylor. We gotta get you ready for bed. Thanks for the tip, Bill. I'll try the leash idea."

Intent on watching the puppy drag Taylor home, Bill had to sidestep an older couple who inched down the middle of the sidewalk, the man supported by a three-prong cane. "Good evening, folks," he said to the senior citizens before turning back to Ray. "Nice family, the Carmodys. By all accounts, he's the driving force behind CCNY's capital campaign, and from what I hear, he's a heck of a fundraiser."

"Yep. He's one of the many good things happening in Harlem."

"Obviously, you've got a pulse on the community. Mind if I ask how I'm perceived? I'm curious, because I know questions are being asked about my decision to buy in Harlem Heights. I wonder if people approved."

"Oh, there were some raised eyebrows, but this wouldn't be Harlem if we didn't have contrarians. Sorry, but it's true."

"No, it's okay. I wanted an honest assessment."

"But, hey, people remember 2001, when the community was going down the tubes and you opened your Harlem office. That was big. Things started changing for the good."

Both men smiled at the memory, then Ray added, "Back in 2011, folks were miffed when you moved the bulk of your office downtown."

"Yeah, I know. I've heard all the conspiracy theories. My charitable work was off the chart and I needed express access to the airports. You can't bring helicopters onto 125th Street when important donors and dignitaries fly in and only have one hour to hear your presentation.

"I hope any ill will from the office move is offset by us buying the house. When I learned the block was once known as Mistress Row, for the city's plutocrats and their relatives, I couldn't resist. Before he was killed, financier James Fisk held the rights to a lot on our street to build a hideaway for his mistress, Josie Mansfield, and their illegitimate daughter. Supposedly the daughter briefly lived in our house in the 1920s."

"Yeah, I'd heard some of that, but mostly about Striver's Row, on 137th and 138th. Harlem went a little nuts in the Roaring Twenties: wild orgies, scandals, even a sensational murder."

"Oh, hell, yeah. The Evelyn Nesbitt murder was part of the story in Ragtime. I remember gobbling up that book."

"Chief, today it would be hard to throw one of those all-night garden parties that spills over to the rooftop. Craziness and crime is way down. Too many unmarked cars now patrol this neighborhood. That keeps your neighbors happy and makes my job easier, if you know what I mean."

"Yes and no, but connect the dots, in case I'm missing the

obvious."

These days, the 30th Precinct mainly worries about traffic jams from tour buses and rubberneckers trying to peek in your window."

"If I'm making that kind of difference, I don't know what to say; it's humbling."

"Don't say a thing. C'mon, let's get on campus before we get rained out."

The work day was over, and a mostly empty number-three bus rumbled up the tree-lined avenue as Bill and Ray passed under the Alexander Hamilton Gate onto the northern part of City College campus. In front of Shepherd Hall, a few evening students braved damp chill to smoke and compare notes. At the Administration Building, a noisy quartet of backpack-laden kids burst through the door, their arms playfully linked. Bill felt Ray tense and shift his weight as the kids skipped past them.

"What was that about?" Bill asked. "Don't you guys ever relax?"

"Just instincts kicking in. They blasted out of that building pretty damn quick."

"But those girls were just goofing around." Bill checked behind them.

"We know that now," Ray agreed, also looking back. "This seems like a light-duty assignment with me dressing down and all, but when I'm with you, it's still the real deal."

Bill thought about his security from the other man's perspective. "I appreciate how the Secret Service has given me some space, but I'm not sure they had a choice. I'd rather you shoot me now than go back into another tight-security bubble, unless, of course, I'm with Hillary."

"You made that loud and clear after Mrs. Clinton was elected, and I respect that, sir. But just like always, I have a job to do."

"Thanks, buddy. That reminds me. Mattie was off today, and I didn't want to ask the other agents about my place being fingerprinted. I know if they'd found something, you'd have told me."

"You'd not only have heard," Ray replied, laughing in a way that didn't sound funny, "but the Bureau, NYPD—all of us— would be on the hot seat for allowing a breach in your home security."

"If you were so sure the investigation would amount to nothing, how did Mattie persuade you to dust for prints?"

"What? Her threatening to quit on the spot wasn't enough?" Sensing an undercurrent to the flip comment, Bill waited.

In time, Ray responded. "Harlem is filled with women like Mattie who navigate by gut instinct and mother wit. You don't brush them off. They're survivors, not scaredy-cats." Ray studied his boss. "Sure you can't remember how the TV got on or if anything unusual happened lately?"

"Just what I already told you about that reporter, Brad Davis, who approached Mattie on the street and asked how she liked working for me. If I know Mattie, by the time she finished dressing him down, he regretted the question. But that's the only thing I can think of, unless ..." Bill laughed. "... it was a ghost."

"In his defense," Ray said, ignoring Bill's ghost joke and getting back to a more likely suspect, "Davis lives around here. After you mentioned that incident with Mattie, I had him checked out. Lately he's been freelancing. He has trouble finding work because of some bad judgment calls. Otherwise, he came up clean."

"For the most part," Bill said, "I can't complain about the media. Around here, they've been treading lightly, but one bad apple can spoil everything."

"If you feel that way," Ray offered, "I'll dig a little deeper. My little brother still shoots hoops with some of these local dudes. What they know would put my mother and her gossipy friends to shame. I'll find out what I can."

It was another half block before Ray broke a companionable silence to point out Aaron Davis Hall, the university's performing arts center. That prompted Bill to ask, "Didn't there used to be a famous outdoor theater on campus?"

"Yeah, through the 1960s," Ray explained, "before they conceived a real performance center, Lewisohn Stadium was used as a summer amphitheater for classical concerts. When the mood around here was turning to 'Burn Baby Burn,' white folks still rode the 'D' train to Harlem to hear the Philharmonic play Beethoven. When my mom told me that story, I didn't believe her."

Bill zipped his jacket against a damp wind that stirred up a small eddy of remaining fall leaves. After pondering Ray's comment, he said, "Yes, I see why whites would still come here during troubled times. A long time ago, when I discovered this place, it got hold of my heart and wouldn't let go."

"Is that why you bought your house?"

"That's part of it; something drew me here. I love my house, but my soul tells me I'm meant to be here."

"I guess that explains it."

"What?"

"Why Toni Morrison called you the 'first black president.' You've got soul." In the waning light, Ray didn't notice Bill's loopy grin.

"Chief, let's cut through here. What I want you to see is down this way."

About thirty yards ahead, the men emerged onto a quiet, tree-lined terrace that overlooked St. Nicholas Park. Leading Bill to the fence, Ray pointed to the Hamilton Grange, sitting below them. "That's odd," Ray said, about the back windows on the third floor. "Since you're in residence at your place, the National Park Service couldn't be planning an event at the house or we'd have heard, so I guess one of the rangers left a few lights on."

"Probably," Bill said, more interested in the view of Harlem's lighted streets that stretched before him. "Once, when I was in college," he said, "a buddy and I blew off Friday classes and took the train up here from DC to hear Miles Davis perform at a jazz club. When he played 'My Funny Valentine,' the tonal quality was so true, it sounded like words, not notes, tumbling out of his horn. I'll never forget it."

"Miles is one of the anointed; he's immortalized in the annals of jazz. Sir, you're a better student of history than I am but, with all due respect, many historians have been slow to disseminate information about significant black people." Ray stopped talking and held out his hand. "The rain is falling a little faster. Come on, I'd better get you out of this weather. On the way back I'll fill you in on more details about the upcoming August event."

CHAPTER 5

A HOUSE BECOMES A HOME

Once the phones stopped ringing and they decided to invite friends for dinner, their New York getaway was falling into place. Now, as he watched Hillary sip a cold glass of Chardonnay, Bill could almost see the tension slip from her shoulders.

Resting on the couch, bare feet on Bill's lap, Hillary murmured, "I'm glad you insisted on this house."

"Me too, but I wish you'd tell Gordon that tonight. He still thinks you're mad at him for encouraging me to buy it."

"Well, he's way off base. My issues with Gordon have nothing to do with owning this historic home."

"Oh? Don't I recall you claiming it wasn't presidential enough?"

"Well, it wasn't," Hillary said in her defense. "And now it is."

"That's what a couple of hundred thousand dollars will do; make my wife happy."

Pulling her feet back, Hillary sat up and hugged her knees. "Bill, we're out of debt now and more comfortable than I ever imagined possible, so what's that comment supposed to mean?"

"Nothing. I guess all that talk about decorating the White House left me in a sour mood, but I'm serious about Gordon. Try to say something nice to him, okay?"

"Gordon's ego is large enough to weather a little bruising. Besides, I was never mad at him, just panicked at the thought of buying a new house during the campaign. The way politics works now, you can hardly go to the bathroom without it causing a scandal."

"I told you, whether the election was a win, lose, or draw, I wanted this house and even agreed to work with the contractors."

"Sometimes it's not that simple. And just out of curiosity, do you know how many times we've moved?"

"Six, maybe seven?"

"Try twelve on for size. Of course I'm not complaining about being back in the White House," she said, smiling.

Just then, Mattie appeared with a tray of stuffed mushrooms and tiny quiches, prompting Hillary to sit straighter, smooth her hair, and stare at the bright blue thing in their housekeeper's hands. While she tried placing its origin, Bill checked out the mushrooms, helping himself to two fat ones.

"Mattie, I haven't seen that before," Hillary said, laughing nervously. Where'd you find a plastic flowered tray? Is it one of ours?"

"Nope. Couldn't find one in your pantry. I barely had time to run to the deli for dinner and taxi to Costco for these hors d'oeuvres. I asked the cabbie to swing by my house so I could grab a tray. If you like it, you can keep it. I bought it last summer at Dollar More."

While Hillary seemed at a loss for words, Bill stood up and gave Mattie a hug. "Mattie, I love you. You're a woman after my own mother's heart."

Their housekeeper was dressed in her usual finery, a stipulation she laid down when Bill and the Secret Service first vetted her for the job. Tonight she wore a gold lamé pants suit with coordinated gold slides.

During the initial interview, Mattie had taken a firm stand. "I've done domestic work for many years, and never have I worn a maid's uniform. I don't plan to start now," she'd explained, "so if you can't handle a black working-class woman who dresses up to do housework, say so now." Mattie was a constant thorn in the Secret Service's side, but as far as Bill was concerned, her wardrobe comment had sealed the deal, and he never looked back.

After she left the room, Bill whispered, "Stop being anal, Hillary. You're supposed to be enjoying yourself. Mattie takes good care of the house. So what if she's a little unconventional."

Hillary sighed. "You're right. Forget protocol. Maybe I should try being more like her."

When the doorbell rang, Mattie popped back in. "Does Mr. Vernell still drink Chivas on the rocks?"

"Loves the stuff," Bill knew to answer, "and if I'm not mistaken, Angie takes white wine, same as Hillary. When you bring drinks, I'll have a small glass of Merlot. A little red wine helps keep my blood pressure under control. I'll get the door," he added.

"Mr. V will have to settle for Dewars tonight. I'd have sworn there was a full fifth of Chivas in the liquor cabinet," Mattie said accusingly. "Now there's barely two fingers remaining. Sorry."

"Dewars is fine," Hillary said and hurried to catch Bill, who was greeting the stylish twosome in their front hall.

"Good to see you, pal. It's been a while." Bill offered his hand to Gordon, hugged Angie, and collected their jackets since Mattie had disappeared.

"You two are a sight for sore eyes, and sweethearts for coming on short notice." Hillary pecked Angie's cheek and brushed against the buttery softness of her friend's cashmere sweater set, which was similar to the one she wore. "Angie, you're as pretty as ever, and I just love your cowboy boots."

Turning to Gordon, she shook his hand. "Always a pleasure," he said, agreeably.

"Hillary, you're getting rave reviews ... and those surprising cabinet appointments!" Angie gushed and clasped her hands. "I know it was a hard decision, but thank heavens you decided to run, despite the constant attacks and double standard that's always applied to you. The country is impressed with your out-of-the-box thinking. Every president before you has been too pigheaded to be so original. Leave it to the first woman, right?" Angie then turned to Bill. "What do you think about all this? Isn't your wife something?"

"She's something," he agreed. "I think—"

"Bill's understandably a bit envious," Hillary chimed in, then grimaced. "What I mean ..."

Annoyed, Bill faced his wife. "For Pete's sake, Hillary, what are you talking about? I believe your new job is to speak for your country, not your husband."

"Honey, I only meant ... I mean, all the meetings you've endured on my behalf, the protocol updates you hate. But I just can't do all that stuff anymore. You know what I mean?" Bill just stood there.

After a few seconds, Angie asked loudly, "Aren't those hors d'oeuvres?" and moved toward the living room where the mushrooms and untouched quiches awaited. She popped a quiche in her mouth with a satisfied, "Yummy."

Her mouth full, she said, "A fabulous retreat, Bill, and I love that piece of kitsch." She pointed at Mattie's tray, eliciting a snort from the hostess.

"Pure Americana. If Warhol were alive today, it's just the kind of thing he'd be into. Instead of soup cans or Coke bottles, he'd immortalize the twenty-first century's two-pound megaburger and the profusion of *tchotchkes* like that."

Though still annoyed, Bill appreciated Angie's effort to wipe Hillary's comment off the floor. After a while, he said, "Don't leave out America's best-selling vegetable, large fries, and a thirty-six-ounce cola to wash it down."

Everyone laughed longer than necessary. Then they waited for Bill, the usual life of any party, to toss off another one-liner, but he appeared lost in private thought. Mattie rescued them by coming to freshen their drinks.

Hillary dutifully steered the conversation to the simple beauty of their New York living arrangement. "Can you imagine having a last-minute get-together like this in Washington? Here, they let me slip in and out without all the fanfare we have in DC. If only I could come more often. It took me a while to buy into this piece of property." Pointedly looking at Gordon, she added, "I didn't think we needed this place, but now I'm grateful to be part of a community that has welcomed us so warmly."

When her husband failed to speak or acknowledge that

she'd kept her promise to play nice with the company, Hillary switched topics.

"But enough about me. As you know," she joked, "the press is happy to acquaint you with my every move. This evening is for having fun."

After dinner the couples helped Mattie clear dishes. Angie, a gallery owner and "reformed attorney," as she referred to herself, shared her excitement about a promising new Midwestern artist. Conversation drifted from art galleries to the Chagall exhibit at the Guggenheim, and everyone chatted amicably.

Despite the evening's informality, the Vernells were well acquainted with presidential protocol. As hands on the mantle clock reached ten o'clock, Gordon, who usually made timely noises about departure, stayed hunkered in the corner nursing cold coffee while studying his buddy, the ex-president.

"Bill," he said finally, "if we're not wearing out our welcome, I'd like a quick word with you before we go."

"Sure, why not? You can try one of my Ashton cigars; it'll blow you away." Bill stood, straightened the crease in his slacks, and, beckoning Gordon to follow, led him into a small, formal office where he sometimes held meetings. Neither man noticed the women exchange looks. "Ladies, excuse us a moment," Bill said.

"Of course you're excused, gentlemen, but if memory serves …" Hillary smiled stiffly. "Last time you two had a private chat involving cigars, it ended with an impeachment."

Stopping in his tracks, Bill spun around. "For God's sake, Hillary. What the hell's going on here? Must you keep poisoning the atmosphere? Come on," he snapped at Gordon.

Inside his office, Bill angrily flipped switches before bright overhead light flooded the book-lined room. Settling in the leather chair his host indicated, Gordon surveyed some of Bill's awards, plaques, and photos, including one of him at a party, jamming on his sax, with Stevie Wonder at the piano.

"Once you navigate the SWAT team stationed outside," Gordon said, "the setup in here is near normal."

"Sorry about all that. The heavy hardware follows Hillary around. Like her, they'll blow out of town in the morning."

"Well, good. I'm glad this place suits you. I thought it would."

"I like it. What's on your mind?"

"You were uncharacteristically quiet tonight. Everything okay?"

"I'm fine. I'm great."

"If you say so. But tell me, while Hillary runs the country, how are you spending time?"

"Doing anything I can to avoid that 'first gentleman' crap at the White House. Right now, the best thing I can do is stay the fuck out of Washington until they get the message. Since our situation is unprecedented, the staff is figuring this out. Unfortunately, I'm the guinea pig.

"Other than that, I stay busy with the foundation. Our Schools Project in Haiti is doing pretty well, but like everything nowadays, I suddenly have to "get approval" before making a public appearance on behalf of education in other countries." Then remembering his book, Bill added, "And I write a fair amount."

"Last week," he said, "I ate lunch with Mary Townsend. I'm sure you remember Mary."

"Vaguely. But, listen. I need a favor. You remember I'm board chair of the Harlem Hospital Foundation."

"Vaguely," Bill said, but the sarcasm was lost on Gordon.

"You probably don't know I'm also honorary chair for one of their upcoming events. It's a fundraiser, but we're also raising awareness for sick kids who need foster and permanent homes. I thought this might be a cause you could rally behind, and, based on what you said about traveling to Haiti, I'm right. This is something that will benefit you and the kids in Harlem. Besides, I kind of let things slide and need to recruit a spokesperson with name recognition."

"I don't know, Gordon. Things are kind of unsettled right now. Maybe some other time."

"Ah, come on." Standing and walking across the room, Gordon playfully punched Bill in the chest. "It's no big deal; you've got the time. All you have to do is show up, wave to the crowd, perhaps make a little noise in a month or two."

Moving to his desk, Bill switched on a table lamp and pulled a box of cigars from a drawer. "When is this thing?" he asked.

"Next Thursday night."

"Damn late, don't you think, for an important cause? How many people already turned you down?"

"Look, it's not what you think. Pure and simple, time just got away from me. You know how I am. I'm on too many boards to keep all my obligations straight."

Bill put the cigars back and slammed the drawer. "My answer is no."

After an awkward silence, Gordon said, "Okay, if the tables

were turned, I might do the same thing. But I'd say no because, unlike you, I don't take to kids. They don't like me; never have and never will."

"Then I guess that's another one of your shortcomings."

"Look, man, can you cut me some slack? I'm being straight with you. This'll be the fourth fundraiser I've chaired in the last six weeks, and I don't have the United States government and a large office staff at my disposal. Nobody's keeping score, but if you want to figure who owes whom, remember I tried everything in my power to bail your ass out of that 1998 mess before it exploded."

Turning to face his old friend, Bill said, "If you're trying to win me over, you have a helluva way of showing it."

Gordon sighed and rose to his feet. "Sorry to bring that up. Extending his hand, he asked, "Will you at least consider it?"

Instead of taking Gordon's hand, Bill punched him lightly on the shoulder. "Call me tomorrow. I'll see how I feel then."

Ten minutes later, as the door closed on their guests, Hillary put her arm through Bill's, and when he didn't respond, she looked at him. "I have no idea what got into me. I acted like a jerk."

"Yep, you could say that."

After a beat, she said, "Earlier, I used the word 'envious,' but that doesn't describe what I detect in you, although I'd be hard pressed to come up with the right word. And will you ever forgive me for speaking so carelessly in front of company?"

Hugging her back, he rested his chin on her head. "Hillary, the sad part is not that you called me envious, but that it's true."

She let go and stepped back. "It is?"

"Yes," he confided, "but I don't covet your job, not that I don't sometimes fondly recall my days in the Oval Office."

"Honey, it's natural to look back."

"Natural, maybe, but counterproductive, although that's what ex-presidents do. No, I don't envy your job. What I envy is your purposefulness, how you can be in charge. And, by the way, you exude the utmost confidence, despite being so new. In a way, my eight years in office were like an internship for you, and that's another one of my legacies.

"As for me," he continued, "for the last ten to fifteen years, I could pretty much do whatever I wanted. Now I have to constantly be aware of the presidency again, but without being president. That's weird. It's also hard to do right, although for some reason, buying this place has restored some balance. Harlem is the real world. It's grounding."

Anticipating more, Hillary didn't interrupt and followed her husband into the living room. With Mattie gone and the house locked down, their footsteps on the terrazzo tile suddenly sounded loud.

Reclaiming his seat on the couch, he kicked off his loafers and placed his feet on the table. "By the way," he said, "you can relax. Gordon only asked me to put my name behind some kind of Harlem Hospital children's cause."

"That's sounds perfect," she concurred. "Despite gentrification, there are still thousands of children in Harlem who need services and better schools." Reaching for her wine glass, she found it empty. "Hmmm, that's odd. I thought I'd topped it off." Somewhat distracted, she said, "I think you hit on something vital a moment ago."

"What?"

"What you said about Harlem, balance, and the real world."

"What about it?"

"Your optimism was one thing that attracted me to you. That, and your commitment to the greater good."

"Not my good looks and sex appeal?" he joked.

"Oh, you had plenty of that. Still do, but seriously," she said, plopping down next to him. "You've never lost your optimism, even during the worst times, so please don't ever lose it. Joining Gordon's charity would be good for you. It's mission-driven for the homeland. What did you tell him?"

Yawning, Bill rubbed his eyes. "I said I'd think about it."

CHAPTER 6

BLESSED ARE THE CHILDREN

The security team ushered Bill and Gordon through a set of the hospital's double doors. The event, already underway, was being held in a large multi-purpose area that was now filled with guests seated at rented chairs and tables.

Because of a robbery in the area, Bill had been advised to skip dinner and now arrived while dessert was being served. He and Gordon were directed to a reserved table near a side exit where they quietly slipped into two empty chairs awaiting them. Neither they nor most of the other guests noticed the small group of children who'd also gathered in an adjourning room that was separated from the diners by folding screens. Before the business end of the program began, an animated young man with a guitar walked out on the portable stage and commanded the audience's attention.

"Ladies and gentleman, welcome to Harlem Hospital, and thank you for coming. It is my pleasure to emcee this important fundraising event for the children who live here at the hospital.

For those of you who may not know me, my name is Christos, and in a few minutes I'll tell you a story, because I was once a boarder baby at a neighboring New York City hospital called Bellevue, just down the road. Many of you know it. But now, if you look to your left, you will see that our guests of honor have briefly joined us this evening."

"Are you having fun yet, kids?" He directed his question to the room on his left. Cupping his ear, he listened until a barely audible chorus of tiny voices answered, "Yes."

"Come on. You can do better than that," he coaxed the group of children who had been allowed to come downstairs for dessert and listen to Cristos play a half-hour concert. But the children were also there to make a point with the well-heeled crowd concerning the need to do more for foster care. Feigning an exaggerated frown, the singer yelled, "Hey, let's get the grownups involved, and everyone tell me in louder voices if you're having fun!" This time, a resounding, "Yes!" filled the room.

"That's better!" he shouted, cheering the second-joint effort. Then, with restless jeweled fingers, he strummed a chord on the gold-toned guitar slung around his neck. "Okay, now, I'm going to sing one of my favorite songs, and if I don't hear you clapping and joining in on the chorus, I'm coming down there to get you. "So listen up, kids. I'll tell you when ...

'La Paz en el mundo

Peace in the world

We the people pray for peace

America, Mexico, Greece.'

Here we go. Say it, boys and girls, ladies and gentlemen: 'America, Mexico, Greece.' That's the way," he told them, as a sweet cacophony echoed the words.

Without missing a beat, Bill joined the spirited gathering that swayed and clapped to the lively rhythms as Christos went into a medley of songs. Though off to the side, Bill and Gordon had a clear view of the young entertainer, a dreadlocked artist of indeterminate ethnic origin, whose baggy outfit facilitated the loose-limbed ease of his dance steps. Bill leaned toward Gordon. "Psst, who is this guy? He's terrific." Gordon shrugged, palms up. "Some guy named Christos is all I know."

"Okay," Bill said over the music. "I'll check it out later." As the brief set continued, Bill's admiration grew for a style of funky music that fused jazz, rap, reggae, and soul. When the music ended, the crowd roared its approval, and Bill went right along with whistles and hoo-hoo-hoos pouring from young and old. Damn, that kid can play some music, he thought, suddenly feeling better about attending this event. Christos then told the crowd, without noticeable emotion, about his abandonment and two subsequent years of living at Bellevue until he was lucky enough to be adopted.

The audience was subdued when the lights came up, and waiters finished serving coffee. Before the next speaker began, Gordon, in a loud voice—the one Bill recognized as standard fare when a bunch of attorneys gathered—quickly introduced Bill to six other people at their table.

In his practiced way, the ex-president energetically shook hands with three Woolbank and Mills litigators and their spouses. "The pleasure's mine. Honored to be here. Great cause we're supporting tonight," he told them.

Bill avoided eye contact with one guy named Frank, whom he remembered meeting two summers ago at a beach party on

Martha's Vineyard. The stout, gray-haired Mrs. who presently accompanied Frank definitely wasn't the same luscious, thirty-something redhead who had played kissy-face with Frank that night on the beach.

Bill was saved from further awkwardness with Frank when an exuberant full-figured woman in a bronze wig startled his security team and popped over, from two tables away, to smother him into her bosom. After years of deftly fending off supporters, he laughed good-naturedly and cleverly untangled himself, as his embarrassed bodyguards escorted the woman back to her seat.

"So happy to see y'all," he said and waved to the woman's table, blowing kisses at her giddy friends, before settling back into his chair that Gordon held out for him.

Up on stage, Christos introduced a woman, Mabel Upchurch, who was the hospital's head social worker. "Ladies and gentlemen," she said, "put your hands together in appreciation for Christos Barton Herrera, a rising star and one of America's most generous supporters and spokespersons for needy children."

After the thunderous applause died down, the noise level on the floor failed to quiet. "Ladies and gentlemen, boys and girls," the woman continued, "from the commotion around table two, I see some of you have already discovered that we have another very special guest with us this evening.

"Please welcome President Bill Clinton, who is also an ardent supporter of tonight's cause." After a gasp of surprise and a collective craning of necks from those who hadn't spotted him, a whoop of joy erupted from the Clinton-friendly audience. The silver-haired ex-president acknowledged the applause by flashing his famous grin and vigorously pumping both arms in a campaign-style victory wave.

"Now I must ask you," the woman rushed ahead, trying to quell the stir, "to please take your seats. We need," she said, struggling to be heard, "we need to get to the most pressing part of the evening. Remember that our young patients, tonight's real stars, have a curfew." At the mention of kids, Bill, red-faced with appreciation, sat back down, the room quieted, and Mabel began her prepared words.

Bill noticed for the first time that the kids in the adjoining alcove were not all ambulatory or healthy; a few were in wheelchairs. He marveled that for this special occasion, two others had been brought down in their hospital beds. Bill watched as Christos circulated among them, offering soft high fives, then posing for pictures.

Suddenly, Bill felt an urge to get into that room, but he also knew that Christos' special moment with the kids shouldn't be interrupted, so he refocused on the social worker, who was reciting a series of statistics. "… thousands of youngsters in foster care … the majority are black and Hispanic … approximately one quarter are eligible for adoption …

"And the children in the next room …" she paused, using a fountain pen to direct their attention to what Bill was already observing. "Some of these children are medically fragile," she said, exhaling in a labored way that made Bill wonder if the woman herself was ill.

"At Harlem Hospital they're known as 'boarder babies.'" Listening intently, Bill was struck by the speaker's appearance. Her sunken chest, lank hair, and the floppy scarecrow quality of her movements added urgency to the message. The woman also had a whiff of the same lonely abandonment she so ably described in her young charges.

"Yes, we want you to open your checkbooks tonight," she continued, "but if you could also open your hearts and consider becoming a foster or adoptive parent, that is our greatest need."

As she concluded her remarks, Gordon, who was also table captain, reached under the centerpiece and produced a folder with 'Foster Care Cooperative' colorfully scrawled across the front in a child's uneven handwriting. Inside were pledge cards, postage-paid envelopes, and slick three-fold flyers reemphasizing the crisis in foster care. The back page had a non-descript photo of Bill Clinton standing in front of a podium. There was also a flattering picture of Christos surrounded by children.

Bill picked up the flyer and wondered who had authorized the use of his photo so quickly.

Having done his part, Gordon sat back down and answered a few of his partners' questions. Frank, in a hurry to leave, immediately pulled out a checkbook. Bill didn't carry a checkbook, but wrote a generous amount on his pledge card and passed it to Gordon.

"So what do you think?" Gordon asked, interrupting Bill's reading of a handout.

"Think about what?"

"Are you willing to lend your name to the cause? The name Bill Clinton could make a big difference in fundraising efforts."

"It's a done deal, Gordon. I'm already in. You even used my photo."

"Yeah, Gertie cleared it for us, and I'm glad to hear you're in on this one." Gordon beamed and clamped a hand with its manicured nails on Bill's shoulder. "You just made my day.

Landing you means I've closed the door on at least one project."

"Look here a minute." Bill waved the information he held. "It says that this Christos fella is an active spokesperson for foster children. The guy gives concerts all over the globe, often donates the proceeds, and connects with all ages. If he can't attract more foster and adoptive families with his music, youth, and personal story, what do you think I can do?"

"Trust me, you can do plenty." Changing the subject, Gordon asked, "You want to stick around to shake hands, or are you ready to take off?"

"While everyone's filling out pledge cards, I'll take a minute to visit the kids. I see that it's a restricted area over there, but I think they'll let me near them. To get this project off on the right foot, I need to at least meet my constituents. I'd also like a few words with Christos; he's an impressive fellow."

Upon entering the makeshift pediatric ward, Bill counted eleven children ranging in ages from preschool to about ten, in various hues of brown; a few appeared to be mixed-race.

Immediately, he was humbled by the spirit of a child walking around while rolling the IV drip attached to his arm. Drawing closer, he realized that this room was ordinarily an employee cafeteria; the back wall, lined with personnel announcements, also had vending machines and folded-up tables pushed to the side.

The most active child in the bunch was a little guy who screeched, "Zoom zoom zoom!" while hell-bent on racing his wheelchair-bound friend around the room. Both boys had freshly cut, close-cropped hair, identical khakis, and white shirts marked by chocolate stains.

With Christos apparently departed, Bill shook hands with

two assistants who came over to ask for autographs, then settled his attention on an efficient-looking young lady whose name tag read, "Lorna Johnson, RN." After she corralled the race car driver, Bill caught up with her, needlessly introduced himself, and asked, "Who's the budding NASCAR star?"

Lorna, as distracted as any classroom teacher with active charges, chanced a quick shy glance at the ex-president and said, "Excuse me, Mr. President. There he goes again."

When she returned a few minutes later, he saw dewy perspiration on her pretty face.

"Is this bunch always so active?"

"It's been very busy over here this evening." She spoke in a friendly manner, but kept her eyes peeled for trouble. "Sick kids can be just as wired as healthy ones."

"So these are the children who need foster or permanent homes?"

"Yes, though a few are too sick to leave just yet."

"What's the story with the speed demon you just banished to time-out?"

"Oh, thanks for reminding me. That's Alonzo. His three minutes are about up." She hurried toward the child who'd remained where he'd been placed, but who now appeared subdued, his motor having run down.

"I'll bring him to meet you."

Lorna coaxed the boy over. "Alonzo, say hi to President Clinton."

"Hi, I'm Alonzo," the boy recited automatically, extending his hand and flashing a rehearsed smile, the way he'd been coached to respond to prospective foster or adoptive parents. "But, you're white," Alonzo added knowingly. "You can't be a daddy to me, so you must be a new doctor."

"Well, you're a pretty smart boy, but I'm not sure you're right about that." Bill covered his surprise at the young child's piercing candor.

Figuring he knew a doctor when he saw one, Alonzo turned to Lorna. "Can I go now?"

"Go ahead, sweetheart. Cindy will be down to get you in a minute. But no more running."

"Bye," he waved, remembering his manners.

Unsettled, Bill returned the child's wave and turned to Lorna. "Whew. That's quite a kid. Are they all so frank about their situation?"

"For the most part, yes. But Alonzo's extremely verbal. I think he skipped baby talk and went straight to adult conversation. He's bright and doesn't suffer fools."

"I can see that, but what's wrong with him? He looks healthy."

"Headaches. Today was a good day, but sometimes he screams in pain because his head hurts."

"Good Lord," Bill uttered. "Is his condition physical or emotional?"

"The doctors think it's physical, but they're still running tests. His young, single mom couldn't cope with the screaming. Neither could his foster parents, so for now, he's staying with us."

In the main room, the thinning crowd had finished filling out pledge cards. Bill couldn't see Gordon, but he knew his host had another engagement and was probably anxious to leave. What Bill also couldn't see was the apparition that had been tailing him all week and that was now hovering above the sound technicians as they broke down electrical equipment.

Bill turned to Lorna. "I know it's near the children's bedtime, but do you have a minute to tell me how a few of these other kids came to be in Harlem Hospital?"

"The staff has been told that you'll be helping the children, so I've been instructed to answer your questions and am happy to tell you what I can." She beamed, obviously pleased. "It was quite an undertaking getting them down here, but if they're a little late getting back upstairs, I think we both know," she said and winked, "the children won't mind a bit."

Lorna was well versed in clinical descriptions but also adept at adding a positive spin to her charges' difficult lives. She directed Bill's attention to Markita, a skinny pinched-faced girl listlessly propped up on her bedcovers. She appeared to be about eight years old and possibly the sickest patient in the room.

"How old is Markita?"

Twelve, and the oldest of our current boarders."

"Twelve? No way. She doesn't look a day older than eight, maybe nine."

"I know," Lorna murmured. "She came to us too late. I'm not sure I should tell even you, but advanced AIDS had already interrupted her growth by the time she came to us."

"Good God. Will she get better?"

"We can always hope."

Bill swallowed the lump in his throat and went over to speak to the sick child. "Want some company?" he asked quietly, but Markita was dozing and failed to acknowledge him. Like Alonzo, most of this crowd didn't see any future in the tall white man who they considered poor parental material, so they ignored him. Lorna briefly rushed through the remaining medical histories.

As he expected, several children with bald heads were receiving chemotherapy; another had a troubling digestive disorder that, for the moment, had doctors stumped, much like the puzzle of Alonzo's headaches.

"What's with the girl in the back corner?" Bill pointed to a light-brown-skinned child sitting on a bench eating a bowl of ice cream while staring in his direction. The front of her hand-decorated black T-shirt had the word "Diva" colorfully spelled in sparkles. The "D" and "i" were crooked, as though the designer needed two tries before mastering a glue gun. Bill supposed decorating with sparkles was this generation's version of tie-dying T-shirts.

"Oh, that's Abby." Lorna sighed, and for the first time a frustrated note crept into this kind woman's voice.

Turning, Bill frowned at the nurse. "Why do you say it like that? Is Abby sicker than Markita? She certainly doesn't look it."

"What she has is hard to even put into words. Abby is what my grandmother calls "an old soul," and sometimes I think that soul has a hole in it. She's so … so willful and stubborn, and for some inexplicable reason, she often gets her way."

He peered at the child. "What would win her over?"

"The right family. She's sabotaged two promising placements. Her exact words were, 'Those homes weren't what my mother would have wanted for me.'"

"Ever think she might know what she's talking about and be holding out for a better deal?"

Lorna laughed mirthlessly. "That's exactly what she's doing, and she can be quite charming in her refusals. But black kids seldom get second chances unless they're infants, and Abby's already seven years old. It's highly unlikely another family will come along, knowing her history."

To Bill's untrained ears, Abby's situation didn't sound all that dire, and on some level, he admired her for setting the bar high. Approaching her perch and aiming for his winningest manner, he said, "Hi, honey." In return, Abby gave him a cool, penetrating stare.

Changing tactics, he introduced himself. "I'm Bill Clinton. Before they throw me out of here, I thought I'd say hello."

The child scrutinized him for several more seconds before surprising both Bill and Lorna. "I know who you are," she said. "You have an office on 125th Street and a house uptown."

"That's right. Did you hear about me in school?"

Lorna, standing behind him, gasped. "How on earth did you manage that?"

"What?"

"To get her to talk to you?"

"I seem to have that effect on women," he deadpanned.

Looking stunned, Lorna waited to see if further conversation might follow. Since Abby appeared to have had her say for the evening, Bill waved goodbye. "It's getting to be both our bedtimes, so goodnight," he told her. "Thanks for inviting me to your party."

The nurse asked, "Will you come back?"

Bill was about to answer when Abby, with a quick intake of breath, said, "Yes, please come back."

CHAPTER 7

A STRANGE PHENOMENON

It was one of those early spring evenings destined to cheer those who'd wearied of winter. Bill cracked open the kitchen door and decided it was warm enough to take coffee on his deck. He looked out over his backyard, then to the right, where he could just see the top floor of the Hamilton Grange Museum.

Behind him, Mattie wiped down the counter, slammed the cabinets shut, then placed a spoon, packets of sweetener, and a creamer with skim milk on a tray. While he waited for the coffee to perk, Bill eased the door ajar for Bootsy, who gracefully tiptoed across the deck and head-butted the gate blocking her way. "I know, I know. You like the yard too," he told the kitten. "Hopefully, by the time you learn to jump, they'll have figured out a way to prevent you from tripping the alarm."

"Here's your coffee, sir." Mattie joined him outside and watched the kitten, who had given up and flopped on her side. You know I don't much care for cats, but this one here has real possibilities. Little devil keeps me company in the kitchen."

"She's a people person, for sure," Bill agreed, and squatted to pet the kitten.

"It's a fine evening to be outdoors, but you need a sweater," Mattie said with her usual lack of deference for what the former president of the United States might want. "I'll just go fetch the one in your study."

"No, no, no." With his knees creaking, Bill slowly got up and gently removed the tray Mattie still held. Her hands were work-worn, each brown knuckle distended by an ongoing battle with arthritis." You'll do no such thing. As it is, you spoil me like a child. Virginia Kelly Clinton, God rest her soul, must be wondering where she went wrong, seeing her oldest son shamelessly waited on by such a good woman. I wasn't always so helpless. Bet you didn't know that when Hillary and I got married, I did the cooking."

"Mr. Clinton, pray tell, what can you cook? I'm still scraping burn off that pot you boiled water in."

"Oh, yeah, sorry," he said sheepishly. "I forgot it was boiling. Guess I didn't do such a good job cleaning it up."

"You didn't, but what did you used to cook?"

"I had a couple of recipes. One was a thing I called 'the blob.'"

"A thing, huh. Will I be sorry for asking what a blob is?"

He laughed. "Maybe. It's two pounds of hamburger meat spread in a pan, then baked for an hour at 350 degrees. Only problem was that Hillary wouldn't eat it."

"Can't rightly blame her now, can you?"

One thing Bill enjoyed about his tart-tongued housekeeper was how she made him laugh, like now. "Mattie, the gross part was that I fed leftovers to the dog and he loved it, but I got sick as a dog. After that incident, Hillary took over in the kitchen, or we mostly ate cold cuts, if it was my turn to do dinner."

When Mattie failed to see the humor, Bill said, "It's almost seven forty. No more fussing in the kitchen. If you don't get going, you'll miss your favorite reality show. The car has been waiting ten minutes."

"Oh, forget him," she said, using her fingernail to rub a sticky spot off the deck table. "He shows up early just to aggravate me. Besides, I told him, 'As much money as President Clinton pays you to drive me, you better sit tight and do right,' as my daddy used to say. But I'll be on my way now, sir." Her plastic tote bag sat waiting inside the door. It was Mattie's version of the carryall favored by women in New York who were experts at being prepared for life's little surprises.

"Leave your dishes," she called over her shoulder. "I'll wash up in the morning."

He waved and picked up the tray with his already cooled decaf and one of Mattie's Duncan Hines brownies. One brownie wouldn't hurt. Just one though, he reminded himself. "Well, maybe two," he said aloud, glancing back at the pantry where extras were stored.

Tonight he needed to stop procrastinating and get to work on the second volume of his autobiography. Bill wished he'd better expressed himself with his agent. Bob assumed his trouble was in finding material. Maybe that was part of it, but in truth, having to now defer to White House protocol left him feeling a little irrelevant. Having had the most vital job in the world was thrilling, but few men in his position wrote honestly about how they felt after leaving office, and certainly never from a first gentleman's point of view.

Out on the deck, he took comfort in the coming beauty of his surroundings. Soon-to-flower shrubs cleverly disguised a sophisticated perimeter alarm system that detected unusual movement. His lot was narrow, but a southwestern exposure would allow bougainvillea and wisteria to thrive on the back brick wall, creating what the landscape architect said would soon be a French garden effect. Daffodils and tulips were already budding, and in June, hyacinths, his favorite flower, would bloom.

He stood up and looked at the back wall, wondering if something other than trellises was out there. A breeze stirred the naked vines, creating shadows along the wall. Blinking a few times, Bill looked from the wall to the sensors behind him, but nothing flashed.

Two security men were posted in the back alley, but Bill stood up and was about to go inside to check his kitchen monitors when a figure passed through his back wall and said, "Good evening, Mr. Clinton."

Staring wildly at a slightly built man who stood ten feet in front of him, Bill willed himself to stay calm. With horror, he realized a nutcase had slipped through the defenses. The guy wore a costume: sateen blue knickers, an old-fashioned jacket, buckle-toe shoes, and a tricorne hat over a wig, in the style of an early American gentleman.

Bill's heart thumped, and blood rushed to his ears. Taking shallow breaths, he strained to recall what the Secret Service told him about red-alert situations. "Look to see if he has a weapon, Mr. President," they'd said.

Good; I don't see one on this guy, Bill thought. So now what? Think. Think. If I don't see a gun or knife, do I assume he doesn't have one?

Cursing himself for always ignoring the portable panic button, he warily sized up the intruder, who obviously appeared to be mentally disturbed. Because he was a small guy, Bill chanced a glance left to gauge how far he was from the wall alarm. Too far. The stranger, likewise, studied the former president with great intensity before being the first to break off their staring contest.

"My apologies, President Clinton. I detect great consternation on your part. Please be assured, you have nothing to fear. In fact, I believe you are already somewhat acquainted with me. The circumstances surrounding this visit are highly unusual, I admit, but I am your neighbor and the rightful owner of the home just south of you."

While the intruder waited for a response, Bill raced through his options. The guy was half his size, but twenty or more years younger. No doubt quicker too although he didn't seem like the fighting type. There was even a bit of refinement about him; he was patrician-like, actually, particularly in his speech, unless it was an affectation. Perhaps, thought Bill, a well-bred Brit might speak like him.

Bill's voice was tremulous and higher than usual when he spoke. "This is preposterous. How the hell did you get in my yard? Leave immediately before the entire federal government and NYPD comes down on you."

"If you insist, but I'll just be back another time. You see, I've taken up temporary residence in my former home." He pointed across to the Hamilton Grange.

Dear Lord, Bill prayed. After all my years in public life, I thought I'd seen every variety of crazy. He was scared, but he'd also inched to within three or four feet of the wall alarm, although something stopped him from lunging for the button. Was it the man's intelligence? His lack of guile? The calm matter-of-fact sincerity? And why did his face seem vaguely familiar?

"I don't know who you are, but how in God's name did you get through that wall? It's solid brick! And what do you want?"

"The answer to your first question," the stranger responded with a bow and a flourish of his ridiculous triangular hat, "is that I levitated. You see, I am the ghost of Alexander Hamilton, first secretary of the Treasury of the United States of America, and I am at your service, sir."

Bill slept little that night, as he constantly replayed the eerie encounter on his deck. Desperately he wished it had been a dream, but he knew it wasn't. He strained to recall every detail of a recent conversation with Ray on one of their walks. "Harlem officials expect thousands of tourists and locals," Ray had said about an event planned for founding father Alexander Hamilton. Bill hoped he'd hidden his skepticism when he asked, "If this is such a big happening, why hasn't it been all over the news?"

"That's kind of the point, sir," Ray said, happily launching into what Bill realized was a vitally important subject to his bodyguard. "The community is undertaking this event because Hamilton has never gotten the attention he deserved. Not only did he do more for America than he's credited with, but he also did more to help African Americans than many other founders.

For that, his enemies taunted him with the term, 'nigger lover.' Even John Adams, who was sympathetic to slaves, referred to Hamilton as that 'Creole bastard.'"

"Was he part black?"

"Don't know, but that question's been repeatedly asked over the ages. Supposedly, a DC lab is conducting DNA tests on some black guy who claims to be Hamilton's descendant."

"Wouldn't that be something," Bill said, thinking of the human interest angle, "if after proving Thomas Jefferson fathered black children, DNA then reveals that one of the other founders was a black man."

Unfortunately, just as Bill got interested in Ray's story, the rain picked up, and they hopped into an official car that had been trailing them. Ray hadn't added much more, and Bill had forgotten about the conversation. Until tonight.

Around three in the morning, bleary-eyed, sheets in knots, Bill stumbled to the window, parted the curtain, and peeked out. The Grange was still there, just as it had been for over two hundred years, and nothing about his yard had changed since yesterday, yet a seismic shift had occurred. I'm not losing my mind; I saw the man, he thought despondently. But what had he witnessed? A clever, quick-change artist, or proof that ghosts do exist?

Rather than going to his computer, Bill suddenly thought to check his bookshelves, hoping the book he wanted was in this house. He remembered that it had several images of the founder. Settling on a task calmed him. He slipped on a robe and went downstairs to his study. Among the far-flung work spaces he'd carved out, this cozy, old-fashioned retreat was the one he most cherished.

Turning on a brighter light, he unearthed his reading glasses and started scanning shelves. Ironically, the book Bill searched for had been a Christmas gift from Robert Rubin, his own former treasury secretary. Though he hadn't read it, he remembered the picture of Hamilton on the cover. Rubin had buttonholed Bill at his and Hillary's annual Christmas party, saying, "If you want to know who to thank for endowing America with an economy that the world still envies, be sure to read this."

Fueled by holiday cheer and an eagerness to show off his gift, Rubin had caused Bill to laugh. "Robert, what about the element of surprise? Christmas isn't for two weeks. Can't I wait?"

"No, no. Be my guest. Open it. It's a new biography of Alexander Hamilton." Once Bill peeled off the wrapping, the secretary thumped the cover and said, "Amazing man, this Hamilton. Damn shame he died so young. Read it. It's all in there."

Scanning the bottom shelf, Bill's eyes now locked on the Hamilton biography, and his heart fluttered. Hefting the weighty tome from the shelf, he struggled to his feet and stared at the book. I may not have read this sucker, he thought dismally, but I've met the man on the cover.

CHAPTER 8

GETTING TO KNOW THE PAST

After having spent half the night and most of the next day scouring websites and books on Hamilton, Bill's head hurt, and his eyes were riddled with red. But his marathon research had yielded a better understanding of the founder. Lookalike lithographs were one thing, but they didn't scientifically explain the person—or thing—from last night. He stared again at a portrait in the book, a John Trumbull painting. There was no denying it. Not only was last night's guy or apparition or whatever a dead ringer for Hamilton, but his jacket and blue satin pantaloons were the same outfit worn by the man in the portrait.

Bill forced down a bowl of chowder that Mattie had prepared earlier. It refreshed him somewhat, but as he waited he grew increasingly tense. Tonight the air had more of a nip to it. To make Mattie leave, he'd quickly acquiesced to her suggestion of a sweater. Now a shiver, either from nerves or chilly weather, ran up his spine, making him appreciate the extra layer. But from a movement in his back bushes, he sensed he wouldn't have to wait long. This time he felt no panic, just determination to seek answers for the bizarre occurrence that had left him shaken and sleep deprived.

"Hello, Mr. President," the stranger said as he walked through the wall. "You appear less shocked this evening. Perhaps I have won your trust."

"I'm beyond shocked, Mister ... whoever you are." Bill was confused anew by the visitor's contemporary attire: plain white shirt, well-cut slacks, and navy blazer, all of decent quality.

"I know it's hard to fathom," the stranger said in an understatement for the ages, "but truly, I am Alexander Hamilton, born 1757, died at forty-seven, my forever age. I am without benefit of middle name or initial ..."

"That's of no consequence." Bill cut him off. "What are you doing here, and how did you get here?"

"If you'll permit me to sit down, I'll explain."

Curiosity was one thing, but this time Bill held the panic button in a death grip. Using his left foot, he unceremoniously shoved a wrought iron chair toward the odd little man. Bill watched, incredulous, as his visitor sat and elegantly crossed one well-tailored leg over the other, as if he'd been invited for cocktails.

"As preposterous as this is," he sputtered, "for the moment let's assume you are Hamilton. But before this goes any further, I need some answers."

"Yes, of course. There are two reasons for this excursion. First, I am to be honored for my contribution to America's early governance. It seems the impetus for said celebration was the relocation and refurbishing of my ancestral home." They both looked in the direction of the Grange, and Hamilton said something else. Hardly listening, Bill strained to think of ways to authenticate this … this figure's identity.

"As for my arrival," Hamilton prattled on, "you're aware that God works in mysterious ways. It's not unheard of that the good Lord grants sabbaticals to heavenly beings. Here on earth, as I recall the custom, when unexplained occurrences happen in old homes, earthlings say the edifice is inhabited by a ghost. Actually, in this case, there are two of us, as I'm traveling with Sarafina, my paramour."

With Bill appearing faint, Hamilton sought to reassure his host. "Some of my less fortunate brethren in the netherworld also return to make trouble in the form of evil spirits. That most surely will not be the case with me. Even were I so inclined, and I'm not, heaven breeds all such mischief out of its inhabitants."

To calm himself, Bill breathed deeply, exhaled, then focused on a knothole in the side railing behind Hamilton's head. It was a technique Chelsea had taught him years ago that ballet dancers secretly used to avoid dizziness. Bill felt as if he'd wandered into a fantasy world and, like Alice, was helplessly tumbling into a wonderland of bizarre characters. A girlfriend? Two frickin' ghosts? In the face of such absurdity, he searched for something to say and could only come up with a ridiculous question of his own. "Do you know Raymond Hairston, the Secret Service agent?"

"Perhaps, if you'll explain 'Secret Service agent.' Its meaning might jog my memory of some long-ago acquaintances named Hairston."

They called me Slick Willie, Bill thought, but if this guy is lying, he's smooth as oil.

Not knowing what else to say, Bill answered Hamilton's question. "They're federal law officers who protect the president and ex-presidents. The agency wasn't established until 1865, sixty-one years after your ... um ... death," he said, feeling foolish.

Gathering himself, he continued on a more pertinent track. "Okay, if you're Hamilton and you're here by some miracle or Godly dispensation, why come into my life?"

"Fair enough, Mr. Clinton." The ghost shifted comfortably, and the gesture drew Bill's eyes to the figure's neatly folded hands. They were unscarred and compact, like the rest of his small body, the nails clean and well trimmed.

Hamilton took his time before answering. "I come to you, because who else but you would I seek out? You—and perhaps John Kennedy—were two of the more notable politicians in modern times. Ronald Reagan was also a robust leader, though I wasn't generally in sympathy with his policies. To those of us living in the above, President Obama's election appeared as miraculous, as I apparently appear to you. Though unfortunately thwarted at many turns, Mr. Obama was a visionary who understood the need to rehabilitate this planet. Sir, if I may say so, Earth has seen better days."

With a shift into more familiar territory, Bill felt less uneasy. Though strange, this personage was spellbinding.

"As you might imagine," Hamilton said, "I've had occasion to converse in heaven with two of the aforementioned gentlemen."

Despite wanting to maintain psychic and physical independence from Hamilton, Bill couldn't help blurting out, "Kennedy was my boyhood idol. Who else, may I ask, are you comparing me to?"

"A good question. I refer to all who were president during your lifetime, from Truman on. Your sensible policies are an established fact, especially on the economy, which, as you know, was my area of government."

While Bill waited, Hamilton went on. "You remind me of myself in many ways. We're both born to single mothers, and thus we grapple with feelings of abandonment. Our greatest flaws come from not having what was rightfully ours: the love and attention of the men who sired us. This deficiency has contributed to our vainglory. In your case, vanity follows you like a dark spirit."

"Now, hold on a damn minute, here! What … what … nerve!"

"Mr. Clinton, permit me to continue." With is hand up, Hamilton spoke with authority. "Despite being charismatic, self-made men, we are also polarizing. Personal indiscretions stemming from our sense of entitlement left a blot on our successful political careers. Sir, you are, as I once was, simply human. With gifts such as ours, man must remember that he is not God-like."

Bill sat slumped sideways in his chair; his face, already strained from lack of sleep, was ashen. The only a hint of color showed in the blue orbs of his eyes.

"Sir, I kindly beseech you to bear with me. I believe you will see that I have your best interest at heart." Though Bill's mouth was agape, Hamilton heard no sound and took that as permission to continue. "We're both undisciplined with tendencies toward loquaciousness, yet we are brilliant strategists. We possess the ability to accomplish much for the greater good of man. But, sir, you endangered your legacy much as I did mine."

"I've heard enough. Is there a point to any of this?" Bill asked dully.

"Yes. In many ways, you have righted your ship, but the point, sir, is that powerful men must continually confront their demons. In your case, it's not too late to address this. Trust me; you don't want to wait, as I have, another two hundred years before assuring your rightful place in history."

Bill jumped up and shouted, "Time—" then quickly lowered his voice to avoid attracting the attention of Billy McManus and his partner, on duty in his alley, "—not individuals, decides how presidents and public servants are remembered. Many Americans already feel that I've atoned for past mistakes. I've made gains in establishing a legacy."

"To a degree, you are correct."

"You ... you, whoever you are, stumble in here and profess to know me and presume to help shape my future?"

"Precisely."

Bill stared at his self-appointed analyst. "Well, I'll be damned," was all he could say.

"Not if I can help it," Hamilton retorted.

For the first time in twenty-four hours, Bill understood that something much larger than personal safety was at stake here, and he turned to his garden, looking for solace. He noticed one mushroom light was slightly askew and threw off an eerie glare. Grimly, he wondered if the strange glare was part of God's work in setting the stage for this macabre night.

No longer concerned about physical danger, Bill laid the alarm aside, put both arms behind his head, and closed his eyes. He felt trapped and, worse, manipulated by forces beyond his control. A paranormal tsunami was rushing in, tossing him who knew where, and he was powerless to stop it. Bill spoke softly. "Other than a commitment to government service, we have little in common."

"You know better than that. If nothing else, enemies hounded us relentlessly for infractions that had no consequence on affairs of state. For you, that misrepresentation of justice contributes to your duality—outgoing but inwardly self-serving."

"Why dredge all this up?" Bill asked. "To make this night more difficult than it already is?"

"Certainly not; rather to help you find the ultimate happiness."

"How dare you think you can just drop in and change me."

"Sir, you misunderstand. You, yourself, are the instrument of change."

Oh, fuck this, Bill thought and stood up, signaling that he'd had enough.

"If my presence is burdensome," Hamilton said, "I will disappear and simply wait for Harlem's celebration, but think of the lost opportunities. Imagine what we could learn from each other."

Someone, maybe a poet, once said you could see a man's soul through his eyes. Bill searched Hamilton's face. Although he was no longer sure of anything, Bill didn't think a transcendent being had a soul, but Hamilton's blue eyes sparkled with intelligence and intensity. Looking away, he asked quietly, "Like what could we learn?"

"Why, history, man! I retrace steps leading up to your modern nation, and you walk me through this life. I suspect we'd have great discussions."

Through the open kitchen door, Bill heard the insistent brrring of the phone, but didn't budge. After a half dozen rings, a robotic-sounding voice switched on. "We are not here; please leave your message." At this point, expecting the worst, Bill was relieved to hear a female voice.

"President Clinton, this is Lorna Johnson. Mr. Vernell gave me your number. Remember me?" He clearly remembered the kind pediatric nurse from Harlem Hospital. "I know this is highly unusual, but could you please call me at 926-74 ..."

Bill would like nothing better than to call the dedicated young nurse, but first he had to do something about the situation here. He turned toward Hamilton, who was staring questioningly in the direction of the telephone.

"One of your talking apparatuses, I assume?"

"Yes, that one's called a telephone; its voicemail allows the caller to leave a recorded message. I suppose we could benefit from some mutually agreeable discussions. But I refuse to be lectured to. Is that clear?"

"Certainly sir. I've had my say."

"All right, then. By your reaction to the telephone just now, I see you have a steep learning curve when it comes to understanding today's electronics. Perhaps I can be of assistance there."

"Indeed. In my prior ... er ... undercover work, shall we say, I encountered a large box in your front parlor that is a talking picture machine."

Bill snapped his fingers. "Of course. You fiddled with the

TV, messed with the liquor … So tell me," he demanded. "What else of mine have you helped yourself to?"

Looking somewhat sheepish, Hamilton answered, "I observed your acquaintances and a few of your activities, sir."

"What acquaintances?"

"For one, your houseguests of a previous evening."

"My God," Bill whispered. "But why?"

"To assist you, I must garner more knowledge of your likes, your dislikes, your foibles, if you will. In fact, might I presume that voice …" He pointed to the wall phone. "… in the talking box, referred to the children's mission you're taking on?"

"I … I … what? How would you know?" Bill recoiled as fear again crawled up his spine. "Besides snooping and eavesdropping, are you also reading my mind?"

Looking highly alarmed himself, Hamilton said, "Please, sir, hear me out. Invisibility is the gift God has given me, not thought transference, sorcery, or any of the dark sciences. Now that we've met, I will henceforth curtail my surveillance of your actions. Would you, perhaps, be more comfortable viewing me as somewhat akin to a guardian angel?"

Grabbing a tuft of his hair in frustration, Bill hissed, "This can't be happening. I swear, shit like this only goes on in the movies. Don't tell me you fancy yourself some kind of Clarence."

"Movies? Clarence?"

Bill closed his eyes, wondering if God, who even in his darkest moments had always been there for him, was still his pal. St. Luke's Episcopal Church was just across the street. He'd never been inside, and he wasn't Episcopalian, but St. Luke's was close. It was too late in the evening, but in the morning he might pop in for a visit. Besides offering solace, would the church provide refuge from ghosts?

Hamilton, still talking, hurried to explain. "Be assured, Mr. President, it was not your mind I attended to, but your manner. After visiting in the hospital with you, simple observation revealed you to be moved by the children's plight. And, please," he urged, "let us return to my suggestion from before."

"I can't think straight. What suggestion?"

"That we look upon my visit as mutually beneficial. Perhaps you could start by reacquainting me with Harlem Heights, which has changed unimaginably since my time. In return, I'll educate you on what this area was like in the late eighteenth century."

"We'll talk about that in a moment," Bill interrupted. "First, I have a torrent of questions, though it's hard knowing where to begin. You mentioned your paramour. The resources I've read make no mention of a Sarafina in your life. Why not?"

"Ah. You've hit on a topic dear to both our hearts, miscegenation. In today's age, I believe it's called interracial consorting, which can now manifest into legal marriage between the races."

Ah, hell, Bill thought. Surely he couldn't know what I did back in high school. Even the special prosecutor didn't dredge that up. "Are you implying that you're traveling with a woman other than your wife and that she's of another race? Perhaps black?" Bill ventured, but figured he already knew where this was leading.

"Exactly, sir. She was an early love of mine, before my marriage."

Though his brain was scrambled, Bill recalled one short

passage from the previous night's reading. "Hamilton," it had stated, "was rumored to go about with a dark lady." At the time, he assumed the line referred to Maria Reynolds, the shady con woman with whom he had the affair that subsequently damaged his reputation.

Pushing the passage from his mind, Bill said, "And now for this encore, the good Lord, knowing times have changed, let you travel with a companion of your choice?"

If Hamilton detected any sarcasm, his expression didn't show it. "Exactly. Perhaps you had a similar, shall we say, 'friend' in your youth, no?"

When Bill blinked, Hamilton reminded him, "Sir, eons ago, while arguing with Thomas Jefferson on how to compose the United States Constitution, I became well acquainted with the inherent bigotry in southern parts of America. Despite my years of arguing against the institution of slavery, biases against the black man only increased."

"But how did you know about me?" Bill leaned across the table.

Grinning mischievously, Hamilton answered, "Sir, I didn't."

Bill had to laugh. "Hamilton, you're a crafty old son of a bitch. But since the cat's out of the bag, I'll tell you something. That brief and innocent relationship with a black woman cemented my determination to do whatever I could to help improve race relations in this country."

"I understand," Hamilton said softly.

"No, I'm not sure you do. It's not like I hadn't seen prejudice all around me, but come on, slavery had ended over a hundred years before. For the life of me," Bill said, starting to pace, the forgotten coffee cup still in his left hand, "I could not understand what was so wrong about going to school with black kids. It's like a light bulb came on inside my brain, and I knew that part of my life's work would be to make the world better for blacks and other disadvantaged people.

"Fast forward ten years, when I met this young lady named Ruth Ann Spanner. We were just two naive kids with active hormones. Like my wife, Ruth Ann was one of the smartest women I ever met. She ran circles around me when it came to math and science, but bigotry and racism were rampant in Arkansas, so it wasn't easy to date a black girl.

"I remember that her parents subscribed to the Sunday *New York Times*. On a few dates, we did the puzzle together, and she was dynamite … that means terrific, excellent. Sports were about the only answers I usually got before she did. Ours was a summer love, a sweet one, but it died a natural death when I left to start college at Georgetown and she returned for her second year at Philander Smith College. I guess we were kind of like you and Sarafina. It wasn't meant to be."

"But, surely life turned out better for Ruth Ann than for Sarafina."

"Interesting that you mention that. Until a few years ago, I didn't know what happened to her. But, I looked her up online. Eventually I'll explain some of that online stuff for you. I knew Ruth Ann went to Harvard Medical School, but we lost track after that. By using Google—um, another of the modern computer technologies that I'll help you with—she was easy to track down. She's retired from her pediatrics practice but spends several months each year in Haiti working with an organization she started called "Do It for Kids."

Heading for the kitchen to get more coffee, Bill was halfway there before he remembered his manners. "Would you like something to drink? This is all a bit overwhelming, but do you imbibe? Can you ingest food and drink?"

"I can and do, although I eat solely for the tactile experience. I no longer require nourishment. Sprits are another matter; I ingest them pleasurably. However, some other evening would be preferable."

"Does Sarafina share similar transformative properties? Will I meet her?"

"Increasingly she enjoys maintaining human form more than I do. When she accompanies me on the street, many men admire her. As for a meeting, that's of her choosing, but I believe so, although she's self-conscious about her spoken word."

"Urge her not to worry about that. With so many immigrants and visitors to this city, New York is awash in languages, accents, and dialogues. I doubt anyone would notice a woman's speech patterns."

Looking down at his person, Hamilton added, "Sarafina learns quickly. For instance, she's taken naturally to selecting fashions. Wouldn't you agree?"

With that question, the weirdness re-enveloped Bill like a heavy blanket. He shook his head, unable to imagine a ghost shopping in Barney's or Macy's. Ducking inside, he poured a fresh cup of hot decaf and contemplated adding some brandy, but decided his brain was fuzzy enough. Sighing, he slid the door open and stepped back into the evening chill.

"Mr. Hamilton," he started, "or maybe I should call you Alex? Would that be all right?"

"Alex, you say? It has a modern timbre, and since I am visiting in the twenty-first century, I might as well make every effort to fit in.'"

He tried to overlook the fact that he'd just asked a ghost's permission to do something in his own damn house. And how, he wondered, did Sarafina pay for her purchases? It was probably best not to know, he decided.

"She and I were both pleased by the items she chose," Hamilton said and, as if to demonstrate, flicked a piece of lint off one wool-trousered leg. "The adventure was not an idle undertaking, mind you. We couldn't very well remain clothed in our arrival attire."

Massaging his temples, Bill studied the visitor, whose maddening composure never wavered. Much like his own, Hamilton's face was centered by a prominent nose, although the other man's was narrower, more flared at the nostrils, and slightly tipped; he was not a bad-looking fellow; had what the ladies called 'pretty boy' looks. His lips were generously full, pouty even, and Bill was willing to bet women had noticed those full lips a lot sooner than he had.

Glancing at his watch, Bill saw that it was eight thirty. Last night's fear and most of its accompanying tension had melted, leaving his exhausted mind brimming with questions. Still, the thought of a decent night's sleep trumped curiosity.

"You will return, won't you?"

"Most certainly. Same time tomorrow. Perhaps then I can propose my list of questions on how government functions."

Bill nodded, stood, and slowly extended his hand. Hamilton understood the gesture and likewise stuck out his right hand. When Bill felt a fistful of solid flesh, he almost swooned in relief. "Until tomorrow," he said, goose bumps running up his arm.

CHAPTER 9

FIRE IN THE BELLY

It was a fine spring day, and Bill and Alex had just managed to spend two fairly private hours on a shady bench on St. Nicholas Terrace, high above Alex's mansion. The simple act of leisurely occupying a park bench was a rare treat for Bill. The real bonus, however, was that Hamilton had unleashed more tantalizing anecdotes about the founding fathers and early Americans than Bill had gathered from a lifetime of study and service to country.

Alex's mind-bending revelations had, for the moment, allowed Bill to forget that the Bureau was stressed out about him being so exposed. Today, at least, to get some breathing room, he had acquiesced and taken a car over here to meet his "old pal" Alex. But now, as they sauntered up the street, the security team scurried around as though he'd already been ambushed by al-Qaeda.

Bill was beyond fed up with restrictions, protocol, and absurd rules. At the moment, despite dragging along a posse, he was determined to enjoy his inalienable right to walk three goddamn blocks without being mugged by guys who were supposed to make his life better, not worse.

Alex, seemingly oblivious to the security, trustingly walked beside him. When they got to 142nd Street, Alex stopped to examine a two-headed gargoyle carved into the stone facade of a townhouse. While he surveyed the building's details, Bill observed the groups of children playing on the block. Not too many years ago, parents in this neighborhood with young children would not have allowed them to play outside. Recalling what Ray said about neighbors appreciating the security he generated made Bill feel better about the men around him.

No matter where he turned these days, his life was complex, but he smiled at the sight of four young boys on the opposite side of the street. With one skateboard among them, they were inexpertly taking turns riding down the last three or four steps of Our Lady of Lourdes Church. He was tempted to say something so the boys wouldn't hurt themselves or the steps, when he saw Father Vasquez come out the rectory and make a beeline toward the group.

Good, he thought. The kids don't know me, but the last thing I need is to bring undue attention to myself.

Bill continued up a few doors where Taylor Carmody and two other girls were playing "Double Dutch." The steady tick-tick of the jump rope slapped the sidewalk in perfect four-fourths time.

"Hi, Mr. Clinton." Taylor stopped turning. "Wanna try Double Dutch? My dad can do it, and he said you're a way more important president than he is."

"Nah, Taylor. Not even close." Bill nodded in the direction

of City College. "Your daddy's doing the most important job there is, educating young people. Plus, he's one of those younger people, so that makes him better at Double Dutch."

Bill had first met Nathan Carmody when he was still a professor, and Hillary had just been elected to the Senate. They'd been at a party with most of the winning New York Democratic candidates. At the time, Bill didn't know that one day he'd become Nathan's neighbor and friend.

Stepping back, as the girls idly started turning the rope, Bill watched for a minute, remembering how he'd skipped rope inside the White House with Chelsea and some of her schoolmates. Once, Hillary caught them and nearly had a coronary when she saw how close they were to the shelf holding a bust of Winston Churchill.

Thinking of his daughter, Bill said, "You know what, Taylor? I used to jump Double Dutch with my little girl, but that was a long time ago."

"Pleeease … ?" a girlish chorus bombarded him.

What the heck? he thought, overlooking the fact that he'd probably be sorry tomorrow when his right knee swelled up. Slowly he rolled up his shirt sleeves. "Maybe you caught me on a good day, but it's been a while." He eyed the two ropes switching through the air. "Can you give it more slack so I can fit in there? And I need to remember the timing for getting between the dang things."

Intent on not making too big a fool of himself, Bill didn't notice that Alex had stopped examining the stonework to follow his interaction with the kids. His first two efforts failed, but on his third try, Bill hit it right and smoothly glided between both ropes. "One, two, three …" he counted, as loose change bounced from his pocket.

"Bravo, bravo, well done, sir!" Alex applauded, spoiling his rhythm.

"Eight is enough anyway." Bill laughed, untangled himself, and bent over to retrieve three quarters.

"See, it's easy. Do it again, faster this time." Taylor ran up and took his hand, trying to coax him back.

"Uh, uh. No more." Out of breath, Bill shook his head. "Tell you what, ladies," he said, leaning against a car. "Show me how you experts do it. Then my friend and I need to finish our walk."

As the girls resumed play, Alex joined Bill. "Quite impressive. These youngsters admire you."

"Kids are the greatest," Bill said, tucking in his shirt and rolling his sleeves down. "I wish we'd had a houseful."

"Why didn't you?"

"You take what God gives you. But the glass was never half full. What we lacked in quantity, we made up for by getting Chelsea. Now, that little one named Taylor, the child in blue with ribbons on her hair, she reminds me of Chelsea; both are only children, daddies' girls. Nathan and Grace have a lot to be thankful for."

Usually a talker, Alex waited for Bill to finish before quietly interjecting, "Indeed, sir, it's never too late."

Waving goodbye to the girls, Bill motioned to Alex to follow and started toward Amsterdam. "Instead of laying on the flattery, why not tell me about your children?"

"Very well. That houseful you mentioned, well, we had it. Eight in all, plus we cared for a two-year-old orphan named Fanny Antill, who came to us when her parents died."

Bill stopped. "With eight of your own, you found room for another?"

"Yes, and the experience was so rewarding, my wife subsequently established a home for orphaned children. And by the way, sir," he added, "there was no flattery intended."

They'd continued talking and were now a few blocks from the Grange and Bill could have listened all day to Alex's stories about his family: their acceptance of wearing unwashed clothing and taking infrequent baths, struggles to feed a houseful of kids, primitive treatments for their illnesses. Despite it all, Alex still conveyed a sense of joy that existed within his family.

What hadn't changed were the tales of sexual intrigue and political buffoonery in government. It was still commonplace and often from the same self-righteous hypocrites. But it wasn't just them, Bill thought; everybody in politics was guilty of something. Well, maybe not everybody.

Before they parted, Bill still wanted to quiz Alex about the neighborhood. He stopped a moment and waited until a woman got out of a cab and entered a townhouse in front of them; he then proceeded to ask his question. "I've seen eighteenth-century lithographs of Harlem Heights, but would you try to describe what this spot and nearby areas looked like in your day?"

Shading his eyes against the sun's eleven o'clock brightness, Alex glanced back in the direction of his house. "There used to be a carriage path somewhere around here. It cut through my thirty-two acres and led to the riverbank."

Trying to estimate the size of a thirty-two acre parcel, Bill asked, "Did your land extend as far as the Hudson?"

"Not quite; my holdings spread north to south, where your City College now stands. Most land west of me remained wild and unoccupied. The exception was Hans van der Linde's cottage, a hovel, really."

"The fellow sounds Dutch."

Alex nodded. "An eccentric descendant of Peter Minuit; he married a disagreeable Wappinger woman. Together they produced their own tribe of pigtailed papooses. A sad situation. Their dear children scavenged food from us. I don't know how they survived before I built the Grange, or what happened to them after my demise. When I was mortally wounded, Eliza had a hard enough time with our brood."

"Were relations always cordial between Indians and whites?"

"The large tribes camped further north, along the Hudson. Occasionally there were tensions with whites, but no one bothered Hans's family, or mine."

In Bill's and Alex's discussions, the topic of Native Americans hadn't previously surfaced. "Did you have any formal dealings with Indians?" Bill asked.

The question caused Alex to pause. Bill was about to repeat it when Alex started smiling. "Except for a journey to my wife's upstate ancestral home in Albany, where I had the privilege of attending a two-day powwow with a tribe belonging to the Iroquois nation, unfortunately not."

"How in the world did you manage such an invite?"

"Since I had no surviving family, my dear wife Eliza and I tried not to lose touch with her relatives. We communicated mostly by post, but on one of our two journeys north, I was asked by her uncle, John Schuyler, Albany's mayor, to try to reason with the local Indians, who were harassing hunters and trappers in the area."

"Why you, a distant stranger, rather than the uncle?"

"Schuyler told the local chief—Many Horns was his name—that one of President Washington's top lieutenants would like to pay him a visit, so an audience was arranged. They knew the president's warfare had not been waged against Indians, but against a tribe of white men from across the big water. They had no animosity toward the American president or me, his stand-in and onetime confidant."

"OK, so you represented the White Chief. Did the Indians treat you well?"

"Indeed, I was received like a king. Instead of bombast, which my in-law believed in, I first-off presented the Indians with some of the gifts originally intended for our relatives. Such items were highly coveted by the natives: a metal pot, a few long-handled axes, two sturdy sewing needles, pepper, some sugar, and a number of other trinkets. With ships constantly sailing into New York harbor, it was easy for me to find necessities and luxuries that Upstate New Yorkers waited months for. Goods arriving at the Boston harbor took an equally long time to travel overland.

"I also had with me a timepiece and a pair of spectacles that were cracked, and I was happy to pass them on. As you know, natives, like the Negro people, were often marginalized and cheated out of rights and property. My intention was to assure Many Horns that the trappers only wanted safe passage north without being molested and weren't after Indian lands. There was more than enough game for Indians and whites, alike."

"Good man. From what I studied about you, I'd expect no less. Unfortunately, Indian land grabs and other abuses went on for ages, just like slavery."

Alex nodded at Bill's comment, and then the hint of a lopsided smile slowly spread across his face. "As Many Horns' honored guest, I was housed in a ceremonial longhouse, a large narrow structure. Bearskin rugs hung upon walls, effectively keeping at bay the damp night air.

"My quarters were tended by a half dozen young maidens clad in soft doeskin dresses with elaborate stitching. Each girl was further adorned in a festive necklace of red, blue, and bright green plumage. A few also wore small beaded bracelets. As they tended to a roaring blaze and served our food, I was touched by their efforts to dignify such elemental accommodations.

"Though we were seated about the floor, Indian style, and used crude eating utensils carved from animal bone, the Mahican cuisine of roasted deer and hen turkey stuffed with greens and dried morels was quite palatable."

He dared not interrupt, but Bill made a mental note to ask if Alex knew about America's Thanksgiving holiday.

"After ingesting a heavy meal and sizable portions of brew concocted from honey, I felt strangely euphoric and would have been content saying good night. Instead, I found myself unable to move, as a dreamlike state overtook my senses. Chief Many Horns remained seated across from me, but his image began to appear through a diaphanous haze.

"Somewhere in the room," Alex continued, "a drumbeat began, whereupon the fire attendants, who'd stolen into the shadows, reappeared and commenced dancing. They snaked around the floor in a slow, mesmerizing way."

Blushing slightly, Alex paused for a moment. "I'm quite sure my euphoria was drug-induced. At the point where the women's sensual movements began to excite me, I looked up and saw that their lovely feathered necklaces, which I had so admired, were one of the few items that remained on their persons. The feathers' purpose, I was about to learn, was not entirely decorative but was used in strategic places on my body. And oh, the way those beaded bracelets could be wrapped around a man's ... a man's ... one's ... Sir, I hope you understand my meaning. It was a memorable night."

The rapture on Alex's face was infectious. In a complete turnaround, Bill was now loving every minute of his company, and good golly, did Alex have some stories to tell! Take this hot Indian sex party, or whatever the hell the Mahicans had going up there. An hour earlier, Hamilton had reconstructed a meeting in Philadelphia, where he and Thomas Jefferson haggled over slavery and how Jefferson should word the Constitution.

"Had you met Jefferson before? I apologize for all the questions, but your revelations are almost as startling to me as cars and airplanes are to you."

"I'd met him many times, but the gentleman was an arrogant sort and not to my liking. Thomas was a complainer, ever complaining about the discomfiture of backwater Philadelphia and its rudimentary boarding houses. Yet the work at hand required us to convene at the seat of government."

"Where did he propose to meet?"

"Thomas didn't propose alternatives. He just wanted to rush

back to the rolling countryside of his Virginia farm."

Having toured Jefferson's Monticello estate, Bill understood its attraction and said so. "Can you blame him? Even by today's terms, the place was awash with luxury and convenience."

"Indeed. But need I remind you, sir," Hamilton said, squaring his shoulders and stretching to his full five-feet-four-inch height, "that Jefferson, a man charged with framing the Declaration of Independence, also found his comfort through the labor of over two hundred slaves and through dashing Sally, a black child concubine, who remained at his beck and call."

Bill knew he'd heard right, but he still felt like pinching himself. Hot damn, he thought, and seeing an opportunity to ask the burning question, he went for it.

"Alex, in your opinion, did Jefferson truly father Sally's children?"

"Bah."

Spellbound, Bill waited.

"Everyone knew it," Alex scowled, his words dripping vitriol. "The affair began when she was fourteen. The little ones started appearing the next year."

"Is your condemnation because Sally was a slave, or because of her youth?"

Alex's cheeks flushed red. "The entire sordid mess was shameful. I damn him now, just as I did to his face, inside the halls of Congress. 'Sir,' I told him, 'considering your conduct, you are a coward and hypocrite for not freeing the slaves.'" Gathering himself, Alex looked at Bill. "The gentleman was well aware that when I said, 'the slaves,' it included Sally and the progeny she produced for Thomas."

Bill wanted to keep talking about Jefferson and slavery, but the subject was distasteful to Alex, who now pointed across the street to the church that had been cleared of ten-year-old boys. "I've noticed an abundance of churches in the area. This one looks quite dissimilar from others. What can you tell me about it?"

"About all I know is that it's Catholic, and I understand it was built in stages, from salvaged buildings. I've met with a coalition of the Harlem pastors, but we didn't discuss architecture, and I've yet to go inside. Sorry." Bill contemplated showing Alex the church's interior. However, a group of tourists from a bus parked at the end of the block, guidebooks in hand, some with cameras around their neck, were waiting to tour Our Lady; they were being held back by his security. Hoping he was too far away for them to recognize him in sunglasses and a Yankee's cap, he quickly moved along. To Alex, he said, "Our Lady, like your home, is a Harlem landmark. Forgive me for not showing you the inside, but perhaps some other time.

"Let's walk ahead. There are a few other things I want to ask you, and then I need to say goodbye. I'm privileged to have had this conversation, but I'd better hop into the car that's waiting for me and let these people around here get on with their day."

The mention of church had given Bill a way to bring Sarafina into the conversation. "If it can be arranged, perhaps you and Sarafina could accompany me some Sunday to Convent Avenue Baptist, the congregation I attend when in the city. It's just up the street."

"Thank you, sir, but even more than myself, Sarafina might be a candidate to visit your church. Just two days ago, she stumbled upon a small spiritual house that comforts women."

"Oh?" Bill perked up. "She's religious?"

"Yes and no. Her faith's been tested, but here among free Negroes, the spark's rekindled."

Having tasted the depth of spirituality in this community, Bill understood how one could be drawn in by some of these powerful preachers, but it was hard to reconcile a ghost being religious. Turning the conversation to history, Bill said, "Harlem is famous for its churches. Since the Civil War, the church has been a backbone of black American life."

"Longer," Hamilton responded.

Bill looked at him.

"Sarafina was an early member of the New Africa Church and found comfort within its doors."

"Did you know her then?"

"Yes, of course. I'd already arranged her shelter and a live-in position with a family."

"Forgive my ignorance, but why a servant? Was that the best she could do?"

"My dear Mr. Clinton, please don't apologize for any gaps in your extraordinary knowledge of eighteenth-century history. I am humbled by your patience with me and with our most unusual partnership. It is indeed my pleasure to answer your questions. Now, about Sarafina: she was comely, vulnerable, and yes, at times, servitude in a benevolent household was a good arrangement for a freewoman. Think of it as akin to the protection European girls received in convents."

When Bill looked doubtful, Alex said, "You must understand the difficulty of trying to create a new democracy." Smiling ruefully, he added, "Slavery, though abhorrent, was legal in New York. The city was a dangerous place. Imagine, if you will, something akin to lawlessness during your Wild West days, which by the way, is a favorite period of history for former president Theodore Roosevelt. Though the country was more settled during his tenure, I believe he fancies himself to be as much cowboy, as ex-president of the United States. At our monthly roundtable discussions, he speaks at great length about his mastery with a rifle and dexterity in the saddle. Much like Thomas, Theodore can be quite pompous."

Teddy Roosevelt? Damn. Alex hangs out with dead nineteenth century figures too?

Bill's senses were so alive, one might think he'd just attended an Upstate orgy. Just like the next guy, he savored inviting stories, but at the same time, he felt strangely unworthy of receiving this gift of their shared humanity. Life repeated itself and the reality was that one's address or date of birth didn't matter. But was this real?

"A hundred years earlier," Alex was saying, "when Sarafina traveled the byways and paths of New York, drunken horsemen still frightened women and scattered pedestrians about. But there were also beggars at your feet, thieves at your throat, venders hawking everything from African guinea hens to spices from the Orient. Amid such noise and chaos, no one would notice a renegade slave trader forcing a young Negro woman onto a skiff about to set sail down the coast."

"Alex, I have so many questions my heart might burst, but for now, I want you to do the talking. I can ask my questions another time. Earlier, you mentioned that Sarafina is your junior in age. Did something untoward shorten her life? How did she die?"

"In a most unfortunate accident. She was crushed to death. Being encumbered by long skirts, her garments got caught in the spokes of a passing carriage. Its momentum dragged her down and under the carriage wheels." Seeing Bill grimace, Alex sighed. "In our era, I'm afraid such mishaps occurred frequently."

CHAPTER 10

A BEAUTIFUL VISION

It was six a.m., and in the Amsterdam Café's early morning quiet, Bill savored his first sip of coffee. Besides Bill and BJ, the kid working the counter, there was only one other person in the store. Just outside the door, a security team waited to check incoming customers. In a perverse coincidence, the third person already in the store was Brad Davis. Anticipating this morning's meeting with Alex, Bill had again been briefed on Davis. Among information Ray learned was that Davis had regularly frequented this café, even before its new owners remodeled it and before Bill moved to the neighborhood. That was cold comfort. Davis was still a journalist and seemingly always around.

Leaning against his chair's headrest and happy for a shadow of privacy behind leafy schefflera plants, Bill wished Alex and Sarafina would hurry and get there before the Service hassled him to leave. At first he'd been fine with Alex's request to meet in a café, something that neither he nor Sarafina had thus far experienced. However, since agreeing, the Bureau had become more adamant about wanting to curtail Bill's ventures. This morning's compromise came with a one-hour limit, from six to seven a.m., before the place filled up.

Technically Bill was a private citizen without salary or official government responsibilities. He was also one of the most powerful men in the world and should be free to make his own decisions, but that battle was lost. Months ago, when Ray first escorted him into this café, it was without fanfare. Now Bill felt harassed, even embarrassed, by the relentless babysitting. The real tragedy might be what his morning's cup of coffee was costing the American taxpayer.

An unexpected twist to this ongoing drama with Alex was that Bill liked him, at least most of the time. Some things Alex had said still rankled, but God definitely had a sense of humor. He'd heard of people snatching glimpses of the afterlife, usually because of a near-death experience, but, in a twist, God had sent the afterlife to him. This was not the first time the Big Guy had thrown him a curveball. There was one in 1998, when he ascended from humiliation and impeachment to become a better man. Then, in 2004, instead of dying from heart disease, he survived and adopted a more healthy lifestyle.

Now, in discussions with Alex, Bill realized that despite all his power and influence, he was simply a speck of matter in the greater universe and, like Alex, would soon be relegated to the history books. He wondered if God had any more surprises up his sleeve.

Today, he realized, might have to be his last public encounter with Alex. The potential for mishap was increasing, and despite the Bureau's history of looking the other way when presidents

lied and snuck around, dallying with a ghost—two ghosts—was
risking too much. He mustn't forget that the Bureau's primary
allegiance was now to Hillary, not him. If he screwed up, they'd
be all over him.

Bill put aside the unread newspaper, peeked at his watch,
then checked the door, willing Alex to appear. On the far side
of the room, Davis was lost in his laptop, and BJ was searching
through the café's CD collection. Moments later, strains of the
Fugees' 1990s hit, "Killing Me Softly," piped through the sound
system.

The café's owners were a baby boomer couple who grew up
in this neighborhood, moved to the suburbs, then returned to
live in Harlem and open the business. Besides strong coffee, a
variety of music, pastries, and a warm atmosphere, their sought-
after back room had become a favorite spot for everything from
children's birthday parties to poetry readings.

A bright flash of color alerted Bill to the door opening, and
he looked over to see a woman in a buttery yellow dress, head
thrown back, neck exposed, laughing softly at something that
Alex, who walked behind her, was saying.

Four or five of Sarafina's leggy strides carried her back
to where the ex-president stood, open-mouthed, by the sofa.
For the moment, neither of them spoke while they made eye
contact and drank in each other's faces. Coming alongside,
Alex launched into cumbersome introductions. "Sarafina, this
distinguished gentleman and scholar has, since my arrival, been
a superb host and savior, preventing me from entering into
numerous awkward situations."

"President Bill Clinton." Sarafina said it like a question, and
a smile warmed her silky voice. "Alexander showed me a paper

likeness of you. Such paper be very much as I now see you before me. My honor," she said, bobbing in a girlish curtsey. Her voice was a tropical melody that made Bill's stomach tingle. He couldn't detect anything in the honey-colored woman that any flesh-and-blood male wouldn't admire. There was nothing behind those softly painted red lips that might reveal her ghostly double existence. Bill pulled his eyes away and managed to utter, "Likewise."

In his peripheral vision, he caught Brad Davis scrutinizing the odd twosome, a tall, beautiful black woman with wild curly hair and her short, conventionally dressed white male companion with long reddish hair pulled back into a loose knot resting at the nape of his neck. It was not the hairstyle one expected on a nattily dressed gentleman, but Alex wore it well. Behind feathery lashes, Sarafina's eyes were hazel, and her skin, amber-toned. Somewhere along the line, Bill saw a white slave owner's strain blending with her African heritage.

Bill tried not to gawk, but Sarafina's body language, the way she held her head high, the correct carriage, the mass of curls, and even those easy, long-legged strides exuded a self-confidence and determination he hadn't expected. After taking in her fill of him, she turned to their surroundings and scanned the room's interior. When she observed the slow spinning ceiling fan, Bill saw a look of puzzlement crease her face.

"It cannot be possible, surely ..." She spoke hesitantly, as though confused. Then looking from Alex to Bill, she said, "That movement. I feel it again, in this place."

"Oh, that." Bill thought the fan, like so much technology that affected Alex, might literally be making her dizzy. "It's just one of a million motorized objects in the world, but it poses no harm."

With Sarafina seemingly fixated on the café's sights and sounds, Bill assumed that she, like most women who valued personal security, possessed a sense of place that men often lacked.

"I hope my choice of seating meets your approval." Then, pushing aside a tall plant's bushy branches, he ushered them into The Cozy Corner, the cheery children's area decorated in Crayola colors. "The sofa and chairs back here are not only comfortable, but the space also provides a bit more privacy."

Now that the shock had worn off a bit, Bill spoke to Alex. "I have to confess, you didn't prepare me adequately."

"My apologies, sir. The dear lady has fully embraced the modern world and has accordingly adjusted."

Bill lowered his voice and directed his next comment to Sarafina. "If I didn't know better, I'd say you'd easily blend in with any woman who frequents this place."

Taking him for his word, Sarafina turned to search for a lookalike. Having been thrown by Sarafina's arrival, Bill hadn't noticed that the café now had one other early morning customer, a short, forty-ish, dark-haired, comfortably padded Caucasian woman. Despite the already hot humid morning, she wore long jogging pants and dripped sweat while standing at the condiment counter, stirring sweetener into her takeout iced tea. Like Davis, the woman was eyeballing the back of the room, trying to figure out what her new high-profile neighbor was up to.

Noting that the tea drinker looked nothing like Sarafina, Bill said, "Allow me to rephrase that. You'd blend in, but as a crowd pleaser." He hoped the compliment didn't sound too forward. "What I mean," he said, backtracking awkwardly, "is that you don't blend in at all, or not much."

She blushed prettily and lowered her eyes. "I understand such praises. But often when I walk about, I cannot catch up with words spoken at me by young boys. Instead of catching daylight and thanking God for blessings, they stand about idly, saying, 'Psst, psst, psst,' like they calling a dog."

Where she sat under the window, sunlight bathed Sarafina's face, and Bill saw color rise in both cheeks. "What they say," she continued, "is not pleasing to a woman's ears."

Surprised by her lengthy speech on sidewalk decorum, Bill asked, "You take walks around Harlem?" The thought of young street corner idlers disrespecting this great man and his lovely companion depressed Bill. Turning to Alex, he said, "In our talks, I never asked how you and Sarafina entertain yourselves."

Before responding, Alex took another look at the woman at his side. "Increasingly, she shows me about, or navigates alone. Don't you, my dear?"

Silently, Bill reprimanded himself for making assumptions. Up to now, he'd thought of Sarafina as a satellite to the brighter star's journey. However, in her spotlight, Alex seemed to pale as many important men did when squiring a beautiful woman. Still, he couldn't help wondering how, indeed, these two ended up together, either in the past or present.

Seeking to engage her in conversation, Bill said, "Women and minorities have made great gains in our society. Does that surprise you?"

"In my outings each day, I listen to the women; I learn what Negro women doing. There be one who have great power to call up the spirits. She trying to tell me something I cannot yet hear."

So far the morning was going splendidly, and Bill had no intention of drifting to spirit talk. Anxious to change the subject, he had a sudden inspiration. "Sarafina, let me show you something." Squatting down, he rummaged through an old pile of periodicals in a wicker basket next to their table.

"A few weeks ago, one of the monthly magazines printed a special edition highlighting black women's contributions to American life. It included luminaries from Harriet Tubman to youthful twenty-first-century celebrities like Beyoncé." Not finding the magazine, Bill rose to his feet. "Well, I'm not surprised that someone probably borrowed it. Too bad."

Hesitating before speaking, Sarafina said, "Mr. Clinton, the written word too often befuddles me, but my eyes see and my ears hear all. That melody," she pointed in the general direction of the café's stereo speakers, "sound sorrowful."

Bill remembered the song on the CD, from when Roberta Flack recorded it in the 1970s. Now he listened and watched as Sarafina swayed to the music. "I hear pain, deep pain in the heart of Negro woman." Seeing him frown, she explained, "It is of loss, a loss of something dearly loved."

Hearing the CD re-loop, Bill wished he'd been listening more carefully. Captivated by this lovely, intelligent woman, he wanted to hear more from her, but outside, he saw the bakery truck pull up in front of the store. Rubbing his hands together, he said, "Sarafina, hold that thought. I'll just get us some fresh breakfast and be right back."

Bill waited while the frazzled driver, who was running over an hour late, talked to the agent on the door and then rushed in to arrange freshly baked rolls, muffins, and apricot and blueberry Danish in the glass case. Standing back, he surveyed his layout. Next, the man counted out five dozen bagels and an assortment of his nut-filled cookies, each approximately the size of a salad plate.

At the counter, something, maybe Sarafina, had lit a spark under BJ. "Pretty lady over there," he said, springing over to wait on the ex-president.

"Indeed she is." Bill followed his gaze. "Three hazelnut coffees. And, in honor of my friends, I'll splurge this morning." Pointing to the muffins and bagels, he added, "Give me three everything bagels, two peanut butter cookies, and two apricot Danish."

"You want butter or cream cheese?"

"I've learned to say no to those, but my guests might enjoy a little of both."

"She's hot." BJ ran a bagel through the slicer. "But what's up with the stiff she's hanging with?"

Never ceasing to be amazed by what popped out of the mouths of today's youth, Bill placed a ten and twenty on the counter. "Whatever happened to respect for your elders? That stiff, as you impolitely call him, happens to be a very famous ... personage. A ... an historian who's played an important role in bringing the upcoming celebration to Harlem. If not for him, both of us," Bill pointed between himself and BJ, "might not be where we are today."

Under his dark complexion, the kid obviously blushed. "Sorry, sir, I didn't mean to alert Homeland Security or anything. It's just that the dude's kind of lame looking. Pretty ladies like that don't usually hang with guys like him, that's all."

"You know what, son," Bill said and grabbed a few napkins, stirrers, and his change, "some things are not anyone's business, and that couple's relationship is one of them."

Eager to make amends, BJ threw in, "I'll be at the Hamilton ceremony. In American history, we talked about how, even before brothers like DuBois, Malcolm, and Martin came along, that Hamilton dude was tight. He was repping how we should do things, so I'm okay with going, although Saturday's my one day to sleep late."

Unclear on exactly what all BJ had just said, Bill nevertheless assured him, "You'll be glad you went. You can sleep in on Sunday."

"Nah, my mom makes me get up for church."

"You're all right, BJ." Bill dropped all his change in the tip jar, carefully picked up his tray, and gave BJ a thumbs-up. "If not before, I'll see you in the park."

Back near their table, Sarafina and Alex were bent over the store's small toy box, examining its assortment of blocks, books, and a battered Fisher-Price clock. Alex pulled out a preschool version of the Noah's Ark story and, fascinated, turned small colorful cardboard pages. Sarafina unearthed a little plump-cheeked black baby doll, its soft-sided face awash in curly eyelashes and its tiny lips painted an unrealistic cherry red. The doll was missing one button eye, and its right arm dangled.

Bill brushed crumbs off the table, doled out pastries and sopped up his spill. "So, Sarafina," he prompted, anxious to re-engage her, "thus far, what's your most memorable impression of our fair city?"

Receiving no answer, Bill tried another approach. "Or

better yet," he said to her back, "what questions can I answer for you?"

"My dear," Alex coaxed, "you seem preoccupied. Didn't you have some questions about the current free education system for Negroes?"

Bill took the cue. "That's an easy one, but also a shameful bit of American history. See," he said, sipping his fresh coffee and eyeing his bagel, "all public schools weren't legally desegregated until the 1960s, well after I was born."

From her utter stillness—even her eyes didn't blink—Bill wondered if she might be having some sort of otherworldly episode. "Our federal, state, and local monies pay for education. We also have private schools," he babbled, hoping like hell this scene wouldn't get any weirder and that she wasn't about to do some kind of ghost thing.

"I know this ... your visit is overwhelming," Bill hurried to reassure her. "I had plenty of uneasy moments after Alex dropped in on me, and that's despite having studied the history of your era. Still, my meeting Alex and now you is a lot to absorb, so I understand." Bill realized he was talking to a ghost, and it was freaking him out.

When she finally turned, Sarafina still clutched the doll. She looked stricken and shrunken into herself. "Who this babe belong to?" she asked, slipping into a thicker patois. "So lone in there," she said, meaning the toy box. "A broke, bitty thing, with pieces amiss, like half a heart."

Seeing her shoulders slump, Bill jumped up, thinking she might faint. Oh, Christ, he thought, willing her not to disappear before his and everyone's eyes, but Alex grabbed her around the waist. "Sarafina, what are you saying? Please take a seat." He eased her down. "My dear, are you all right?"

"I be fine, Alexander," she said from someplace far away.

"Mr. Clinton." She turned away from Alex. "Have you ever had contact with the spirit world?"

"Oh," his voice cracked. "I think I'll sit down, too. And call me Bill," he told her, buying time. What the fuck kinda question is that, he thought, as his heart raced. Was it his imagination, or was there something in the air, like a current passing between him and her? Reaching for his bagel, Bill bit down viciously, trying but failing to overlook how strange Sarafina seemed compared to Alex, who, after all, was also a ghost.

As suddenly as it had come, Sarafina's spell lifted and her former dazzling presence re-emerged. "Mr. Clinton, in my prior life, except for one cruel day, I be granted many privileges for a person of lowly birth." Still rattled, all Bill wanted was to get out of there, but he made himself refocus on what Sarafina had to say.

"There is reason behind that, don't you think? Alexander, why you bring me? Did you know hereabouts be home to my peoples now?"

Alex considered the question. "I suppose I could have come alone," he responded. "I did not know everything about residents in the village of Harlem. However, I did know that President Clinton's office and home were in close proximity to the Grange. Considering the deprivation you experienced in our lifetime, bringing you just seemed like the right thing to do. My wife, at age ninety-seven, had no interest in accompanying me on this journey."

"I remain powerfully glad you renewed our acquaintance," she said, patting his arm.

Despite his desire to put some distance between himself and Sarafina, Bill found this part of their conversation fascinating.

While they all pondered mysteries of the afterlife, including marital relations, Bill fanned his face with a menu and looked at the clock. It seemed as though time stood still, but almost forty minutes had passed since their arrival.

Sarafina tucked a loose lock of hair behind her ear, replaced the doll on the table, and turned to Bill. "A moment before, I hope I didn't too much startle you when I asked about spirits."

"I'm a little beyond being startled, but yes, your question about the spirit world resonated with me."

"Oh, spirits be wonderful and useful beings," she assured him. "They allow you to connect to your dead forebears and let them know you still love them. You have nothing to fear from spirits, Mr. Clinton. They speak highly of you."

"Well, then." He stood and noisily banged his shin on the table. "On that positive note, I'd best be getting home."

CHAPTER 11

A CHILD'S REQUEST

Emerging from the hospital elevator, Bill sidestepped a gurney returning a post-op child to his room. Trailing behind his three escorts, which today included Ray, all four men watched an attendant wheel the boy into his room just as a candy striper came out with the child's untouched lunch tray. Across the way, under a red EXIT sign, four young interns huddled together as an attending physician quietly lectured to them.

"More like controlled chaos than a pediatrics ward up here," Bill commented to Ray, since no one except him and his group paid any attention to the intercom message saying the fire drill would begin promptly at two thirty. Recalling an episode on *ER*, when the linen closet went up in flames, Bill couldn't help but wonder how they managed a drill with so many vulnerable kids and adults in the building.

Moving unimpeded through the hall, Bill heard the familiar strains of "Can you tell me how to get to Sesame Street," then saw a volunteer and two pint-sized patients head into the playroom. After logging a full circle around the floor, he spotted Lorna and asked Ray to wait by the playroom door. With her back to him, Lorna and a gray-haired nurse sat at their station, discussing patient charts.

Not wanting to interrupt, Bill hung back, but his eyes were drawn to the name on the door nearest the nurse's desk: Alonzo Riley. Yep, he surmised. *Must be the dynamo I met after the Christos concert; makes sense to locate him close by so the nurses can keep an eye on him.* Bill peeked into Alonzo's room, but both beds were empty.

"See anyone you know?" a voice asked. "I wasn't sure you'd show up."

Bill turned, and there was Lorna welcoming him with a broad smile. The other nurse just stared.

"You said it was important," he replied, smiling in return.

"In this job, it's always important. Lillian can verify that." She politely drew her astonished colleague into the fold. "Harlem Hospital thanks you for coming."

"It's the least I could do." He refrained from saying that nothing on this fourth-floor children's ward looked especially urgent.

"Oh, dear Lord!" Lillian blurted. "I can't believe my eyes, Mr. President. We talked about you in last week's staff meeting." Lillian tossed her hands about, not sure what to do with them. "But I never imagined a big shot like you standing before me like an ordinary citizen."

Laughing, Bill patted his flat stomach then shook Lillian's hand. "I'm just a regular guy, and I'm happy to say I'm not a big shot these days. But the pleasure's mine." He read Lillian's name tag that identified her as Charge Nurse. "You ladies are truly angels of mercy."

"We appreciate your kind words." Lillian nodded in thanks, her professional demeanor restored. "Unfortunately, I spend more time on administrative problems than on patient care." Sighing, she picked up the phone. "In fact, excuse me while I make another call."

With the other woman preoccupied on the phone, Bill turned to Lorna. "I have to confess, I'm feeling a little guilty."

"Oh? Guilty for what?"

"I think that foster care outfit forgot they rented me out for a year, unless they're too reticent to ask for my help. I made two pop-in appearances: a gala for a retiring child welfare supervisor and a foster care auction at the Hilton."

"That doesn't surprise me."

"What, that they'd hold an auction?"

"No, that they'd waste your visibility on small-time stuff. Oops, sorry!" She winced. "Their department is understaffed and overwhelmed, but they do good work. It's just that their kids aren't usually ill. I was way out of line." Bill thought so too, but before he could follow up, a beeping sound claimed Lorna's attention. He watched her calmly flip a switch to turn it off, but his curiosity got the best of him. "Is everything okay? What's that noise?"

"Just a reminder that it's time for treats." She laughed. "The kids are about to get their fix of Fritos and Twinkies.

Assuming nurses knew a few things about empty calories, Bill didn't say what he was thinking—that kids who eat junk might end up with a bad ticker, like he did. Instead he said, "That auction I mentioned; it raised $37,000. It was aimed at smaller donors and not the jackpot, but I wouldn't call it chump change, either. I'd like to think my attendance helped put people in seats. What do you think I should do for foster care?" he challenged.

"You're right; I was wrong. Funding is vital, and I don't mean to minimize its importance, but money doesn't solve everything. Right now I'm pulling my hair out over one of our boarders. Do you remember meeting the little girl who sabotages her placements?"

Bill clearly knew which child Lorna meant. He also remembered her deep brown doe-like eyes giving him a thorough once-over. "Yes," he answered. "Pretty little thing; curious too. Wasn't her name Abigail?"

"Close. It's Abby, not Abigail," Lorna corrected. "After she was abandoned in our lobby, the nurses named her Abby. It's short for Abandoned Baby."

"And she's been here, what ... seven years now? You must be kidding."

"More like four or five years, and I wish I was kidding. Despite her tiny size when she arrived, doctors estimated her age as close to two years. At her last placement in December, she stayed a week then went on a hunger strike; wouldn't eat a thing. Did the same thing in a group home. Can you imagine a seven-year-old bamboozling an entire foster care system?" Lorna laughed without mirth.

"So what's next for her?"

"The state just informed us she can't stay here any longer. They'll commit her to a place for willful, uncooperative girls. It's breaking our hearts. We're her family."

"Commit her to what? An asylum?"

"Asylum is a harsh word. Let's just say these homes are often the last resort for seriously disturbed youngsters. They're not ideal for any child, but it would be disastrous for Abby. She's stubborn, but all she needs is a family."

"You asked me here, so you must think there's something I can do to help. What?" he asked warily.

"Abby told us you promised to visit. She wants you to fulfill that promise." Had he made a promise? Bill flashed back to the night he met Lorna and a group of kids in the staff lunchroom.

"I may have assumed my spokesperson duties would bring me back. Sorry if the child's been expecting a visit."

Just then, the head nurse completed her conversation and turned slowly toward Bill. "Mr. President, I must tell you, that call was about Abby, the child Lorna is speaking of."

"Okay," he smiled, "and what about her?"

Leaning back in the armchair, Lillian began massaging her temples. "I swear, that kid's going to be the death of me. My call was to Mr. Watson, our hospital administrator. His instructions were that if you showed up, I have permission to fully explain Abby's situation and answer any questions you might have. So here goes," she said, looking up to meet Bill's questioning gaze.

"Abby has not only been asking to see you, but she … um … also told Lorna that she wants to go home with you and … um, President Clinton, of course."

Bill didn't say anything for a few seconds, then he chortled. "You know what, kids used to say that to me all the time when I was in office. 'Can I come see you at the White House?' they'd ask. What can I say, other than I'm flattered?"

The two nurses exchanged looks. "Mr. President," Lorna said haltingly, "Abby wants to come live with you. For some strange reason, she thinks you're the parent—foster parent—"

she hastened to add, "that she's been waiting for."

"Well, it's impossible. Obviously, I'm not. It's insane."

Glad her part was over, Lillian huffed, "That's what I told Lorna, but she insisted on following through with this."

Lorna, not about to give up, tried another approach. "Is it so insane? Look at you, Mr. President. You're certainly not old, and you have so much to offer a child. You could consider it on a trial basis."

"It would never work," he insisted. "She's black, we're white; she needs better role models."

"Now hold on there a minute." Lillian brought her seat back to its upright position. "It might be a bad idea," she snapped. "But, where'd you get the notion that we need a color match?"

"Well," he started, surprised by her vehemence, "don't white families only adopt black children from abroad? Haven't black social workers done studies showing race matters in placements? You know, for role models and stuff?"

"Mr. President, I don't mean any disrespect, but this is the twenty-first century. And," she emphasized, "in foster care and adoption, color stopped mattering years ago, especially with hard-to-place kids. Sure, you're going to find your detractors, but it's not about them."

"Whoa, that's great. I'm glad. I've backed a lot of charities that work with kids; I thought I was up to date. I just didn't know this."

"Same race placements are still preferable—when there's a match," Lorna chimed in. "Besides," she added, "Abby's biracial. We believe she's half white."

"And in Abby's case," Lillian picked up, "if a lime green Martian stepped off that elevator," she pointed with her pen, "and asked to take Abby to Mars, I'd help her pack."

Downing what remained of a cup of water from the cooler, Bill looked at the ceiling, searching for an air conditioner vent. He was right under it. Lorna, noticing the gesture, reached under the desk and pulled an icy bottle of water out of a small refrigerator.

Absently nodding his thanks, he took a big swig.

Lorna spoke. "Lillian just means it would take a Martian, a miracle, or the return of her mother to make Abby happy. She's restless, and I don't mean in an overactive way. Believe me, we have plenty of hyperactive kids, but that's not Abby's problem. It's more like Abby's spirit is restless, and she insists on having what no one's been able to give her."

Nibbling his lower lip and staring at the floor, Bill asked, "Was she abused then discarded, like so many children in this world?"

Lillian took the question. "Abby was abandoned, Mr. Clinton, not abused. After years of observing her behavior, the doctors feel that prior to being abandoned, she was well loved. In fact, they're certain she retains some memory of her mother."

"I don't believe it. Chelsea certainly doesn't remember her first two years."

"Fortunately," Lillian said, "trauma has never triggered such memory in your daughter." "But the brain is an incredibly resilient organ, even in a developing child. They're capable of looking into the shadows and distinguishing good from bad, on a subconscious level, of course."

"I suppose that could be a mixed blessing," Bill said.

"In Abby's case it certainly seems that memory is partly what has stymied all our efforts to get her past that initial bonding experience."

"How can adults do these things to children?"

"Often, when children are abandoned at a hospital," Lillian explained, "rather than, say, in a dumpster or at a remote location, it's a well-thought-out plan, signaling the mother's hope of rescue for her child."

"Well, that's something at least, but I still don't understand how someone could do that to an infant."

"Technically, she was a baby, not an infant," Lorna clarified.

"Baby, infant, whatever; that right there shows how little I remember about parenting." Bill got to his feet. "The only couple I know who're raising an adopted child are my friends, Nathan and Grace Carmody. In fact," he said, pausing, "I'm pretty sure Grace told me they worked with your social service people. Am I right?"

"Since you know their situation," Lorna told him, "I believe it's okay to tell you that Taylor was another one of our foundlings. That year, six children were abandoned in various spots in the building. Most years we get one, maybe two, and when a child is left here, often after twenty-four hours of reflection, family pressure, and other factors, the distraught parent has a change of heart and returns the next day."

Bill stopped twirling his water bottle. "Because of my work, I know a few things about needy children, but I wasn't aware that foundlings were still an issue."

"And," Lorna added, "as you may have observed, Taylor is also a biracial child, and the Carmodys are both black."

"I never even noticed, but you're right. Taylor fits that family like a glove. She couldn't be more real to them if they'd conceived her."

Lillian, who sat with arms crossed over her bosom and hadn't spoken for a while, piped up. "Mr. President, maybe I should remind you that Taylor is the Carmody's real daughter. Furthermore, how she got there is nobody's business."

"Yes, point well taken," he agreed. "Words matter. I understand. Ladies, thank you for your time. I wish I could help you, but I need to get going. Before I take off, though, I'd be happy to visit Abby. Is it possible to see her now before I go?"

Lorna pointed. "That way. Room B16."

Bill glanced down the hall. "Great. Should I go in alone, or is this a package deal?"

Gently touching his arm, Lorna reminded him. "Abby didn't ask for me. And just one thing. See if you can come up with a miracle," she said, without a trace of irony.

Walking down the corridor, Bill suddenly felt nervous. At room B16, he peeked in. The child, wearing capris and a T-shirt, sat cross-legged on a pink bedspread. She appeared to be talking to the sketch pad propped on her knees.

"No way," Abby complained, shaking her head. "You always suggest birds. I don't know what a magpie looks like. How about a pigeon? They sit outside on my ledge." She checked the window, but the blinds were drawn against the midday glare.

Abby's adorable one-sided conversation reminded Bill of Cricket, Chelsea's imaginary friend, who used to live in the top drawer of her dresser. Not wanting to be caught eavesdropping, he knocked. "Hi, Abby, it's Bill Clinton. May I come in?" The child stopped talking and drawing but didn't answer or look over at him.

"Listen, Abby, I think you know why I'm here." He walked

over to the bed. "And I apologize for not coming sooner. Apparently I made a promise, and by not keeping it, I messed up."

Unsnapping and then recapping the cover on her red marker, she mumbled, "I know."

"Okay. I think you also know why Lorna called me, and now that I'm here, we need to talk. Tell me what's on your mind. The nurses are worried about you. Did you know that?"

"Yeah."

"What happened at your placements?"

"Nothing," she said, rubbing more red onto a good likeness of a bird.

"Nothing? You wouldn't eat," he said, striving for the right tone. "That's not nothing. If you keep doing stuff like that, what's going to happen to you, huh?" Without being invited, Bill moved a pile of books from the room's one chair and sat down. One of her books, he noticed, had the word "Teen" in its title.

"Abby, can you stop drawing for a minute and look at me?" Her hand stilled. "What's this about, Abby? You wanted to see me. How can I help, if you don't tell me?"

"It ... if ..." she started. "It's stupid. If I tell, you'll be mad."

"I won't be mad," he said gently. "Just spit it out."

"You'll think I'm crazy."

"Abby, I promise, whatever you want to say can't be any crazier than what's going on in my life right now. And that," he added, "is a promise I can keep."

Chancing a quick, shy look at Bill, Abby said, "Well, see, it all started right after you came to the hospital party that time." Apparently reassured by the neutral expression on his face, she added, "I got a tummy ache, but a good kind.

"Go on," he encouraged.

Instead of finishing, Abby leaned back and closed her eyes, as though remembering something. The gesture reminded Bill of what an older person, with years of memory, might do.

"It was a happy stomach ache," she said, "like I had a long time ago."

Bill didn't have all day, but he felt obligated to hear her out. In a kid's mind, stomach aches were not stupid or crazy. Trying to speed up the process without stymying it, he said, "So far, so good; anything else you want to tell me?"

When Abby opened her eyes they bore into him, and what he saw made his stomach tumble.

"I want to go home with you. Can I come live at your house? You'll be a real father to me. Please say yes. Pretty, pretty please, with sugar on top."

CHAPTER 12

NOWHERE TO HIDE

When Bill stepped awkwardly from Abby's room, he didn't bother to say goodbye to Lorna or Lillian. He just signaled Ray who, with one look, knew something was up and figured the kid had dropped a bomb about her medical condition. Ray remained mute, giving Bill space to digest the bad news, which seemed to have hit him hard. They bypassed the elevator and ducked into a stairwell, surprising the agent guarding the door who followed them.

Exiting a side door, they were escorted to Ray's car but had to wait for a lull in traffic before taking off. Two blocks from his office, Bill remembered the three o'clock meeting with Alex. The realization brought on the burning sensation that sometimes attacked his stomach. Searching his breast pocket, he found the Zantac and popped a pill, wondering how his once peaceful New York getaway could have turned into such a shitstorm. Suddenly, he couldn't put two decent sentences together on his manuscript, the White House people kept bugging him with asinine questions, a ghost—at least it was friendly—was jamming him up, and now a little kid had just sucker-punched him with an impossible request.

Unlike most children, she had gone beyond explaining what she wanted to what she needed. "I want a real father, and I need to come live with you," she'd told him. His immediate reaction had been, "Oh, no, little darlin', you can't be serious."

Well, it hadn't taken long to learn that, unlike kids before who'd asked to visit or even have a sleepover at the White House, Abby was dead serious about moving in. After several back-and-forths, if he hadn't felt so low, he would have laughed at the absurdity of trying to reason with a seven-year-old. Finally, he said, "Look, honey, I'm flattered beyond all heck, but you can't come with me. You need to talk with one of those lovely ladies you trust, Ms. Lorna or Ms. Lillian. They'll tell you how wrongheaded this is."

Back at his office building, he nodded to the guard, took his elevator upstairs, avoided the reception area, and entered his suite through a door marked "Private." Bill knew Alex prized punctuality, but it was only ten to three, and he needed those ten minutes to pull himself together.

"Gertie, I'm back," he announced into the intercom, "but hold all calls." Stripping off his jacket, he tossed it on a chair, stopped, reconsidered the directive, and pressed "Talk" again. "That's all calls except from Hillary, of course." He knew there was about a snowball's chance in hell of her calling, but if he was wrong, he wanted to report that he'd done something different today—very different.

He grabbed a Diet Coke and tried to put Abby out of his mind, but couldn't. Neither today's events nor the soda were helping his heartburn. He poured it out and turned just in time to catch the ghost hovering midair. "Oh, for Pete's sake, Alex. What is it with you and doors, anyway?" he shouted, not caring who heard. "You're on my visitors' list. You can use the goddamn door, like everyone else. But come ahead," he sighed. "I don't have time for games. It's been a crap-ass day."

Uncharacteristically, Alex didn't start gabbing right away. Grateful for the small mercy, Bill waved him into a seat while he spent a few seconds looking at messages. Too unsettled to focus, he turned to Hamilton.

"What?" he asked, seeing Alex's raised brows. "What are you looking at? I'm not the freak of nature in the room," he said nastily.

"Your countenance, sir. Something has caused great consternation."

Less testily, Bill added, "Sorry. It's no one's fault, but this thing just now hit me harder than I want to admit. It's a long story, but tell me, how does a grown man wake in the morning and, before day is done, end up breaking a little girl's heart?"

"Oh, dear. That is a conundrum."

"Yeah, you could say that."

"If it's the child at the hospital, why break her heart?"

"Because she has no family. She wants to come live with Hillary and me and have us as parents."

"And?"

"And what?"

"Why not be her parent?"

Bill started to speak but instead ran both hands through his hair and flopped down in frustration, then popped up again. "Okay, I'll play your game. There are dozens of negatives, but right off the bat I've got things to do, I don't know the kid, and essentially, I'd have to be both mother and father. You recall, don't you, that Hillary just accepted a new full-time position that doesn't allow time for 24/7 mommying? Our daughter is already an adult. At our age, grandchildren are now the priority. Although," Bill paused a few seconds, as if lost in thought, "I will confess to sometimes wishing I had little people around me all the time and not just when it fits my daughter and son-in-law's schedules."

"Sir, Madam labors, but you do not. This child could fill that void. It is perhaps the job you need. Think of it: 'Former president rescues a needy child.'"

Bill cut him off. "Alex, discussion closed. I don't want to talk about this anymore."

"I quite agree, sir. We'll continue at another more opportune time."

"And I'm taking a rain check on whatever it is we've scheduled today. Sightseeing, was it?" Noticing the dubious way Alex glanced out the window, Bill quickly added, "A rain check means a postponement."

"Ah, I understand. Our engagement was to visit a ladies' shop. I hoped to obtain a gift, a peace offering, if you will. It's for a friend."

A ghost needing to make a peace offering? Bill thought. What next? Leprechauns knocking on my door?

"Alex, I guess I misunderstood. I thought you wanted to do a little sightseeing. You know, like driving around New York in a car. I can't just stroll into a store in this busy city; it would be pandemonium. Here, let's check it out," he said and sauntered to the window. Raising the blinds, they took in the street scene, eighteen stories below.

It was too early for offices to empty out, yet the corner of 125th Street was alive with pedestrians and vehicles, many of them trying to get through the intersection. Hotel Theresa sat across the way. Starbucks, where his security detail bought coffee, was on the corner. Other than that coffee shop, he knew little, if anything, about area retail.

"See, look at all those women carrying bags. There must be dozens of shops where they bought stuff they're lugging around. Just go into one, browse, act natural, and buy something you like. If you become a bit overwhelmed, trust me, that's how many men look when they shop. You'll fit right in." Still curious about how Alex obtained his money, he was again prevented from asking when his secretary buzzed him. "Sir, the president is on line one."

Mouthing, "Excuse me," Bill hurried over to his desk, grabbed the phone, and pointedly turned his back. "Hillary," he cried, "I'm glad you called. I thought you'd still be closeted with the business team."

"I needed a break. Way too many numbers rattling around in my head."

"Yeah, I remember well."

"Actually, things haven't gone too badly." Bill thought Hillary sounded fired up. "We're making progress. These young hotshots are leading me out of a thicket of red ink, especially Jim McAtee."

"The fella from Georgetown?"

"Yep."

Young? Bill thought he remembered McAtee being in their class. He was about to clarify that when Hillary said, "Honey, how was your day?"

"Pretty weird," he answered, and for the first time in over a month, he wasn't thinking of Alex or Sarafina. "I visited a kid named Abby at Harlem Hospital. Remember, I told you some of them live there."

"Good for you. If I ever had a few spare minutes, I'd drop by too."

"You would?"

"Oh, honey, don't you remember the stump speech I gave last year up there in Harlem, outside the uptown offices of the children's division?"

"Hillary, you gave over a hundred speeches."

"True, but in that one I told the crowd that I couldn't imagine anything worse than for a child to not have a family. I said the loneliness and despair must be crushing. Don't you remember?"

"Well, no, I mean yeah, I think so."

"Every day feeling abandoned and hoping the right person will come along. Remember?"

"It's funny you say that, Hillary. At the hospital today, Abby seemed to have the idea that she wanted to come live with us."

"Bill, what a novel idea! With the grandkids arriving, I'm reminded of how we used to wish for more kids. Now, children seem to be falling out of the sky and right into our laps. Life is funny, isn't it? Maybe this is a sign from above. Of course, I couldn't possibly handle the day-to-day responsibilities, but perhaps you should consider doing it. I'd support you wholeheartedly."

"Well ... the very notion of me taking care of a little kid ... I mean, I'd already dismissed the thought, but ..." From the corner of his eye, Bill saw Alex make a gesture. Momentarily distracted, he looked over to see him absurdly bobbing his head up and down.

Bill turned his back again and spoke into the handset. "Hillary, what'd you say?"

"What race is the child?"

After a pause, he replied, "She's black, maybe biracial, but the nurses explained that race matching no longer matters in foster care, especially for kids who badly need homes."

"Everything matters in politics. It's a wonderful idea, but we can't do that. I've worked so hard to get to this point. It would be a major distraction. Everyone—black, white, and purple— would make our lives and the child's miserable. They'd accuse me of doing it for politics or to curry favor with minorities."

It took Bill a moment before he felt he could trust his voice. "Hillary," he finally responded, "I don't believe what I just heard. You might as well have said you've spent half a lifetime supporting children's rights, but only the rights of white children."

"Oh, Bill, don't be ridiculous," she scoffed. "You know that's not what I meant, and it's nothing personal. But here's another thing: would we want to get an already vulnerable child caught up in today's twisted politics? Look, the number crunchers are returning. I have to go."

Bill hung up, slipped behind his desk, and slowly lowered himself into the leather seat. This time, Alex, out of eyeshot, kept his distance. After a few minutes, Bill leaned back, tented his fingers, and slowly rotated his chair until he spotted Alex by the window, looking on anxiously.

"Sir," Hamilton finally spoke, "correct me, please, if I'm mistaken, but did I not initially detect Madam's approval of becoming a guardian to the child?"

Alex stood framed in the double window, but Bill stared beyond him. "My friend," he said, sounding tired, "we still have a color problem in this country; it permeates every goddamn thing we do.

"But Hillary's right," he added, "and even if I wanted to— and mind you I don't—taking in a black child could scuttle any hope of a second term for my wife."

"Oh, bosh. That's manifestly ridiculous. At the moment, Madam is simply thinking like a politician. I too have examined the president's platform on child care. It's a record to be proud of. I assure you, she'll come around."

Emitting a mirthless laugh, Bill responded. "Like I said before, Alex, discussion closed."

CHAPTER 13

BEHIND THE CURTAIN

Issa, a popular new restaurant, was the latest addition to Harlem's thriving Malcolm X Boulevard. Like so many uptown clubs and hot spots, Issa attracted not only locals, but downtowners, tourists, and late-night hipsters. The evening was still young, so the boulevard was several hours away from what would become a vibrant night scene.

Just left of the restaurant's entrance, a small easy-to-miss side door led upstairs to a second-floor apartment. Faith, who owned the restaurant and five-story building housing it, used her second-floor unit as an office. In her front room, she held palm readings and tended to broken spirits.

This evening, a small group of women had gathered in Faith's front parlor where a heavy scent of eucalyptus hung in the air. The room was furnished with an ornate round oak table, matching chairs, and bookcases that lined one wall of the small room. Besides an old two-volume encyclopedia and a vase of plastic daisies, the bookcase contained an assortment of photos, Samburu baskets, and a family of African elephants carved from the wood of an ebony tree. The room's only lighting was powered by four tall candles in glass jars, the kind sold in Professor Abdul's religious store on 125th Street.

The candles faintly illuminated the faces of three women whose skin tones were a palette of soft pine yellow, honey, and the warm chestnut brown of the young fidgety one, who chewed off a fake blue fingernail then gnawed her glue-stained nail bed to its nub.

Behind a curtain of glass beads, in the center room, in a language that two of the women had never heard, a throaty alto sang what sounded like a verse from a love song:

"Coro Baay Samba,

Ngga nakk sa yaay, jel ma ..."

The singing stopped, and a few seconds later, Faith, the priestess à la restaurateur, a large woman with a closely cropped Afro, emerged. Clapping three times, she unleashed a joyous paroxysm of jingles from a dozen silver bangles lining her fleshy forearms. "Welcome, my darlings," she cooed in a velvety voice.

With one hand cupped around her ear, she asked, "Hear that? The spirits are active this evening." Looking up at nothing anyone could see, she added, "There is chatter in the air; plenty of time to learn what's being said."

Faith bustled about breathlessly. "Always something. I regret a business matter delayed me this evening." Unwrapping a brown paper package, she removed a long punk, struck a match, then relit an assortment of burned-out candles on top of the bookcase.

Still not satisfied, she repositioned the table candles, carefully placing one in front of each seated participant, then gathered up her flowing orange silk caftan. With movements as graceful as a doe's, Faith eased her generous frame into a waiting armchair of crushed gold velvet. "Come, come, girls." She clapped again, waving them into a tighter circle. "The stage is set, so let us begin.

"Tina, Keisha, and the new girl, I see. Say your name, darling."

"I am called Sarafina," the girl whispered, almost inaudibly, but her voice caused her candle to flicker.

Faith eyed her from lowered lids. "In a moment I will come to you." Reluctantly she turned away. "Tina, we best start with you." Glancing down and to her left, Faith did a once over of Tina's tiny skirt. "I don't have to consult with spirits, child, to know your troubles. You're walking on the devil road with Ndiaye."

"Miss Faith, I don't know no Ndiaye," the girl whined, sullenly rubbing her arms against the window air conditioner's chill.

"Did you take the potion I prepared for you?"

"Yes, ma'am," she lied.

"You can call it jungle juice if you want," Faith said, seemingly interpreting the girl's true thoughts, "but, unless you mend your ways, such old-fashioned potions might be too little, too late for cleansing your spirit."

"Come here," Faith ordered, reaching out. The girl, frightened now, was young—maybe seventeen—and had heavy breasts that intentionally overwhelmed a too-small tank top. Though not endowed with natural beauty, Tina had high cheekbones, dimples, and large eyes, but her flawless skin was overly made up, coarsening her best features and cheapening her overall appearance.

Faith patiently waited for Tina to place one small brown hand inside her own larger one. Before turning it over, she studied a faint blue vein that snaked from the finger where Tina was missing a nail.

"Though you're playing with fire, girl, your troubles are only a grain of sand in a world gone out of order, and you're wasting my time," she said. You're no longer in school and, despite my giving you a starting job, you didn't show up to clean the restaurant. I can't help one who won't help herself."

"Miss Faith, I ain't doing nothing wrong," she whispered, trying to pull back.

"Shhh," Faith hushed her. "With each lie you come closer to sleeping with the devil of death. Your mother, Odelia, is my friend, but friendship only goes so far." The priestess turned the small hand over to read the palm. "I've already warned you, and now I see." She squinted, using a small magnifying glass to get a better look in the dim light. "God will punish you; the living will forsake you, and the walking dead will welcome you. Go now." She dropped the girl's hand and Tina stood up, tugged down her skirt, and scampered gratefully out the door. The three women listened as her five-inch heels clattered down old marble steps.

"Darling Keisha," she said, turning to the short, plain young woman flashing an infectious smile and wearing elaborate African twist braids. "My little worrier. They should all be as cautious as you. Come, darling, I don't need your hand, just a hug." Keisha stood, and Faith placed two ample arms around the girl's thin shoulders. "Something tells me your little son's much better this week, no?"

"Yes, Miss Faith. Your medicines helped. He only had one seizure this week." The priestess had given the epileptic child, who was being monitored by a Harlem Hospital neurologist, nothing more than a placebo. But when she saw that Keisha's anxiety was not helping the fragile child's situation, nor her own, Faith had mixed a mild sedative for Keisha.

"I don't need to stay tonight, but I wanted to thank you in person. Here's the twenty-five dollars you lent me." Shyly, she held out the bills.

Folding the money back into Keisha's fist, Faith said, "Put it away. The first twenty-five is a gift."

"Oh, Miss Faith, my manager gave me more hours, at the store. I'm okay now."

"Spend it wisely, child. Leegi leegi. I'm here if you need me." Faith hugged her again and walked with her to the door. "The gods be with you, and you come back anytime, darling. I'm holding regular sessions on Tuesdays. Come to one, if you care to."

"Thank you, Miss Faith."

The priestess bustled back to the table. "Sarafina," she said, pleasurably rolling the syllables like a four-part melody. Without speaking, Faith studied the girl for a full minute before finally asking, "How did you find me, child?"

"I heard a dove's lullaby calling to me, Mother. I followed her song."

Sarafina's answer mildly surprised the woman who dropped her smile, extended her hands, palms up, and signaled Sarafina to place hers on top.

When they touched, the priestess jumped back, eyes wide, startled. For her part, Sarafina sat very still, looking hopeful.

"Eshu," Faith whispered. "The spirit chatter I heard tonight was Eshu," she said wondrously. "It spoke not to me, but to you. What are you, child?"

"They've always called me Sarafina, Mother. I come from the Other Side."

Warily shifting her interest from Sarafina's hands to her face, Faith swayed slightly as their eyes met. "Yes, I have heard of those like you," she finally said. "What is it you desire of me?"

"Tell me, Mother, why have I yet to meet one I love on the Other Side?"

Smiling now, Faith said, "We all seek answers, child. My powers are not eternal nor boundless like the heavens from which you come. I will try, but you are an Other and not like our Tina, who makes man and god cry out." She took Sarafina's hand again and ran her index finger along the palm then closed her eyes. Faith took her time and, after a few tense minutes, finally said, "Your heart is not blessed with peace, but I cannot see the cause, only that you are still on the path of a journey."

"Please, tell me what you seeing."

"There are three men; one like you comes from the Other Side. You still have many stops and starts while on your journey."

"What awaits me at the end?"

"That," Faith said, gently placing Sarafina's hand back on the table, "is what I cannot see. You must have patience, my darling. Only with time will you discover what awaits you at the end."

CHAPTER 14

SARAFINA

Sarafina stood at the window, reflecting on her relationship with Alexander, who was such an innocent. He thought he knew her story, but he didn't know the half of it and certainly not the events occurring the day before they reacquainted.

She'd been tending the big cauldron while sorting peas—precious green peas that had just arrived upriver from Carolina. There she was, shaking the separator back and forth, dreamy like, in front of the cook room fireplace. Judith, just fed, played on the floor at her feet while chewing on her rag doll.

Sarafina heard the soldiers outside. They'd been in the city all week and were starting to spread to outer parts of town. Master didn't tell the workers his troubles, but all workers—black, white, freed, or slave—knew Master Shields had drawn the ire of the militia. Ugly ragtag army men who claimed to be patriots were hounding innocents thought to favor the enemy. Red Coats, they called them, although Master and Mistress Shields hadn't dared wear the color red since war talk filled the air.

Sarafina heard rumbling down low in the lane near the gateposts. At first it sounded like the terrible autumn from a year before, when cruel winds blew away the main house roof. Only on this clear, cold day in January, there was no rain or wind in the air. The discordance was from the footfalls of a search party marching on red-coated devils. Master made his people work hard, but he and Mistress Shields weren't any kind of devils. Before that day was done, Sarafina saw the devil in the flesh. The Bible said Satan lived in a far-flung place below. In truth, the devil walked on earth among the people.

It was around noon when a band of ragtags kicked in the door and Sarafina dropped the peas. Peas went everywhere, rolling all around, with everybody running and hollering. She grabbed her baby to her bosom and would never forget the baby's sweet milky breath on her cheek.

Other rabble came running with their flintlocks and fixed bayonets and pushed in the portico's French doors. Though there were only women and little ones inside, the intruders ordered everyone to line up along the parlor room wall. Moments later, their partners in evil came down the lane, prodding the bound brewery workers before them. With Master being forced to run, he kept getting caught up in a length of becket rope and got dragged, running and falling along the road.

Roughly they threw their prisoners in with the household folk. Sarafina watched the rabble, men of no more refinement than their billy goats, ransack the shelf room, despoil their family larder, and boldly sweep Mistress's silver service into a woolen sack. Right in with it went a side of mutton and potatoes meant to tide them over during winter.

Master Shields, scraped and bloodied, his doublet torn, struggled and shouted at his captor, saying by all that was holy to leave some victuals for the women and children. His order got the ragtags a laughing, but it wasn't a sound anyone would choose to hear again.

Enjoying his moment of sport, the leader took a thirsty gulp from a pint of brandy. "Ain't ye the royal one," he sneered, taking the butt end of his musket to Master's head. He accused Master of spewing orders like good King George. When Master went down from the blow, the tormentor rested a boot on his prone figure. "I've a mind to shoot ye dead, but that'd be a waste. The pox on ye women. If I be them, I'd na be worrying none about vittles."

With that, the leader of their band, the stinking lice-infested one, proceeded to belittle Master something fierce. Sarafina remembered how it was right awful to witness Master being pulled outside and stripped to his pink skin, the shame all over his body. For further sport, they smeared him with tar heated in the man's own fireplace. No pillow was spared that they didn't slit open and make one and all watch feathers being dumped on him.

It was a cold day with sun glittering hard off packed ice, but Sarafina still smelled the meanness in those men's sweat. Mistress had her little ones, who'd never known fear, circled and hidden in her skirts. When she could stand no more, it was her whimpering that started up Annie's baby to crying. Though Sarafina and Annie both held babes on their hips, Annie's little child's insistent wailing revealed the ugly truth of the situation.

Sarafina tried to put Judith back on the breast, but she refused to suck and stared transfixed into the face of evil. Despite plenty of movement about the room, the head of the ragtags noticed the fixedness of Judith's eyes, glittering brown pools that shamed his actions. "Ye," he yelled at Sarafina. "Set that one east to the rear wall. Face her about to the fire."

Oh, why'd he speak such? His voice carried like a poisonous echo of hemlock, and it was then that Sarafina knew she'd not witnessed the worst of that dark day. Judith, though still shy of her second year, was like Sarafina's dear Auntie. She possessed the power to hearken onto what others couldn't hear or see, well before events chanced to happen.

Sarafina turned the child as directed and began covering Judith's face with her apron. But then a great draft of wind swept down the chimney, freezing already cold hearts. With the fire dying and the candles aflicker, the ragtag felt Judith's power to condemn. Plucking her from her mother's arms, the bossman stuffed her with the rest of his stealings into his foul sack. The sound of her hiccuping and struggling for breath was forever imprinted into memory.

After that, shadows shrouded Sarafina's soul in misery and later events remained muddled. Sometime during that terrible long night inside Barrow Street Prison, she recalled that they separated women from the men. Dear sweet Annie, amid her own grief and fear from having also been separated from her child, tried vainly to comfort Sarafina.

At light of day, a wagon came and rolled them down to the waterfront auction block. There Sarafina beheld Peter, Joseph, and Pompey, Annie's man, bunched up in leg irons. She had never before stood the auction block. Awful as it was, for a few cruel moments her spirit livened because she was hoping to see Judith, but the child was not to be found.

It was later that morning, after they sorted and labeled everyone and all hope was gone for reclaiming Judith, that Mr. Alexander Hamilton bought Sarafina's freedom and delivered her to the abolitionist people.

Blessed be the good in the world. After such troubles crushed Sarafina, a school teacher named Mary helped fix her outside and taught her well. But powerful as the education was, it couldn't heal a broken heart. Some months later, good Mistress Mary noticed Sarafina pining and called her into her study. Mistress told Sara to sit down then explained that her lessons hadn't wandered into the pedagogy of mind and body; still she wanted to tell a story. Her story was about the fever that took her baby Katherine and how Reverend Corbett sought her out, much as she was now confronting Sarafina.

Sarafina told Mistress Mary that she mourned her little Katherine's loss but was confused by Mistress's big words. In truth, she thought she was being readied to be sent away for absentminded mooning. Sarafina spoke cautiously, as memory and bitterness welled inside her, but she stoutly sympathized and agreed that nothing was worse than losing a child.

Her spirit low, she awaited the chastisement to begin, but

Mistress Mary did no such thing. Instead she explained that the Negroes trusted her because there in her schoolroom and on the outside, she worked tirelessly for their betterment. With that, Mary added that she was disappointed Sarafina had not confided in her. Had she done so, a search might have ensued for little Judith. Only belatedly had she discovered Judith's disappearance to be the source of Sarafina's sorrow. As a result, she'd made inquiries, but there was no sign of the child's whereabouts. However, she now asked Sarafina to listen to what Reverend Corbett had told her.

Reverend said that our heart is the body's handmaiden. It consists of two chambers; one side harbors the darkness of our sorrows. But each tiny tick brings a ray of hope for a better tomorrow. To grow stronger, she told Sara, she must have faith that God will answer her prayers. When you believe, nothing is impossible.

Mistress explained that the heart is made of a strong earth, wind, and fire substance, like the skin of a drum. That made Sarafina remember how Auntie once enchanted her with stories of her young warrior, back in the land across the sea. Until they met again, he kept her heart alive by sending spirit messages through the beat of his djembe. Over treetops and on the wings of a yellow claw, Auntie heard him say he'd await her return. The soft thrill of his drum traveled the sea on a humpback. In spring, when the seabirds flew out to meet the mighty whale, Auntie heard their singing and knew his love had arrived.

Sarafina came to feel the pull of Mistress's spirit-world teachings, which recalled another of Auntie's home stories about the soft green tree land where great god Eshu stood at the crossroads before two doors. Both were open but one led nowhere, and only those who believed in his powers continued through the right door.

Over time, Sarafina learned to forgive herself and walked through Eshu's door. Only then dared she harbor hope that Auntie, who possessed the power to see beyond, would find Judith.

When she was able to discern sun again among the clouds and her sense of feeling was restored, she noted she still drew the attentions of Mr. Hamilton, the gentleman who rescued her from the block.

Mr. Hamilton was the lawyer man who had once come to Master Shields's each Wednesday conveying ledgers and sundry sheafs of paper, helping with Master's requests to sell and export his beer. One time, upon Mr. Hamilton's approach, she clearly forgot her place and smiled at seeing an important gentleman so cumbered under piles of ledgers, like a beast of burden.

"Sir," she said, curtseying and explaining that Master and the other men were still tending to the malt mash, so it fell upon her to gather his bundles and see to his mount.

However, as she reached forth, he drew back and said that she would do no such thing. Somehow their interactions dislodged his great sheaf of papers onto the ground. Red-faced and scrambling on hand and knee, she quickly grabbed a sheet or two when she felt him beside her. She dared not look, as he pulled her to her feet. "There," he said, steadying her about the waist as she almost swooned in fright. On the spot, he confessed to having wanted to touch her for the longest time.

"S-sir," she had stammered in a crouched position, awaiting his blow. Laughing soundly, he said it was okay to open her eyes.

In fact, he added, while opportunity presented itself, he insisted on seeing her eyes close up. "Go on," he'd urged her. Hesitantly, she did as told. With an intake of breath, he described them as brown with flecks of gold.

Three years later, as fate willed it, the gentleman again lifted Sarafina when their paths crossed at the auction. As time allowed her to tuck grief into the recesses of her being, she began to slyly meet up with Mr. Hamilton. By then the war was well on, but his duties sometimes obliged him to journey off the battlefield and into the city, as was the occasion when he came to her rescue. At one of their secret meetings, she learned his lawyerly skills won a trifle of justice for Master and Mistress Shields after the militia plundered their property. Fearfully, she had asked Mr. Hamilton if he knew what had happened to Master's other taken-away slaves. Of them, there was no word.

On this earth journey, Sarafina knew that Alexander, despite his book learning and lawyerly skills, was of no further use to her. Perhaps she would tell him so he could tend to his manly needs with another. It had been weeks since she last felt Auntie's spirit, and never had she received a message from Judith. Here on earth, she had come across a wise woman who was part-touched in the ways of Afterlife. But even she could not tell Sarafina the outcome of her journey, and time was running out.

CHAPTER 15

THE CARIBBEAN CONNECTION

Hoping that a few hours of quality time on his manuscript might clear his head of ghosts and abandoned children, Bill listened to the soothing sounds coming from his Sixto Rodriguez CD. When it finished playing, he approached his computer and sat down with resolve. After forty minutes of fits and starts, he thought he should probably open the manila envelope that lay buried in his desk's clutter. Reluctantly he pulled it out, peeled it open, and flipped through three edited chapters and comments. In that annoyingly familiar large block print, Bob had systematically scribbled, "CUT, CUT, CUT," or slashed through text. In one margin he'd written, "Bill, WHAT PURPOSE DOES THIS SERVE? DO YOU REALLY NEED THIS?" Bill stared at the manuscript for what seemed like forever. Finally he muttered, "Screw it" and returned the pages to the envelope.

Now, hours later, after a nap and two low-fat peanut butter and jelly sandwiches for dinner, some soy milk, and a Granny

Smith apple, Bill felt wide awake. It was too early for bed, but he changed into his robe and pajamas and picked up Through the Looking Glass, the book he'd been reading the night before. He'd stopped reading at one of his favorite parts, the railway carriage scene, in which Carroll makes a brilliant case against any sense of measured time:

"... And a great many voices all said together ('like the chorus of a song,' thought Alice), 'Don't keep them waiting, child! Why his time is worth a thousand pounds a minute!'"

Bill had loved this children's classic ever since he discovered it in a freshman English class at Georgetown. Now that he was experiencing bizarre Alice-in-Wonderland-type moments, he'd increasingly felt a need to revisit the book. Just as he had in 1968, he marveled at how Lewis Carroll turned conventional thinking upside down by employing fantasy to arrive at truth about life being confusing, mysterious, and strange.

Reclining comfortably, he kept one hand on the small hardback and instinctively lowered the other to rub behind Bootsy's ear where cartilage formed a tiny trumpet. "Quiet, girl." He hushed her mewling. "It's just wind banging that loose gutter brace," he said to the cat, feeling the slight draft of air blowing through the cracked window. In response, the cat popped up, stood rigid, and hissed at the emerging swirl of luminous, off-white energy.

"Sir, my apologies," said Alex. "I know I'm overstepping the tenets of hospitality and appreciate how terribly rude I appear. But I have a problem."

Slamming his book shut, Bill brought his recliner fully upright. "Oh, for Christ's sake. Haven't you disrupted enough evenings around here?"

"Kind sir," he said. "I need assistance. Sarafina's gone."

"Gone? As in gone back where you two came from or as in gone out?"

Seeing him hesitate, Bill continued. "You've spoken of Sarafina mirroring contemporary Americans and exploring her surroundings. At the time, you considered that a positive, remember? Is that what she's done?"

Looking miserable, Alex nodded.

"Young people, including my own daughter, stay out late in New York. Instead of barging in here, maybe you should try it. Get out and meet other people."

"Well, I would consider doing so, if …"

"If what? New York is one big party town; just do it. Sarafina has earned the freedom to do as she pleases. Let her be. From a few things you said, I think she needs some space. Alex, I appreciate our unique situation, but you can be tedious as hell. Sorry to be so blunt, but it's true."

"But it's going on nine o'clock. She's never been about this late."

"I'm well aware of the time. Look, it's Thursday night; essentially the weekend has begun. Harlem doesn't close down until three or four in the morning. She's fine. She's a ghost; apparitions are invincible. Right?"

"Well, yes, but she wants to replicate the manners of a human. People don't disappear, so she's unlikely to do so." Hamilton walked over to the window and drew back the drape as if expecting Sarafina to appear behind it. With his back to him, Bill noticed the beginnings of a bald spot under a fringe of red hair. "There's something else," Alex whispered. "Since we arrived, Sarafina has changed."

"Be happy for her. She's relishing what she never had before: freedom. That's a powerful emotion. She can no longer be denied the right to move about. You're aware of her history and previous life. I'm not, but I imagine that Sarafina endured terrible deprivations."

"Yes, there were many. Conditions for Negroes were even worse than you'd imagine."

Since first meeting Alex, Bill had envisioned dozens of scenarios explaining his involvement with Sarafina. Now he saw an opening to ask.

"Your relationship with her is private, but perhaps you'd share what prompted your commitment to help blacks in general and Sarafina most particularly."

"As a youth in the West Indies, I recognized that life on sugar plantations was uncommonly cruel for Negroes. I swore if ever I gained power, I'd work to reverse the injustices."

Having had similar thoughts while growing up in the segregated south, Bill nodded.

Alex, seemingly eager to talk, continued. "At age eighteen, I emigrated to New York, attended Kings College, then began practicing law. I first met Sarafina while representing the legal interests of a certain beer brewer, Conrad Shields. Some three years later, I encountered her again, but not within the confines of Shields' household; she stood upon Wall Street's auction block.

"By then, I was an officer in General Washington's army and in the city on a mission for the general. Slavery, of course, went against every principle for which the colonies fought." Looking over at Bill, Alex asked, "Sir, did you ever have occasion to witness the selling of a human being?"

Grimacing, Bill quickly shook his head no.

"Consider yourself blessed," Alex said bitterly. "No man should witness such degradation of another. During the Revolution, it was bad enough that southern states, while espousing democracy, continued to hypocritically trade in human property. But to witness northerners engaging in the odious practice was indefensible.

"Seeing Sarafina on that platform was akin to observing a fox hunt with the poor beast cowering and cornered as the pack moved in for the kill." Fascinated, Bill sat very still, listening intently.

"The auction scene," Alex recounted, "brought back memories of Mirabel, a slave girl I'd grown up with in St. Croix. In fanciful fits of whimsy, I planned to rescue Mirabel and set her free."

Just above a whisper, Bill inquired, "Did your parents own her?"

"Certainly not. I was destitute, orphaned. At that point, my existence depended on the kindness of outsiders. And because of my pecuniary state, boys and girls of my own station spurned me."

Remembering the path to the White House and all the times he'd defended his modest Southern roots against blue-blooded politicians who often had everything handed to them, Bill couldn't resist interjecting. "Alex, I salute your climb from poverty to the pinnacles of power. Believe me, I know it wasn't easy."

"Thank you, sir. Ironically, while I was ostracized, Mirabel labored under similar censure from peers. A neighboring plantation owned her, but island-wide house servants such as she were often shunned by other slaves. As a result of our social isolation, we sought each other out. Yet, in my naiveté, I dismissed her grandmother's objections to our friendship."

Having been briefly in a similar situation with his high-school girlfriend, Bill understood exactly how a grandparent would condemn such an alliance.

Bill had resumed sitting, and Alex walked over to stand before him. "Sir, my purpose in disturbing your privacy was not to relate long ago events. I rather hoped, with your considerable resources, you'd help me search for Sarafina. I have reason to believe she's taken up with strangers and I fear for her."

Bill looked at the clock: nine fifteen. "Alex, I really don't think you have anything to worry about. And since you've kinda put me in the middle of this venture, I'd like you to finish explaining how Mirabel's situation led you and Sarafina to my back door. Afterwards, we'll talk about this search business."

"Thank you, sir. I can ask no more from one I've come to call a friend. Mirabel's grandmother," Alex picked up the thread of his story, "was an old crone to be avoided. Negroes on the island feared her sorcery, and deep down, I suppose, I wondered if there was truth to their talk of her being possessed. Being in my fourteenth year, I was a heady, bold fellow and had been about one evening when the old woman stepped from behind a mandevilla bush, startling me.

"Were you following me?" I asked, squirming, as I was retreating from a rendezvous with her granddaughter. "Paying my discomfort no mind, she held me in her sights, then, spewing island patois, admonished me: 'Be gone from the girl.' For the longest while, with her eyes locked onto mine, she remained silent then lapsed into a strange, unintelligible mumbo-jumbo.

"A breath of moonbeam illuminated the crone's black face with its wandering milky eye, and I confess, sir, it unnerved me. With all my heart, I wanted to run, but the heavily perfumed air and the old woman's magical cadence impaled me. Then, switching again into patois, she said, 'I be warning you; stay away or a curse upon our heads.'

"Mustering courage, I protested. 'I've taught Mirabel her letters. Soon she'll be reading and doing sums. You can't prevent my visiting her.'

"Giving no sign of hearing, she wagged a bony finger in my face. 'I be done warned you, boy.' With the defiance of youth, I told her, 'God didn't make any race superior. Mirabel is like one of my own kind.'

"At those words, the old hag's eyes blazed, and I expected to hear a curse or a hex. Instead, breathing her foulness on me, she muttered, 'And for such, our peoples reap great sorrow.'"

Despite the passage of centuries, the old woman's words sent a shudder down Bill's spine. "I wish I didn't sense that something awful happened to the girl. Tell me, was the old lady's prediction as ominous as it sounded?"

"To answer your question," Alex suggested, "allow me to back up and start at the beginning. Early in life, I understood the importance of sugarcane to the West Indies economy. Island slaves outnumbered whites twelve to one, and their labor fueled massive plantations. Yet, to my reasoning, a necessary evil did not excuse the barbarism inflicted on slaves."

Again recalling his youth in Arkansas, Bill despaired to think how much the long-ago legacy of slavery continued stunting generations of black people.

"It was a sultry August day," Alex continued, "several weeks after my encounter with the old woman, and I'd ridden up island to a distant relative's boiling house, hoping to prevail on him to help pay for my next year's schooling. Heat and humidity bathed the still air, and a hurricane threatened. Momentarily, there was no trade wind for cooling nor a passing cloud for protection, and my skin was burning. Seeking quick relief, I took a shortcut and cantered across a neighbor's property, encountering motionless windmills and occasional gangs of naked caners toiling in fetid, bug-infested fields.

"As mature stalks thickened and hovered higher than my horse's head, I was forced to slow down and seek a trail opening. I almost missed it, but some miles from home, hidden among a vein of ten-foot stalks, I stumbled upon a slave woman who had passed out from exhaustion and a vicious beating. Her crazed taskmaster stood over her, snarling like an attack dog. Seeing my approach, the man spoke familiarly.

"'Too much time up at the big house has this one acting high and mighty. They sent her to me to set straight.' Then, directing his ire on the poor woman, he said, 'Up, you lazy, worthless whore.'

"'I say,' I offered feebly, reining in for a better view of the downed figure. 'Let her be. Can't you see it's a lass? She's sick from sun and needs water. Some of these lassies can't handle such harsh work conditions. Stop, or you'll kill her.'

"'Why you impudent young squit,' the overseer exploded, revealing a ribbon of rotten, tobacco-stained teeth. 'Already had a dip in the ink pot, have you? And now,' he said, nudging the prone figure with his boot, 'you thinks to tell me how to handle the likes of she.'

"Suddenly realizing the man's intent, I ducked as his whip,

stiff with blood and sweat, bit like a snake, glancing my shoulder and slicing my shirt. The leather's awful impact caught the horse square on its withers, sending it bolting across the narrow passage as I held on for dear life. Fighting tears, I looked back futilely as the man's demented hahahahahaha became forever imprinted in memory.

"Only then did I understand the grandmother's warning. The next night, fearful that Mirabel, already marked from association with me, might also be beaten, I choked back further tears of frustration and told Mirabel that we could no longer see each other."

"Thank you for sharing that story. Those are not easy memories to recall. Now, if you'd like, we can discuss what you want to do here tonight about Sarafina."

Softly, Alex said, "I think I'm losing her. She's become more attached to this world than to me."

"I feel your pain, Alex, but sometimes relationships just run their course. It sounds like the lady wants to be alone."

"Yes, but why does she insist on maintaining human form?"

"It's kind of hard to interact and experience what the world has to offer, if you're flitting around like a ghost. It tends to freak people out."

"I must find her. I fear she's in danger."

"Alex, it goes against basic survival instincts not to protect oneself. If she doesn't want to disappear before someone's eyes, can't she just excuse herself to the restroom or something and then vanish? People do it all the time, especially if they're wanted by the authorities. And believe me, there's nothing otherworldly about some of these disappearing acts. Does she have money to take a cab, like many women do at night?"

"Well, yes."

"Which reminds me," Bill added. "For weeks, I've been meaning to ask what you two use for money."

Reaching into a pocket, Hamilton pulled out a mass of loose tens, twenties, and fifties; several fell on the floor.

"These."

Bill bent down and helped gather a few, then examined a dog-eared ten. "How did you come by these, may I ask?"

"In heaven, money is plentiful; it just doesn't mean anything once it gets up there."

Bill looked at Alex to see if he was trying to be humorous. Realizing he wasn't, Bill said, "That might just be the funniest thing I've heard in months."

With Alex looking like he didn't get the joke, Bill added, "There's an old comedy from the 1930s called You Can't Take It With You. The title stuck around and became a common expression, suggesting that people share and enjoy their money while on earth, since it doesn't do them any good once they die. I wish I could tell someone what you just said about money in heaven."

Knowing that wasn't feasible, Bill instead passed Alex a smoothed-out ten. "Take a look at this."

Alex took the money, examined it carefully, and read aloud what was written on the back: "'In God We Trust.' Pray tell, whose idea was that?"

"It's a long story." Bill laughed. "I'll fill you in later. But look at the picture on the front. Anything seem familiar?"

After a moment, Alex waved the ten and looked questionably at Bill.

"Your name and face is stamped on every sawbuck coming off the press. Oh, and sawbuck is a just a nickname for the ten dollar bill."

"Sir, I'm humbled. I had no idea."

"It's the least the government could do in appreciation for your service. But back to Sarafina. Do you realize she could be anywhere?"

"Not anywhere, sir. Of late, Sarafina speaks of a new acquaintance who gave her one of these. Bill watched in surprise as Alex pulled a number of business cards from his breast pocket. "These are not as artful as ours were, but your practice of distributing such identifications reminds me of how, in my day, we announced ourselves with calling cards."

Alex handed him a small, unadorned, dog-eared buff-colored business card. On one side was written the word "Faith." The other side said "Issa." Beneath Issa was an address on Malcolm X Boulevard. Oddly, there was no phone number or website. Bill figured that street number was south of his office, in a booming upscale area of eateries, boutiques, and night spots. Maybe, he speculated, it's a private club. He'd heard of them but didn't know how such places operated.

"Why two names, and is it a restaurant, church, or what? It's Thursday, and some churches hold Thursday night prayer meetings." He eyed his watch. "But it's late. Most services would be ending around now. What time did she go out?"

"Hours ago. As for a description, Sarafina describes it as a sheltering abode for women."

"A shelter? I hadn't thought of that, but I doubt it; not

around there. Let me think a minute." Bill pondered calling
Ray. After so many years together, it was hard to deceive him.
For that reason, he had twice bypassed Ray when Alex was
around and instead used agents from the NYC field office. His
guts, however, were warning him to not try sneaking out on his
own. Ray would be suspicious about the purpose of running
around Harlem, but he was also loyal. And discreet.

"My bodyguard," he said, deciding to err on the side of
caution, "knows Harlem like the back of his hand. Since I'm
flying blind here, I'd best get him in on this." Reading the card
one last time and still making no sense of it, Bill walked to the
phone and punched in Ray's number.

◆

CHAPTER 16
GOOD NIGHTLIFE

Hamilton, suddenly oblivious to anything but taking his first car ride, scrambled into the SUV's back seat after Ray opened the door for him. Hovering on the sidewalk like a mother hen, Bill watched Alex switch seats and regretted not giving him more pointers on how to ride in the car. Unlike the other Secret Service agents, Ray was not hesitant to ask probing questions about impromptu assignments. He was nobody's fool, and from the grim, down-turned set of his mouth, Bill already sensed Ray's wariness.

Fumbling for the right tone, Bill said, "Alex is an old friend; he's an historian. If you've read recent activity reports, you know the two of us have ventured out a few times. He's here studying Harlem's economic turnaround and will stay for the upcoming gala. And, after burying himself in research, he's damn excited to see the outside world," Bill ad-libbed.

"Look," he added, when Ray didn't interject, "Let's be honest. We both know the Bureau's giving me a hard time about going around in public. About this thing tonight: it came up suddenly. Alex and his lady had a misunderstanding and she took off. That's what this is about. Neither of them knows the area well. He's worried and asked my help. And, goddamnit, I don't want the cavalry on my ass, just because I'm going out with a friend." Bill snapped on his seatbelt, hoping his speech, which was more or less true, didn't sound like a crock.

Having already warned Alex, Ray nodded politely, but he still wasn't taking anything for granted. When he got into the car, he immediately raised the bulletproof barrier, cutting Alex off. "Sir, remind me of Alex's last name."

"Of course," he mumbled. "It's Hamill, with one M, two L's." Oh, shit, he groaned inwardly, trying to remember if he told the field office that Alex spelled his last name with two M's. He made a mental note to ask Alex which spelling they had agreed on. When he was first caught up short by that question, it was bad enough that he couldn't think fast and foolishly blurted out Hamill. Even Smith or Brown would have been preferable. At least he knew how to spell those.

Ray looked straight ahead. "Chief, you haven't said where we're going."

"Oh, sorry." Bill exhaled slowly and passed him the business card. "We'll start here. This came from a friend of Sarafina's." Turning on the overhead light, Ray scanned both sides of the card and read, "'Issa.' I've heard of the place; that street number is around 117th or 118th, on Malcolm X. If I'm not mistaken, it's a restaurant. Somebody, my mother maybe, told me that Faith owns it. She's a big wig around there. Among other enterprises, Faith has an old-fashioned yarn and general store called Faith's Notions and Potions. Two days a week, she holds an after-school program for neighborhood girls. Volunteers teach them how to knit, crochet, sew from a pattern, that kind of thing. Essentially, they learn the craft of sewing."

"Sewing? How did you come up with that piece of minutia?"

"Pure coincidence," Ray said laughing, "and no, I don't crochet. But my mom is a knitter and learned about the program when she started buying her supplies there. It was a big deal when she and other women in Harlem no longer had to go downtown to buy yarn.

"Is there anything about Harlem that you don't know, buddy? So what exactly do you hear about this Issa?"

"Just that it's a pretty dope—sorry—pretty nice new hangout with good food and decent entertainment."

Bill rapped on the glass divider and spoke into a small nickel-coated receiver. "Alex, would Sarafina likely frequent the bar scene?" Catching himself, he quickly rephrased the question. "Does she imbibe? You know, drink wine, beer, any type of spirits?"

"To the best of my knowledge, she's acquainted with sherry, and perhaps other potables as well."

Glancing at Bill, Ray put the car in gear and drove off. In the city that never slept, there were surprisingly few people or vehicles about. They cleared the light at 141st Street, where motor and pedestrian traffic picked up. Ray slowed at St. Nick as two men, both in maroon-colored uniforms, emerged from the IND station and jaywalked in front of their car.

As their SUV sped through Harlem, its darkened windows and muscular antennae drew a few stares. At the next traffic light, Ray broke the silence. "Chief, see those dudes?" He meant three rangy young men who were passing money to a

fourth man. They stood under a street lamp and stopped what
they were doing when they noticed Ray's car.

"Barely. They don't have a spare pound of flesh among
them."

"Yeah, that too, but those dudes are bad news. Looks like a
drug deal to me. They made our vehicle and figure something's
up. Look at them hunching and balancing on the balls of their
feet, ready to take off."

Squinting into the night, Bill said, "Okay, I'll have to take
your word on that one."

"If I wanted to mess with them some," Ray added, "I'd let
'em hear the locks pop up, and Slim Shady, the one in the middle
who looks like he has something tucked in his already sagging
waistband, would outrun us down to 117th Street." Pulling
out his phone, Ray said, "Looks like something could be going
down. I'll give the 30th Precinct a holler and a description.
They'll ease over here and see what's up."

Shifting uneasily, Bill sensed the agent's dark mood. "Ray,
it's okay, you don't have to take anything out on a few street
corner kids. We're just looking for the lady. Alex's lady. That's
all."

"Chief, I'm cool. I'm driving, but you're in the driver's seat,
if you know what I mean."

Damn it, Bill thought, scowling in his visor mirror. "Look,"
he sighed. "I know sudden late-night business smells funny and
my friend's a little odd, but I swear I'm not dragging you, or
myself, into a mess. Those days are long gone. I promise."

"You're the boss, sir."

"And you were one of my closest confidantes during my last
two years in office. We've been through thick and thin. Have I

ever lied to you?"

"No, sir. But to be perfectly honest, at times the truth was more than I cared to know."

For the next several blocks, neither man spoke. Finally, Bill said, "Way back then, I deserved that assessment. But you're just gonna have to trust me on this one." Suddenly feeling better for having spoken up, Bill leaned forward and fiddled with the knobs on a wide-angled mirror that panned the rear seat section.

Alex, enthralled, his eyes bright with the reflections of oncoming headlights, sat perched behind Ray.

"Everything all right back there, Alex?"

"Simply splendid, sir. I cannot thank you enough for the opportunity to—"

"Great. We're almost there," Bill said and quickly snapped his mike off.

At the Harlem Hospital complex, Ray moved to the curb as an ambulance, its siren shrieking, roared up behind them then cut sharply into the ER driveway. Bill glanced up at the fourth floor where Abby still lived, at least until they sent her to the Castle Girls' Home. Just yesterday, Alex had been on him again about making a return visit. Alex could be annoying, but sometimes he was also right. What harm would it do? Also, he wanted to tell Alex that Hillary had apologized for her knee-jerk reaction about mixed-race placements.

Ray, noting his boss's interest in the hospital, pointed at the building. "If you take a bullet in this borough, that's where you want to go. Yep," he said. "Harlem docs can sew you up better than an Armani tailor."

Bill had heard enough doomsday talk. "Ray, why don't we try

to have a good time tonight, okay? But, I'll tell you something. If you want to know what Harlem Hospital can do for the sick and wounded, try visiting the fourth floor. It's full of homeless kids, sick kids, and boarder babies, whose maladies and hurts run deeper than a nine-millimeter slug from a handgun."

"Sure, Chief. I'll do that sometime. Boarder babies, you say? That's a new one on me. In a softer voice, he added, "Maybe you can tell me about the kids, sometime."

Absorbed with memories of his turbulent last years in office, Bill didn't notice Ray's sideways glance meet his hard-set profile. He also didn't notice the smile playing on Ray's lips, or that his bodyguard's shoulders relaxed as he sped through the yellow light.

Over on his side of the car, Bill didn't particularly care about Ray's feelings, even though he knew what was bugging him: his 1998 summons before the grand jury. Ray had never forgiven the prosecutor, or Bill, for putting him in a situation that meant squealing on his boss. Still, Ray's bad memories paled in comparison to what he'd been dragged through. And now, with this current tragicomedy taking over his life, he didn't need a bodyguard busting his balls.

They continued in silence until Ray got within a few doors of the restaurant. Rolling to a stop, he quickly explained that since Bill didn't want a heavy federal presence, he'd been obliged to notify NYPD. They'd already swept the premises and would act as his backup for the evening. Two off-duty cops stood outside Issa's door. An unmarked police car was double-parked across the street. Bill and Alex watched Ray flip down his visor with the "US Government Business" sign, then flagrantly ignore the "No Parking Bus Stop" sign and back his heavy vehicle smartly between two other illegally parked cars, a Beamer and new Lexus SUV.

A few seconds later, Ray said something to the cops, flashed his badge, and also ignored the "No Weapons" sign as he led the small entourage quietly into Issa. At this time of evening, lights were dim and the sound system was pumped up high, allowing them, at least for the moment, to move unnoticed around the curved wooden bar.

The room was large with an updated but old-timey, speakeasy feel. Square oak tables were scattered around the floor; booths were lined up along an exposed brick wall beneath an array of iconic Harlem photos from the 1920s to the '50s. Some, like the picture of a young, smiling Sugar Ray Robinson leaning on his pink Cadillac, had been colorized and enlarged. The back of the restaurant was open to the kitchen, where high-energy cooks, wearing Pope-like Toque Demagny high hats, went about the sacred chore of filling empty stomachs.

Nice, Bill thought, turning his attention to Alex, who gaped at a room full of lovely twenty- and thirty-year-old women.

"Alex," he hissed, "if this is going to work, you have to act like you've done this before. Close your mouth. Glance at the ladies; don't fixate on one person. Keep your eyes moving, look around, then occasionally turn back to say something to me."

"Certainly, sir," he said to Bill's face, before doing a comic slow-motion back toward the room. Who could blame him? Bill thought, also appreciating the mostly young, ethnically mixed crowd of couples, groups, blacks, Hispanics, and whites.

Ray, on Bill's right, signaled the barkeep who, elbow-deep in suds, was rinsing martini glasses but gave an "I'll be right with you" high sign. When he realized his customer was Bill, he abandoned his chore, dried his hands, and hurried to place napkins in front of Bill and his party. Several other customers were now pointing and looking Bill's way.

"Sorry for the wait," he apologized, flashing a gap-toothed grin at Bill. About fifteen minutes ago, we got a heads-up that a celebrity would be in tonight. Big shots come in all the time. Last week it was Cindy Crawford and Spike Lee, but never someone of your status, Mr. Clinton. I'm honored, sir."

"Thank you, but these days I'm just regular folks. Sometimes live in town, work in town, and every so often, I try to get out on the town."

"Well, you're more than welcome in here," the bartender said. "What can I get you?"

"I usually have club soda with a lime, but lately I've had a taste for wine. How about a Merlot? Do you have something from California?"

"Sure, hang on. We just started carrying Grouser, a new Napa Valley vintage that's been popular. Let me know how you like it. Also, would you do me the favor of an autograph?" Grinning like a kid, he put the wine in front of Bill then pushed a pen and two additional oatmeal-colored cocktail napkins toward him.

"My pleasure." Bill took a sip of wine then drank the rest before picking up the ballpoint. Thanks. Good choice, not too dry."

The server topped off his glass. "And what about you two gentlemen?"

"Ginger ale for me, but we won't be staying long. We're looking for a woman named Sarafina. The name ring a bell?"

"Sorry. I wish I could help, but it doesn't sound familiar."

"And, you, sir?" he asked Alex.

"Chivas Scotch whiskey will work just fine. Alternately, I enjoy a Bordeaux," he elaborated, appreciating the extensive selection of whiskeys and wines displayed behind the bar. "Since the third century, the area of Bordeaux has produced some of the best ..."

Bill cleared his throat. "My friend happens to be an expert on early French wines." Easily satisfied, the bartender said, "Cool. I'll get the other drinks." Ray noted that Alex seemed to be not only peculiar, but an expert in everything.

When the bartender returned with Scotch and a ginger ale, Bill asked, "What's your name, for the autograph?"

"It's André."

"You French?"

"I'm from Senegal."

"Thought I detected an accent."

"Everyone in New York has an accent, even you."

"*Touché*," Bill laughed and dashed off André's greeting, then handed over the napkin. "This is a classy establishment. How long's it been here?"

"A year and ten months." André carefully folded the paper memento and tucked it into his shirt pocket. "Thanks a million for this."

"You're welcome."

"The place," he said, resting his elbows on the bar, "was a hit from day one. It's like magic; everything the owner touches turns to gold. Excuse me a minute while I check on a few other drinkers."

"You were explaining something about the owner," Bill reminded André when he made it back to refill their glasses. "By any chance is her name Faith?"

"Yep. Faith. She's quite a lady."

"I can appreciate that. She's left an impression on me."

"Sir, this bar is not the half of it."

"What's Faith's claim to fame?"

"Wow, where to start?" André seemed perplexed, as if he'd been asked why the universe has black holes.

"For one thing, she owns much of this block and is the force behind a lot of new development around here. The shops are closed now, but you should see the bustling businesses in daylight. We have a large African community in here now. Faith's married to a Senegalese guy; that's how I got the steady job."

Listening, Ray piped in. "Where does she get her money?"

"Hard work, investments, who knows?" he shrugged. "Faith's a bit of a mystery, but the lady's revered in this community."

Time passed pleasantly. A three-man reggae band arrived and started setting up their drums, keyboard, and amps. Around the room, patrons, some newly arrived, whispered about Bill's presence but politely resisted intruding on his evening. André got back to them as often as he could. When he next went to serve a group of women who had walked in, Bill and Alex followed the movement, wondering if Sarafina might be among them. Not seeing her, Bill looked away, while Alex's fascination with the comely new arrivals only increased.

"Stop drooling," Bill told Alex, but he laughed and twirled his glass by the stem then took a few sips. "Now, do you see what I mean? Unescorted ladies really do step out on their own."

"It is indeed as you described."

"And like I also suggested, you ought to try it."

"Perhaps," Alex agreed tentatively, "complexities of the social order are less daunting than imagined."

"Atta boy," Bill affirmed, glancing again at the cluster of people bunched near the door. "No doubt, some in the crowd will take cabs home, maybe call a car service," he explained then suddenly stopped mid-sentence, gawked, turned to Ray, tapped him on the shoulder, and blatantly pointed.

"Do you see what I see?" Bill asked darkly, zeroing in on a reveler with a loud high-pitched voice who, despite the smoking ban, drew on a lighted cigarette before mashing it out on the wooden floor. Behind her, grasping the bottom folds of her fringed skirt in his tiny fists, stood a bewildered little boy, about four years old. He was dressed in a Spiderman T-shirt and pajama bottoms with too-short legs.

"That kid shouldn't be in here." Sliding awkwardly off his stool, Bill stretched to his full six-foot-three and signaled André. Seeing the ex-president's scowl and taut body language, the bartender hustled over.

"Sir, is something wrong?"

"That woman and child," he said, bristling with presidential authority, "need to be sent home."

Bill's ominous tone had alerted Alex of something amiss, and like André and Ray, he watched tensely.

André didn't even glance toward the door.

"Sir, I understand your concern, but … I'm afraid the woman's a chronic problem." Twisting the bar towel in his hand, André explained. "The law stipulates children are permitted in our dining room or the designated waiting area." He tilted his head at some vague space to the left but wouldn't look in that direction. "Our kitchen closes at ten thirty, and it's only ten fifteen or so."

Pushing up his jacket sleeve, Bill checked his watch. "Shouldn't matter," he mumbled. "It's after bedtime."

"We serve late supper at this establishment, and she knows how to play the system." Increasingly uncomfortable, André added, "She might have a plate of oysters or a shrimp cocktail, then, in a half hour or so, she will head to her next party and probably put the kid to sleep in someone's apartment."

"Well, if you can't do anything to help one little kid, then, by God, I will." Bill took a step.

Ray stood up. "Take it easy, Chief." At the same time, he moved Bill's wine glass off to the side and out of reach. Imperceptibly, Ray shook his head at the two detectives across the room to indicate he had this under control.

Alex, who'd retreated into silence after witnessing his affable host's uncharacteristic behavior, suddenly perked up and attempted to peer around Ray's broad shoulders, which were partly blocking his view of Bill.

"Excellent, excellent," Alex said to the uncomprehending ex-president and his bodyguard. "The sentiment of claiming a needy child lurks in your heart."

Momentarily distracted by the dissonant sound of musicians warming up, Bill asked, "Alex, what are you talking about?"

"I'm remembering a previous conversation. Perhaps now, if you'd kindly retake your seat, sir, we might resume the discussion on the benefits of rescuing young children."

Despite his dignified bearing, Ray thought Alex had the characteristics of an annoying gnat and felt like swatting him. Instead, he stepped in front of him but spoke to Bill. "Chief, let's go. It's time to leave. The lady's not here."

"Listen, you two. Don't humor me. Two or three drinks haven't blinded me to the fact that there are too many neglected children in this city. And, for the public record," he said, spraying spittle that Ray ducked, "the only persons who need to vacate these premises are that woman and the little boy who deserves a lot but wants nothing more than to sleep in his own bed.

"Chief, we're outta here," Ray said, and without removing his left arm from around his boss's shoulder, he reached into his own back pocket. Grabbing his wallet, he got it open and partly used his teeth to fish out some bills and throw them on the bar, hoping they were enough.

"On second thought," Alex said, taking a step back from Ray, "perhaps your man has the right idea. I shall reiterate my point at a later time. And, might I add, it seems ever more unlikely that Sarafina will appear."

With Alex trailing close behind, Ray nudged Bill toward the exit just as the drummer of the band, his rubber-tipped mallets poised midair, yelled, "A one and a two ..." With lightning speed, he struck his steel drum, drowning out Bill's voice.

"Easy Chief."

"Now see here," came Bill's slightly slurred protest into a whirl of music. "That little kid, all the little kids. It's a damn shame. I need to speak to that woman and let her know it isn't right for her to be here."

"Sir, that's not such a good idea."

Around them, the happy crowd was now pleasurably toe-tapping and bobbing heads as the group broke into "Buffalo Soldier."

CHAPTER 17
A LADY NAMED LIZ

Alex hesitated. The sign said "Crystal's," and he debated several more minutes before walking in. After all, he'd recently patronized a bookseller's tiny store without drawing undue attention. And, thanks to his evening with Mr. Clinton, he knew the practice of visiting public houses for a taste of spirits had changed little over centuries—except now, women joined men for a nip. Another thing about today's women, beyond public drinking and boldness of dress and speech, is they were easy on the eye.

"It's all in our improved diet and hygiene," he remembered Bill saying about healthy skin and hair. Yes, that makes sense, Alex thought, looking around, but whatever the cause, he thrilled at modern femininity's comely attributes.

"Chivas on the rocks," he ordered like an expert, before the bartender even asked.

"Sure thing, buddy. That'll be twelve bucks, upfront."

Hamilton nodded, put down a ruffled twenty, got his drink,

and headed for the far stool where he would draw the least attention to himself.

"Hey, thanks, man," the bartender said to his back, "thanks a lot."

The gold liquid had a spicy almond scent and went down smooth. Taking another sip, he debated pulling from his pocket a new book, Harlem Highlights, that he'd borrowed from Bill's bookcase. However, a quick glance around the room showed that, unlike the bookseller's friendly confines, no one here appeared to be reading.

Instead, Alex nursed his drink and thought about how much he missed Bill, who was traveling with Mrs. Clinton. He also missed Sarafina, who no longer sought his company and now immersed herself in the new African-American community. The void left Alex feeling alone in this alien world, but Bill was right; he shouldn't begrudge Sarafina's bold new independence.

Consumed with his own thoughts, Alex didn't notice the woman until she was seated next to him. "Sweetie, are you always so obvious?"

"Obvious, madame?" He shied from the perfumed presence.

"My, my. Madame. A real gentleman." She nodded in approval, an unlit cigarette between two fingers. Her lap held a large collapsible leather bag, the kind so many women in this city carried.

"Well, madame is the moniker most appropriate in this situation," he stated awkwardly. "It signifies respect for the gentler sex." Encouraged by the incredulous smile and spray of freckles across the woman's unmade-up face, he warmed to the topic, happy to make conversation. "It's French, as you may know, and, despite their capacity for barbarism, the French must be afforded equal credit for introducing the masses to social refinement."

"Wow," she said. "And you haven't even answered my first question, but here's a follow-up. Are you always full of such scintillating fact?" Seeing him about to answer, she rolled her eyes and waved him off. "Never mind. Let's get back to the obvious."

He stared blankly.

"Your eyes were locked on that woman's boobs." She nodded at a couple having lunch. "It's good I saw you before her husband did, don't you think?"

"I-I-was …" he stammered.

"See what I mean?" She laughed easily as Alex tried focusing anywhere but on the deep V of her sweater's neckline. "It's okay," she assured him. "When you have big tits," she looked down and sighed, "you get used to dealing with chest men."

Seeing that she was making him uncomfortable, she changed the subject. "You're cute, you know; a little nerdy, but cute. Whaddaya do?"

Composing himself, he followed Bill's prescription. "I'm a scholar in the history of early America."

"Why doesn't that surprise me? Do you have a name, Mr. Early American Scholar?"

This earthy woman befuddled him. Timidly, he responded, "Alexander, but my new friends call me Alex. What, if I may inquire, is your name?"

"You may. It's Elizabeth Wellington, and I don't have any friends, but when I did, they called me Liz."

❧

Because of generous portions and moderate prices, Crystal's did a steady lunch business, and neither Liz nor Alex noticed the handsome brown-skinned man observing them. Brad Davis, finishing a late lunch, wondered if his eyes were deceiving him. He chewed slowly, wishing he hadn't ordered buffalo fish—too many bones. Trying to hurry his meal, he felt another bone slide toward his windpipe.

He spit it out and pushed his plate aside. Wiping grease from his fingers, he swiped at table crumbs and pulled out his ever-ready laptop. Now that Harlem was a wired hot zone, he could go online in mere minutes. "Come on, baby," he coaxed his MacBook Pro, willing it to boot up faster to www.societyphotos-info.com before the couple left.

About two years ago, wild child Elizabeth Wellington, daughter of Gordon Wellington, Davis's old boss at the television station, scandalized her social-climbing mother. She also shocked her closest friends and threw her powerful father's nose out of joint by calling off her six-hundred-guest wedding extravaganza two days before the nuptials.

Instead of marrying, she ran off to Harlem and moved in with her true love, an African American actor. Gordon squashed most of the story, but it was a well-known secret that the boyfriend dumped her after learning that daddy had cut her off. And now, for reasons Davis hoped to discover, here she was hanging out with that weirdo he'd seen with Clinton.

Bingo, that's her. He smiled nastily and looked up from Elizabeth's seventeen-inch image, just long enough to make sure she hadn't split. A pity, he thought, that little miss-newsworthy-Wellington wasn't still into her black thing. New Yorkers, despite their sophistication and laissez-faire attitudes, loved titillating sex scandals, and if race and class were part of the formula, all the better.

If Brad Davis had a real bone to pick, it was with Wellington for not only firing him after he tried scooping Liz's story to a rival, but also for savaging his reputation as a journalist. The SOB must have called in every chit, from Maine to Miami. The only work Davis was able to get was his current gig with a struggling new cable channel that specialized in cute animal stories. Maybe, just maybe, the worm was about to turn.

Across the room, Hamilton contemplated what to do about Liz's cigarette. On Mr. Clinton's television set, he'd seen a gentleman suavely produce a small personal lighting device for a lady's cigarette. Alas, he had none. Instead, he asked, "May I offer to buy you a whiskey?"

"No. No thanks. I don't drink."

"Well, that's a relief," he blurted out. "For a minute, I thought you might be a lady of the night. They're known to imbibe."

"Me, a whore?" She threw her head back, enjoying a raucous laugh from deep in her lovely throat. "I've been called a lot of things," she said, still laughing, "but that's a first. Even my father doesn't think I've sunk that low." Tensing suddenly, a thought occurred to her. "You aren't one of my father's stooges who he sent to spy on me, are you?"

"I've not made the acquaintance of many New York gentlemen, so I haven't had the pleasure."

"No. Never mind; you're not the type. Not macho enough. So why did you come in here? If you want to pay to get laid, it's the wrong kind of place."

"Get laid what?"

"Laid. Like fucked. Jesus, where're you from, Alex?" She stared at him sideways. "Some place on Mars?"

A little defensively, he replied, "I was born in Nevis but emigrated to St. Croix before settling in this country."

Liz raised an eyebrow. "Now that, I didn't expect. You mean the Caribbean islands?"

When Alex nodded, she continued. "Nebraska would be easier to believe, but Nevis, no kidding?" Discovering he was serious, she said, "I do detect an accent, but I wouldn't have called it Caribbean. You are full of surprises, baby." She puffed on her cold cigarette.

"So why're you in here? You don't look like a regular." She noticed the expensive weave of his linen shirt, compared to the dotted pilling that marred the front of her tired cashmere.

"If it's sexual intercourse you're referring to, I-I-I didn't. I came in to think things over."

"It's okay," she replied, patting his hand. "You don't have to justify anything for me. I was just curious. Me, I came in to ask for a job, but the day man over there," she indicated the bartender leaning against the cash register, "says the manager, who I know casually, doesn't come in until four. So I wait."

"Why do you seek employment?"

"For money, of course. I'm having a wee bit of trouble getting to my trust fund." To emphasize the wee, she squinted one eye partly shut and squeezed her right thumb and forefinger together. "Daddy, bless his money-loving soul, says 'my performance,' as he terms it, violates its conditions."

"A trust fund, you say? I once knew a bit about those."

Then you may understand how my father has tried to get the trustee to revoke it, even though it was originally set up by my grandfather. Everything's in limbo at the moment. I'm between acting gigs, and last week, the restaurant where I wait tables fired me when I skipped a shift for an audition. I didn't get the part, by the way. So I'm broke."

"May I ask you something?" he said shyly.

"Fire away. In case you haven't noticed, I'm not that easy to offend."

"Why are you holding that cigarette?"

"Because," she exploded, glaring at the NO SMOKING sign, "they fucking won't let you smoke any fucking-where in this fucking city. That's why." She shuddered and took another puff.

"Oh, I see," he said, not really seeing at all.

"Plus, this is my last smoke, and I'm an actress, right? So I'm playing this tragedy for all it's worth."

Hamilton thought Liz's conversation every bit as fascinating as it was difficult to follow.

"How much money do you need?"

"I'm fifty dollars short on my rent." Again using her fingers, she ticked off a litany of woes. "My fridge has practically nothing in it except Grey Poupon and mayonnaise. I'm behind on my phone bill, and without a cell phone, I can't get callbacks, right? And ..." she paused, looking at the cigarette in her hand, "even though I'm trying to give them up, I'd kill for a pack of Marlboros."

"Would two hundred dollars help?" he offered.

She whirled on him, annoyed. "Granted, I don't offend easily, but I already told you I'm not a whore."

"Understood," he bowed deeply. "But you're in a bit of a

bind, and I'm offering a gift."

She cocked her head again. "Are you for real?" she asked, less hostile.

He started to say something else but settled for "Yes, and my dollars are quite reliable, though a little undervalued on the world market at the moment. I'm a bit alone. My lady friend has forsaken me, and frankly, you've been kinder than anyone I've met, except one gentleman." His thoughts turned to Bill. "What you said a while ago about being different, well, yes, I am a bit. Certainly, I'd enjoy speaking with you at length, but I'd also be honored to help a lady in distress. Money no longer means what it once did. Here," he said and started digging into his pocket.

She watched him root among a mess of wilted greenbacks. "For the lady's rent." Smoothing out a fifty, he placed it on the bar, then followed with a second bill of the same denomination. From a breast pocket he found a hundred, folded it crisply lengthwise, and in a tender gesture, plucked the cigarette from her hand and replaced it with money.

Liz was afraid to glance down. Instead, she took a deep breath and turned in search of a looking glass, some small, behind-the-bar optic that might record this moment. She focused on a Guinness spigot: brass, shiny, distorted. It reflected a girl in another body, exactly the way she felt. Good things like this no longer happened to Elizabeth Ann Wellington.

"Alex," she said softly, clearing her throat, "when I was a little girl, some cable station ran old episodes of The Millionaire. Do you know it, by chance?"

Alex shook his head, straining to understand a connection between cables, nostalgia, and millionaires.

"For the longest time, those reruns were my favorite show. See, every week this nice rich guy named John Beresford Tipton, a total opposite from my father, had his secretary give some poor sap of a stranger a million bucks. Viewers never saw his face, but I imagined him in heaven, sitting on clouds of angel hair like my grandmother used to decorate her Christmas tree. Know why I loved that show?" she asked earnestly, sounding like the little girl she once was. "Because I desperately needed to believe in angels, and every Monday night I had living proof they did exist.

"Then one day, all my angels were replaced by demons, and I stopped believing. But you know what?" She swiveled to face him, touching knees. "I think my belief in angels has just been restored."

He was relieved to have gotten the gist of her millionaire story, but also taken aback by her references to heaven. "Are you saying that I somehow remind you of your earlier belief in heavenly powers?"

"I am, Alex; that's exactly what I'm saying."

"Oh my, that's quite extraordinary."

Liz hurried ahead. "And I suppose the next thing to say, besides thank you from the bottom of my heart, is where does this leave us?"

Hamilton wasn't sure what to think about all this, but he had the good sense to remain still and let her question breathe. For a few moments, Liz wrestled with her thoughts, then said, "Promise you're not an ax murderer?"

Astounded, he reared back as if struck. "Madame!" he exploded. "I too have been called many things, but never such as that!"

"Oops," she winced, biting her lip. "I guess we're even on insults. Sorry, but a girl can't be too careful these days. I'm dealing with a lot, but an ax murderer is one thing I don't want to take on." His look of genuine astonishment eased her mind. "Besides being a little clueless, Alex, I'm not sure what you are, but a slayer of women is not it, I don't believe. In the past, every time I hooked up with a shit, I walked into him with my eyes wide open. Good angel / bad angel scenario, one on either shoulder telling me what to do. Know what I mean?"

Liz could tell by Alex's wrinkled brow that leaping from ax murderers to angels perplexed her new acquaintance. Rather than a murderous air, he had an innocence about him, so she demonstrated by patting herself on each shoulder and said, "Invariably I listened to the wrong angel.

"I like you, Alex. You don't exactly light my fire, but you have a certain charm. That's a good thing, baby. Maybe my luck is changing." Having made a decision, she stuffed the money in her purse and started gathering her things.

"First," she said, crooking a ringed index finger at him, "let's get some groceries. My apartment is just up the street."

With his lunch tab already settled, Davis slipped out after them.

CHAPTER 18
MODERN PLEASURES

Alex followed Liz's shapely legs as they scissored across the room. First she made space on the coffee table for the small bouquet of blue limonium and baby's breath; then she walked over to replace several stray DVDs in the bookcase. Alex, assuming they were tiny books, watched as she plucked another one of these items from the bottom shelf.

"Sweetie, why don't you have a seat?" From the kitchen, she called, "You'll notice I'm really into Feng Shui. A little balance and harmony around here offsets some of my other shortcomings." Returning with a tray of hummus, pita, and sliced green apples, Liz laughed, "I have lots of shortcomings, but neatness isn't one of them."

Downstairs in the vestibule, Davis searched for Wellington's name on a mailbox. Most labels, he discovered, held only the apartment number, including whichever one was hers. Inching further into the hallway, he glanced around at all the first floor doors, which told him nothing.

Taking a chance, he crept up to the second floor for a quick peek. More brown doors, one with a small orange Post-It notepad and pen placed under the knocker. That was no help either, since nothing was written on it. Plus someone's television set was blaring, killing any chance to pick up voices. He nervously sprinted up the remaining three flights, remembering how unpleasant it was the last time he got caught snooping at someone's doorway. Hearing and seeing nothing helpful he backtracked, went outside, and scanned the street for a good stakeout spot.

Alex, meanwhile, increasingly adept at emulating modern men's behaviors, sat with both arms stretched along the back of Liz's sofa and his left leg atop his right knee. "Your home has a calming presence," he complimented her, noticing the lack of clutter and simple lines of her pale green chairs and the white settee. Except for wooden table lamps and a framed photograph of twenty foot waves, there was little decor. It was a warm day, and the afternoon light softly illuminated the corner of the living room where they would eat.

A buxom sort, Liz walked around barefoot and, instead of artifice and paint, relied on her natural attributes: a full, flared nose, sensual lips, and a tussled mane of thick red hair.

"Modernity abounds with complex gadgetry," Alex commented.

"Amen to that. Everyone has too much stuff," Liz agreed, peeling off her outer sweater and assessing her handy work. "Hmm, smell the garlic?" She sniffed the hummus. "I hope this isn't too spicy for you. After all, it's your treat. That new deli seasons its dips very liberally. Well, dig in." She hesitated, not sure whether to take the couch next to him or a chair.

By popping up like a Jack-in-the-Box and startling her, Alex made the decision easy. "After my lady," he waved gallantly, indicating she be seated first.

Liz just stared at him then dropped into the far chair. "Alex, you're killing me. I swear, if I didn't know better, I'd guess you rode in from some other century or galaxy or ... something." As if in defense of the unknown, she crossed her arms. "Nobody, I mean nobody, acts like that. But whatever." She readjusted the scrunchie holding back her hair. "The air was cool this morning, but it's gotten hot," she said, fanning her face before dipping a piece of pita bread into the hummus.

Pondering her "other century" comment, and far from certain what he'd just done to displease her, Alex settled for watching the V in Liz's sweater expand as she bent over for a smear of the garlic concoction.

Finally, unable to resist, he asked, "Suppose I told you I was from another century; would you believe me?"

Attacking the simple meal with gusto, Liz, with her mouth full, murmured, "Maybe. Hmmm," she added, "this is good. All I had today is coffee and toast."

Maybe? The word echoed in his head, and he filed it away for further consideration.

"What were you tidying?" he asked next.

"A few old movies. I study them for acting tips." She walked over and pulled a copy of *Peggy Sue Got Married* from the shelf. "They're cheaper than acting lessons, which I can't afford right now, and they help.

"People tell me I look a bit like Kathleen Turner when she was young. Even I see a resemblance. I think she's really good in this movie." She passed Alex a DVD cover with the actress's photo. "Ever see it?"

He limited his answer to a simple "No," hoping a DVD had something to do with television, a technology Mr. Clinton had demonstrated then explained in great detail. As she talked, he studied the item she'd handed him. It was an image of a pretty round-faced woman with a widow's peak whose smiling confidence lacked the vulnerability he saw in Liz.

"There's even a movie over here that I'm in," she said, "but it was never released or shown to the public."

"I'm sure it's delightful," he replied, knowing he wouldn't be expected to have seen it, whatever "it" was.

"Not exactly." She glanced his way. "It's a skin flick," she said, waiting for a reaction. Getting none, she continued, "I count myself lucky that it never got released. Not that my acting was any worse than that of other blue movie divas, but those films don't exactly help one's career. Besides," she said, rearranging the folds of her skirt before tucking her feet up under her, "the production company went bankrupt. They were all a bunch of sleezebags, so it's not surprising they went under. I shot it a few years ago, when I was mad at the world, or maybe just mad," she qualified.

Skin flick? Shot it? Alex recalled Bill explaining that these things called films and movies fit into categorizes such as history, adventure, romance, and comedy, but he couldn't remember a subgroup called "skin flick."

"Well, are you going to do me the honor? I'm sure it's excellent," he said, still grateful that Bill had taken time to explain so much to him.

"Alex, how nice of you." She beamed. "Not five minutes ago, I thought I'd never met a squarer guy. But anyway," she said, "after two years, I'm still deciding if I'm proud or ashamed of my brief movie career. Still, I don't know," she demurred, "I shouldn't have even brought it up. It's pretty ... um ... graphic, if you know what I mean, and we hardly know each other."

"Nonsense." He remembered Bill's presentation on movie-making, including his explanation of the G, PG, and R rating system. "Gritty dramatization is simply the manifestation of another character," he said confidently, "not who one truly is. What better way for me to get to know more about you."

Hours later, when Alex staggered from the apartment, he feared that he and Liz had not only sinned in the eyes of God, but had watched and performed unnatural acts like no man or woman before them. Now he prayed for forgiveness. But he couldn't block the memory of Liz on the screen, Liz everywhere ... under him, over him. Those strong tanned limbs gripping him tight, the flaming hair down there. And, oh, the thrilling shame of mounting another human being from the rear, like a horse covering a mare, and the poor animal collapsing from the assault. Except he and Liz were human beings, not animals.

His despair kept making him forget the words to the "Our Father." He tried again. "Thy Kingdom come ... hallow be thy name ..." Giving up, he interjected his own words. "My dear beneficent Lord, though my time on earth nears its end, I pray you consider readmitting me to your heavenly abode."

Trying to calm down and feeling some of his senses return, he prayed harder. "Thy will be done on earth ... and lead us not into temptation ..." He managed a somewhat accurate finish, but it didn't help; he still felt miserable and wonderful at the same time.

Darkness had set in, and Alex, in turmoil, didn't notice Brad Davis, who was ten paces behind him and following on the opposite side of the street. Alex took a few seconds to get his bearings. He knew he was on 148th Street and remembered traffic on even-numbered streets flowed east, the way he wanted to go. Good, he thought; so that meant his home on 141st was south, then several streets east of the river.

Absentmindedly stepping off the curb, an oncoming car swerved to avoid him. "Oh, dear," Hamilton muttered, knowing an accident could prove awkward with constables, requests for identification, and much consternation should he opt to vanish before their eyes.

Dismissing accident scenarios, he focused on what he should say the following evening when he returned to Liz's home to partake of her dinner invitation. It was of the utmost importance that he apologize for his flagrant carnality. And now that he was fully aware of the vixen's secret wiles, he'd certainly not be drawn in again. With that consoling thought, he made himself invisible.

Stopping in his tracks, Brad Davis, sore-footed and in a sour mood, rubbed his eyes. "What the fuck? Where'd he go?"

CHAPTER 19

SO HOW DO THINGS WORK?

For this visit Bill had invited Alex to the house, but now he wished he hadn't. He'd forgotten that the Interleague Yankees-Mets series started today, and now he just wanted to watch the game.

"Alex," he said irritably, "at the moment you aren't invisible, and you keep blocking my view. Besides—" Bill made a motion, intended to shoo him to the right. "Your pacing makes me nervous."

Alex, who was also snatching glances at the screen, stopped moving about and stepped off to the side. "Ah, yes, the truly amazing magic box. But why are those men just standing around?"

"It's a game. They're waiting for the ball to be hit to them."

"Their performance doesn't appear to match that of players in *The Ten Commandments*, that magic box epic you kindly shared, or the new form of film I've become acquainted with."

"These guys are some of the best athletes in the world.

They're superstars, just like Charlton Heston and Yul Brynner in Ten Commandments. If you follow baseball, you understand that they perform at the highest level of their profession."

Alex was barely listening, and Bill thought he seemed more sprightly today. For one thing, his usual fascination with the television was missing. He almost seemed smug, plus his cheeks were flushed. After a moment, he asked, "What's up, anyway? You don't look like you came to pick my brain again. What's so important this time? A few weeks ago, you led me on a wild goose chase and didn't seem all that broken up when we came back empty-handed. Is this still about Sarafina?"

Alex took a chair and fidgeted with the TV remote, which Bill immediately lunged for. "If you don't mind?"

Deprived of a tactile stimulant, Alex resorted to cracking his knuckles, a habit that creeped Bill out.

"Sarafina remains occupied, but I-I need to know the implications of initiating an affair of the heart with an earth being. Yesterday I met a lady named Liz. It's Elizabeth, actually," he said, digging into his pants pocket. "Here, she gave me this." He handed Bill a card that read: "Elizabeth Ann Wellington; Actress, Singer, Dancer."

If nothing else, Bill realized, Alex had a knack for collecting women's business cards. Elizabeth's included a thumbnail photo of a good-looking redhead, along with a phone number, email address, and a QR code, a technology he'd not used.

"She's been beyond kind to me," Alex blushed. "I'm intrigued, but being unfamiliar with modern courting ..."

Realizing that Alex was telling him that he got laid, Bill was tempted to say something sarcastic but couldn't think what, since the woman's photo, though small, indicated she was clearly a babe. He gave the card back and, from the corner of his eye, caught a Mets runner sliding safely into second.

"Alex," he started, "there's a Southern expression that an old black gentleman once shared with me. He used it to describe folks ... beings ... whatever, like you and me, or at least what you used to be or ... or currently are pretending to be. Oh, never mind all that. The point is, he told me, 'Mr. Clinton, you're free, white, and twenty-one.' Do you get his meaning?"

Seeing that Alex clearly did not, Bill enlightened him. "It means you can do whatever you please. And so can the lady." As an afterthought, he added, "assuming she's of age. Race, of course, doesn't much figure into the equation anymore." Taking a deep breath, Bill asked, "She is at least eighteen, isn't she?"

"Of course. She's a grown woman, well schooled in the art of love and willing to engage in a short-term relationship. Elizabeth advised me that she is temporarily unable to access her trust fund, so I accommodated her immediate needs then escorted her home. We became friends."

Hmmm, interesting, Bill thought. She might be running a con, although she did show him her place. Maybe she is a woman of means, someone with connections.

It wouldn't hurt to remind Hamilton of one other thing. Reaching for his soda can, Bill took a swig, while formulating the right words.

"Alex, you know what sometimes happens when fellas stop using their brain and start thinking with their pecker? We've both caused train wrecks in the past, and trust me, you can't imagine how today's media can savage reputations."

"I hadn't thought of that. Frankly, sir, my concerns were more focused on the celestial, but I will take your words to heart and be mindful of the lady's reputation."

"And here's another thing: you're ... um ... different. You tend to draw attention. You've been associated with me, and a few people are already wondering who you are. You don't know anything about this woman. Suppose you create another screw-up. This time, you can just disappear, but she can't. Know what I mean?"

Despite the jargon, Alex thought Bill's message was clear and said so. "I believe you're referring to my Mrs. Reynolds and perhaps your Miss Lewinsky?"

"I am, along with a few other judgment errors. So, first off, is this lady married?"

"Not at all." He straightened up taller. "She's rather a free spirit, really, describes her nature as 'will-o'-the-wisp.' It's quite apt; she's an earthy sort, of Scottish ancestry like myself."

Bill couldn't help wondering what the attractive redhead saw in Alex who, anyway you cut it, was odd. "According to the Southern gentleman's standards, you both pass the test. I'm sure you and Elizabeth make an excellent match," Bill diplomatically fibbed. "The lady sounds swell. Good for you, and good luck with the relationship."

At the mention of luck, Alex emitted a noise like a crow strangling on his caw. "Sir," he said, his ebullience gone, "I don't consider myself lucky. If so, in my former life I might have curbed two self-destructive impulses that sealed my fate."

Removing his eyes from the screen, Bill probed, "Which ones? Your biographers detailed numerous such impulses, as did you when you were lecturing me on my shortcomings."

"Surely you know my ill-conceived affair with Maria Reynolds left me muddle-headed, which, in turn, led to an even more self-destructive action: a duel with Aaron Burr.'"

Bill's eyes flew open. Did the infamous sex-capade lead to the duel? Curious to explore the topic without seeming ghoulish, he said casually, "Interesting you bring that up. Over the past two days, I've reread the last hundred pages of Ron Chernow's biography of you. It's a scholarly piece of research and was well worth reading more carefully than I did on my first rushed go-through."

Alex nodded. "In studying the copy you kindly provided me, I must agree. It's a fair assessment and captures me quite well."

"I'm glad you think so," Bill said, "because you deserve a better legacy than time has thus far provided. But since we're discussing affairs of the heart, I want to ask you about a quote in the book. None other than your great admirer, Martha Washington, called you a 'lascivious tom cat.'" Letting the phrase play over his lips a few times, Bill couldn't help chuckling, as he visualized prim, white-haired, pink-cheeked Martha tossing out the ribald comment while sedately doing needlework. Tickled by the incongruous image, Bill added, "If that's the first lady's assessment, I can just imagine what detractors called you."

Hamilton, now somewhat accustomed to being teased, mustered a faint smile. "Sir, lest we forget, the Lord also spoke these words: 'He who is without sin may cast the first stone.'"

"Well, yes. Yes, He did," Bill offered. He hoped the conversation wasn't turning to him. Looking away, he saw the Mets had the bases loaded and the Yankees were making a pitching change.

"If you recall, sir, this biography you so aptly quote," Alex persisted, drawing him back into conversation, "in commendable detail, explains how I fully apologized and took complete responsibility for my culpability with Mrs. Reynolds."

Inwardly, Bill groaned. Aloud he said, "Alex, you not only apologized; you did it in a ninety-five page pamphlet that had forty-one words in its title. A bit excessive, weren't you?"

"Indeed, sir, but to receive forgiveness, one must go to great lengths."

"Alex, let me be candid here. Apparently some of your contemporaries speculated that by not firing your pistol, you were toying with suicide. Any truth to that?"

Hearing no protest, Bill figured he'd hit a nerve. From the slight pulsing in Alex's left temple, he saw which one it was.

"But why?" he asked, stunned. You had everything to live for."

"Sir, despite confession and remorse, I never forgave myself and could not pretend to carry on when my most estimable asset, my character, had been impugned. It was a difficult time; my law practice suffered and creditors hounded me. Additionally," he added in a clipped tone, "that scoundrel, Burr, a thorn in my side and a grave threat to our young nation, continued using the Reynolds affair against me.

"The custom of dueling was falling out of favor, thus a true gentlemen did not shoot to kill. Had I hit the mark, it would have only furthered my fall from grace."

Leaning back, Bill placed both hands behind his head and tried to fathom how someone could seek revenge by letting the enemy get the upper hand in such a lethal way.

"It's true that after shooting you, Burr became a pariah and ended up leaving the country in disgrace."

"That, I learned, was indeed a satisfying development. Unfortunately, Burr soon returned and married Eliza Jumel, an unsuspecting widow, whose fortune he then frittered away."

"Yes, at least in his later life, it seems he was a nasty piece of goods," Bill agreed. "Do you know that he and his wife lived here in Harlem in the Morris-Jumel Mansion? It's an historic structure that I'd be happy to show you."

"No need, sir. I know it well. General Washington headquartered in the mansion during the autumn of 1776. Its picturesque hilltop location was a bright spot during those hellish months of war. Your offer is most kind, but I've already revisited the site and surrounding area. Like all of New York, much around the mansion has changed. However, the interior is strikingly reminiscent of what I remember."

"Of course you would know the home's history firsthand. But for the moment, I'd like to follow up on the last days of your life, your former life. Having already apologized excessively for the affair, you didn't need to flirt with death—and lose—to prove a point."

"When expressing contrition, verbosity can be cathartic. If it fails, death can be ennobling."

"Nonsense. What you did was pointless. It proved nothing and deprived your children of a father and your country of one of its sharpest young minds."

"Perhaps, but if we may for the moment turn to you, my kindred spirit." Suddenly on the defensive, Bill looked warily at Alex.

"In your case," he continued, "when confronted, you simply uttered, 'I did not have sex with that woman.' Many Americans did not believe you. Furthermore, your lack of contrition was viewed as arrogance." Alex wasn't finished. "I also contend that you've never forgiven yourself."

Instead of responding, Bill looked at his feet resting on the rich maroon border of his Oriental rug. Pulling his eyes away from the pattern, he looked directly at Alex. "You may be on to something there."

"Indeed. I surmise that you're still troubled by the events of 1998."

"I said you may be on to something, but if you're implying that like you, I am—or ever was—suicidal, forget it. I'll concede we have similarities, but suicidal tendencies are not among them."

"Metaphysically speaking, they are. Actions of the heart are revealed in different ways."

"Oh, bullshit." Bill whirled on him. "And, if you're going to start harping again on how I can suddenly become Saint Bill by taking Abby into my home ... well," he stammered, "you can ... um ... save your breath."

"Sir?"

"I've seriously considered doing it," he said, again meeting Alex's eyes.

"To parent the child?"

"Well, yes, but it would be as foster parents, and nothing's final, so hold your horses. I mean, slow down." Bill scowled. "Of immediate concern is the time factor. Even Hillary can see the clock is ticking; institutionalizing Abby would be a great waste. Our interest in the child has temporarily put a halt to her being transferred upstate. That gives us time to figure this out."

"So Madam President has no objections?"

Bill thought a moment before answering. "She and I are sorting out details, such as when to have Abby come here for a trial visit or two, how to announce it, details like that. Also,

Mattie, our housekeeper, will play a role. Naturally, I needed to share this idea with her. She never had kids of her own, but was a foster mother for twenty years and raised four children to adulthood. One, in particular, thinks of Mattie as her mother. Mattie is the salt of the earth. As for Hillary, she's softened to the idea and has undergone a change in attitude. Sorry, I failed to bring you up to date on all this."

"Might I inquire what caused Madam's reconsideration?"

"Oh, Alex, other than Chelsea's enthusiastic endorsement, I'm not sure. I guess some of us are lucky to catch a star before the world spins by. Maybe Hillary sees a way to help a child but also potentially help the world."

"Do you think it was for political reasons?"

"Yes and no. Hillary has a long history of promoting children's causes, and she now has the opportunity to do something about it. Who knows, perhaps she can get legislation through Congress? Others have failed, but that doesn't mean she will. One former president, I think it was Truman, famously said that he held the most powerful position in the world, but all he did was kiss ass … or words to that effect."

"How has Madam viewed the practical concerns?"

"After the US presidency, parenting runs a close second to being one of the most impactful responsibilities a man or woman can have. She's had occasional moments of panic, but she's talked with Abby via Skype, and she's flying up for a visit. Visits are required for all potential foster parents, even presidential applicants."

Alex, delighted, raised his bushy eyebrows, waiting to hear more.

Checking the date on his watch, Bill said, "Hillary knows

that in exactly forty-five days, if we don't do something, Abby will be shipped to a facility that also houses juvenile offenders. And, God rest their souls, those youngsters need help and intervention. But all Abby needs is a family, and it looks like we're it."

"Then you are to be commended, sir. My congratulations."

Bill smiled. "No need for that just yet, but I appreciate the sentiment. Since I'll be undertaking new responsibilities, I've broadened my recreational reading. That's what some of this stuff is here on the table." He waved at a stack of periodicals and what looked like an official report lying next to several paperbacks about parenting and child care. "I also dug up a speech Hillary delivered last year about America's overburdened, underfunded child care programs." Searching through the pile of papers, he said, "Here. I have plenty of other copies. Read that when you have a chance and tell me if, by wanting to give Abby a home, I'm not doing exactly what Hillary has long urged the rest of the world to do.

"And speaking of uncovering stuff," Bill said after a few moments, "a few days ago, when I was still researching you and your contemporaries, I came across a sentence that John Quincy Adams penned in his memoir. It really struck a chord. I quote: 'There is nothing in life so pathetic as a former president.'"

Both men seemed to think about that for a moment before Bill asked, "Did you know the younger Adams, by chance?"

"I did, sir. John Quincy was my senior by several years. He was an honorable man who fought to abolish slavery, plus he was less prone to fits of temper than his father."

Laughing, Bill said, "So I've read." Then, more seriously, he added, "My post-presidency has been fulfilling, especially the foundation work, so I don't believe I'm one of the unenviable figures John Quincy described. I've given this a lot of thought lately. As politicians, we spend our lives wheeling and dealing. It's hard to cede the limelight, but I'm planning to do more of that now."

"I too was guilty of reclame eclat. For you see, sir, publicity is the bedfellow of politics."

"Point well taken. However, bringing Abby into my life won't be another project. I hope to turn this into a labor of love."

CHAPTER 20

MELANCHOLY IN THE FACE OF GOOD NEWS

Within seconds, an elated Hamilton levitated the short distance separating Bill's property from his. He then slipped through the locked northern door into the grand foyer of his estate. While the lower level underwent a minor renovation, this original entry was now functioning as the museum's reception area. Upon arrival, he almost did a double-take to discover Sarafina confidently seated in the receptionist's leather desk chair.

He quickly changed into human form and, after carefully readjusting his clothing, was struck anew by Sarafina's beauty. Her hair was pulled back the way he'd always preferred it, and she wore a gold-colored shawl and a pair of stylish trousers that he'd not seen before.

More and more, he had difficulty reconciling her former status as a bondservant with the woman she'd become. If he didn't know better, seeing her behind a cluttered desk full of brochures, binders and tiny slips of yellow paper, he might think she was mistress of this manor.

"Do you return from nearby after an audience with Mr. Clinton, or have you been further afield?" she asked.

"The former," he said. "I approached him with a minor question, but he quickly allayed my concerns." Glossing over the nature of the question he'd raised with Bill, Alex continued. "During the discussion, we digressed into issues touching on our past troubles."

Smiling mischievously, she peered into his flushed face. "From your rosy look, sir, neither present concern nor past trouble appear foremost upon your countenance. Perhaps you and Mr. Clinton conversed on other gentlemanly merriment?"

Despite the gulf that had opened between them, Alex was pleased by Sarafina's spark of sly humor. Patting his cheeks, he said, "Often, my humor is reflected upon my face. But in truth, dear lady, your supposition nears its mark. Any appearance of felicity is purely due to Mr. Clinton's glad tidings, not merriment on either of our parts."

"Our earth visit is nearly ended. How pleased you must be that your audiences with the gentleman go well."

"Indeed. My hopes for Mr. Clinton's legacy have come to pass. He has decided to take a parentless child into his home."

Plucking absently at the fringe of her shawl, Sarafina looked in the direction from which Hamilton had just come. Suddenly somber, she whispered, "Would it were I reaping such satisfaction. Alexander, tell me how is it that Mr. Clinton, and not I, discovers the child of his desires?"

Surprised by her comment and question, he said, "Though I'd like to take a small measure of credit, I believe God brought Mr. Clinton and the child together. Some weeks ago, the president expressed the notion that God, not man, despite our act of procreation, decides what child or children we shall have."

Aware that Sarafina's anguish had returned and not wanting to appear insensitive, he spoke with caution. "Your rueful comment about a child of desire prompts me to ask if you regret not becoming a mother?"

"My ... regret," Sarafina began, but she stopped speaking when she was suddenly drawn to a sound on the street. Standing abruptly, she stalked across the room to peer through a chink in a shuddered window where daylight leaked in. Joining her, Alex spotted the source of noise: two chattering youngsters passing on the sidewalk, presumably on their way to the playground on St. Nicholas Avenue.

Hoping for some positive conversation to rid Sarafina of melancholy, he asked, "Do you find consolation in observing Negro youth partaking freedoms that a child of yours would not have enjoyed?"

With her eyes still on the scene before her, she spoke quietly. "A mother dwells not just on freedom's precious gift, but on the freedom to stroke a daughter's soft skin and smell her baby breath. Oh, Alexander," she sobbed, turning to him. "I mothered a dear, bright-eyed baby girl of strong will who were named Judith."

Stunned, Hamilton stood immobile. "A child? Great Scot! Will you ever cease to amaze me? What came of her?"

"In 1777, that year of brutal plundering at Master Shields's, Judith was lost, cruelly stolen from me."

Assisted by scant light coming through the window, Alex studied her anguished face then gently led her back to the chair and kneeled alongside. "For the love of God, why did you not tell me this?"

In a strangled voice, her head bowed, she mumbled, "Motherly shame and grinding grief rendered me mute and inconsolable." Feeling her tremble, Alex wished he could warm Sarafina's heart.

"The terrible desire to see my child at peace has never gone from me."

"Yes, yes, now I understand." He recalled those first weeks after rescuing her, when Sarafina was too despondent to speak. "That explains my puzzlement over your initial lack of joy at gaining freedom. For the longest while, I attributed your heartsickness to tortured memories of the auction block and what the jailers might have done while they held you at Barrow Street."

Alex was formulating additional questions when Sarafina's next comment cleared them from his mind. "Though my time on earth is nigh its end, I hear Judith somewhere out there calling me. It is she I search for in my wanderings on earth."

He was not completely surprised that a grieving mother would utter such an unfathomable statement. However, for her own good, he felt her words could not remain unchallenged. "My dear, the male species forfeits the unique parent-child bond that comes with birthing, but as you know, my good wife, Eliza, bore me eight fine youngsters."

"Yes, of your children, we have spoke."

"What you don't know is that we lost Philip, our first born, in a tragic and untimely death when he was only nineteen." The image of his son's body flashed before him; Philip racked with pain, the bloom of youth fading before their eyes, as the blood drained out of him.

"Sarafina, I understand your despair. Eliza and I endured great anguish when Phillip was killed. My wife, who lived many years beyond me, grieved until her dying day, but neither she nor I could alter God's plan."

Sarafina raised her hand to her mouth. "I did not know. I am sorry for your Philip. He was your eldest, but why so young?"

Alex took a deep breath. "In truth, the circumstances of Philip's death torment me still. Like many a rash young man, he was foolishly, though valiantly defending my honor in a duel against George Eacker, a fiery Jeffersonian who practically accused me of plotting to overthrow the president.

"But in time," Hamilton hurried on, wanting to relay his message rather than receive sympathy for which he was undeserving, "we both accepted our son's passing, as you must accept Judith's."

"Alexander, you are honest and wise, but you know not the ancient wisdoms of our African gods who say when a mother does not properly see her dead child into the ground, she is never set free of its restless spirit. Always I pine for Judith, but of late I hear a girl-child calling to me, and I must try to find her."

Unable to shake Sarafina's conviction that her long-deceased daughter was sending messages, Alex tried a new approach. "My dear, your thoughts spring from the extraordinary experiences you've had here on earth. I too am much taken by the wonders of communication. The human voice," he said, swaying slightly as he remembered Liz's brief, husky speaking parts in her movie, "now has the capacity to be immortalized inside the glass talking box. Perhaps it is this technology that confuses you as it often does me. But, might I remind you, while alive, your little child had not fully mastered the spoken word. So it is not clear she would do so now."

Angrily brushing his hand from her shoulder, she said, "You become wearisome with repeated attempts to explain what you do not know."

Though her disdainful reactions were happening more frequently and she no longer welcomed him into her bed, Sarafina's indifference saddened him. He also realized his intervention was further distressing her and briefly debated the wisdom of leaving her alone. He feared she'd venture out again and land in the arms of charlatans whom, he surmised, must be responsible for her delusional thoughts.

Alexander hated being late, but his extended interaction with Sarafina had caused him to lose track of time. It was two hours past when he should have been at Liz's home. Dusk was descending over the city, the workday had ended and lamplight now glowed in the windows of many tidy brownstone and brick houses. Hurrying through the darkening streets, he followed the setting sun, its glow still visible in the low western sky. Once he reached148th Street, he had no trouble finding Liz's residence. Entering the building, he quickly ascended the stairs and knocked on the door. Getting no answer, he tried again. After three attempts, Alex pondered his options. He dismissed the thought of entry-by-levitation but contemplated returning to Bill's home to inquire about contacting Liz over the speaking box.

Turning away, he was about to leave when he noticed the

notepad affixed to her door had writing on it. Leaning closer to examine the small cramped script, Alex realized the dispatch was addressed to him. Then, to better see, he pulled at the top sheet, which came off in his hand.

"Alex," it read, "though you were a little weird, I really thought you were different from all the others. By not showing up, you proved me wrong, although I was right about one thing: angels no longer exist.

"Don't contact me again. I'm tired of waging the good fight, so I've decided to heed my father's request to join a family confab this weekend in Connecticut. As you read this, I'm likely on the Metro-North, on my way to Westport. And, while I'm there, here's a suggestion. Why don't you just go back to that planet or galaxy or wherever it is you flew in from. In fact, you can just plain go to hell."

CHAPTER 21
THE PRESIDENT SPEAKS

As always when Bill had the dream, he awoke with a start, his heart racing. Trying not to disturb Hillary, he lay still, waiting for his heartbeat to slow. He realized that until a few months ago, the nightmare hadn't bothered him since the late 1990s. God, what a train wreck those years had been. But, why would the dream return now?

On the other side of the king-sized bed, Hillary lay curled in a fetal position, blonde highlights poking above the covers. Pulling the blanket over her head, she mumbled, "Go back to sleep." Instead, Bill stuffed another pillow behind his head and eased back against the cushioned fabric of the headboard.

He'd turned off his reading light around 1:30 a.m. and then slept well. Why would the dream bother him now? He hadn't been the only mouthy kid in Arkansas to butt heads with a stepfather. Shit happens. Could it be related to something Alex said about fathers that night on the deck? Bill hadn't cared for the adjectives Alex used to describe him, particularly "vainglory."

He was long beyond that chilly April conversation—at least he'd thought so—until a few days ago when, like a fool, he actually checked the thesaurus for synonyms matching vainglory. For a word with such pleasing, soft-sounding vowels, nothing about vainglory was flattering. One match was especially distasteful to him: narcissism.

To ease tension in his shoulders, he placed both arms behind his head and surveyed the bedroom. He understood why this was Hillary's favorite spot in the house. "Calm inducing," is how she described the mix of chocolate and taupe colors. At first he thought the room was too dark, but now he agreed with her: it was calming.

Last night, he and Hillary had talked for hours. But now he had another question and was tempted to shake her awake. Instead, he got up, slipped into one leather slipper, then felt around for the other. After taking a quick pee, he went down to the kitchen, switched on the coffee machine, and wandered down the hall to peek through the bulletproof sidelights on either side of his front door. His block was cordoned off, cars were detoured, and people expecting to walk up or down 141st Street were politely re-routed to a path through the park. In the near distance, police helicopters droned. Three communication tents were set up in front of the house. In a few hours, all this hardware and all the officials and officious pains in the ass would fold their tents and blow out of town. Good riddance, he thought, hating that his neighbors didn't get their usual preferential treatment when Hillary was here.

Back upstairs, he entered the bedroom, and Hillary stretched languorously. "I'm awake," she said. "Lord, I wish I could lie here forever. I guess it's just as well that I no longer command the deep, worry-free sleep of youth. Ah, youth," she sighed, kicking away covers. "Speaking of which, Abby's an adorable child: smart as can be, the whole nine yards. Although something about this situation reminds me of David and Goliath. Another little guy outwitting the stronger one."

Bill kept silent. He knew Hillary's nervous prattle was a way to keep working through her doubts. Despite their lengthy talks, the decision to become a foster parent weighed heavily on his wife. He understood. A few months ago, he felt the same way.

"Abby's a very intense child, Bill. It's so sweet to see how she adores you in that unfathomable way kids have of making you the center of their world. At least," she added, "until the terrible teens set in; then a parent can't do anything right."

"It was a good weekend, though, wasn't it?" Bill didn't want to sound like he was asking for Hillary's reassurance, but he could have used it. The social worker had toured the house, and Abby would have one more home visit. If that proved successful, and if Hillary didn't balk, then it should be a go.

"Bill, considering her history of intransigence, it's odd that she bonded with you. She's a bit tentative with me, but did you notice how she perked up when I fixed her hair? That seemed to break the ice somewhat."

"No, I didn't pick up on the girlie stuff, but that's a good sign. She's not used to much affection," he reminded her. "Maybe she craved a little contact: close, but not too close."

"Could be, but I think I gained a few points when she realized I was an expert at untangling kinky, knotty hair. It brought back sweet memories of school mornings when I had to tug a comb and brush through Chelsea's thicket of curls."

Hillary stopped talking and looked at her husband. "Bill,"

she said softly. "I'm trying. God knows I'm trying to get my arms around this thing, but it's very scary. There are so many details to work out, and you know I'd prefer her to attend school in DC. For this to work, we'll need to be a more conventional family now. With a young child, we can't keep running back and forth."

"I've thought of all that. More normalcy is a good idea, and families make those kinds of accommodations. We'll do it. I already have feelers out for January openings in the DC schools we considered for Chelsea. Meanwhile, Gertie is compiling a list of well-recommended homeschool tutors for me to interview here in New York."

"I see you've been busy," she said, then turned to examine her face in the mirror behind their bathroom door. "Yes, we'll be more normal and conventional, but no one will ever mistake me as a mother of a young child. Now that I have all these wrinkles and extra pounds, there's a mirror at every turn. When I was young and thin and cute, I would have killed to have a full- length mirror in my bedroom."

"Hillary, you're still cute, you're brilliant, and you have a womanly figure that I'll always love. But would you really want to be young again?"

"Maybe not, but I'm no spring chicken, and I want a second term in office."

"I want that too, and it'll happen. Even with today's ramped-up election cycle, the next presidential vote is a long way off. You can't control every last thing. With Abby, I'll handle as many details as possible, but this can't happen without participation on your part."

"Instead of Skyping, I'll do my best to be here for the next meeting on the fifteenth. After that, we're free to bring her to DC as often as we like. But right now, I need to take a shower, then get back on the plane."

She walked over and checked the thermostat. Frowning at its sixty-five-degree setting, she slipped into her robe, a Mother's Day present from Bill. The soft cream-and-gold silk paisley matched her knee-length gown but didn't offer much warmth. Hillary pulled the robe's sash tight around her waist. Noticing the thin material clinging to his wife's hips, Bill realized it had been a while since he'd paid attention to Hillary's shapely backside. It was only eight o'clock, and an image started forming in his head. He was about to ask his wife if she wanted to slip back into bed, maybe fool around a little, when she dispelled the idea with a question of her own.

"Honey, do you remember how scary it was to wake up on January twenty-first, after your first night in the White House, and realize you were president of the United States? Becoming a foster parent feels a little like that."

"I never told you that about January twenty-first."

She laughed. "Now you won't have to."

"Fair enough. So can I ask you something?" he said, watching her open a drawer and rummage around. Settling on a pair of blue panties, she hung them on the doorknob next to a black bra.

Not hearing anything, Hillary faced him. "What is it? What'd you want to ask me?"

"Hmmm. Do you think I'm vain?"

"Oh, for God's sake. What kind of asinine question is that?"

"No, seriously. Am I?"

"Seriously? Are you kidding? I hope you don't think of

yourself as some kind of shrinking violet, because you're not. Why'd you ask?"

"Someone implied that I might be a bit self-absorbed. I hope people don't hold that against me."

"Sorry if this comes as a surprise, but you've always been Mr. Center of Attention. It's what you do best. I thought your skin was tough enough to not give a damn what people thought of you. So, yes, there is a certain vanity, even arrogance to you. If it makes you feel any better, it comes with the territory. Public life can suck. To stay relevant, to be heard over the noise, you have to elbow your way to the front. That can bring out certain unflattering characteristics. We're all guilty of it, but you're especially adept."

"Okay."

"Is that all? That's what you wanted to know?"

"Pretty much, but I want to do better. I will now, because of Abby."

Hillary paused for a moment, as though thinking what to say next. "You know, when Chelsea was born, you loved her more than life itself, but you didn't have much time. Now the tables are turned. Are you sure you're ready to assume primary responsibility for a child who comes with baggage? This decision could blow up in our faces."

While Bill pondered the Clinton family's future, Hillary, in a softer tone, said, "Despite a demanding schedule back then, you did some fatherly things very well."

"Did I?" he asked hopefully. That was a long time ago. Remind me."

"Being a night owl, you eagerly took on two a.m. feedings and diaper changes. Baby poop didn't faze you in the least."

"Glad I was good for something."

Hillary stepped back. "Sorry, honey. You know I meant it as a compliment." Throwing her head back, as though calling on patience, she waited a few beats, searching for more suitable words. "Lately," she tried again, "I've been watching you closely."

Bill pictured I-95 and the two hundred-plus miles that often separated them, but he waited to hear her out. "And what I'm observing," she continued, "is a new Bill; one I haven't seen before."

"That's because we finished your grueling campaign, and I got the hell out of Washington."

"Perhaps, but what I'm trying to say is that although your plan to parent a needy child is slightly mad, it's also the most unselfish thing you've ever done. At speaking engagements, you advise young people to focus their energy on what makes us alike, not the tiny amount that differentiates us. It's easy to talk, but with Abby, you're taking the walk. Everything is on the line. Your generosity makes me proud. I just hope you don't end up taking me down in the glory."

Despite the qualifier tucked at the end, he was touched and caught off-guard by Hillary's naked compliment. They didn't come often.

"You're a big-picture guy. If someone could devise a plan to save the world, you'd be in the running for chief architect. Yet, with Abby, I somehow see you doing this to save yourself as much as her. Does that make any sense?"

"Um ... um, I'm not sure, since it's—"

"And what I was trying to say before," she interrupted, "is that you're good father material, and you'd better be. This is a personal decision, but our personal is also our public. The press, the public, all our enemies will zoom in; every move we take will be examined ever more closely."

"They already scrutinize us at every turn, and let's not forget Mattie. She can fend off just about anything and will be my right hand. Already she's clucking like a mother hen."

"That woman is more bull dog than mother hen, but I'll admit, she's perfect for the job: bossy, overbearing, and territorial. I have no doubt how she she'll handle herself."

"I might call on Ray more often if need be."

"He gets along with kids. I'll give him that. Unlike most of the other agents, Ray never scared Chelsea half to death." Always good at multitasking, Hillary checked her phone while making a U-turn around the bed, looking for her briefcase. Clicking off the phone, she bent down and unearthed her bag from the fluffy folds of their duvet that had slipped to the floor. The scratched and weathered brief bag, a mainstay since law school, traveled everywhere with the president.

"Ray's okay," she continued, gathering a pile of documents from her night table and stuffing them in the case, "but, sometimes you treat him like a friend. Not a good idea. His job description doesn't include 'friend.'"

Bill didn't say anything. He knew she harbored a grudge against Ray and anyone still around from1998, blaming them for not putting the brakes on his affair. His professional competence aside, Ray's loyalty and discretion was precisely why he loved the guy and considered him a friend.

"Also," Hillary said, "I wouldn't let the NYPD get too used to your independence. Don't worry about stepping on jurisdictional toes. You can carry this 'Mr. Ordinary Citizen act' just so far. You're not ordinary."

Bill wasn't sure how to respond or interpret "not ordinary," but he settled for, "Of course. There's always the unexpected." He was thinking of his first terrifying moments with Alex. "Overall, the neighbors have been respectful of our privacy. Inviting them in for a private viewing of the house was a stroke of genius. Ray told me folks really appreciated that."

"I'm not only thinking of neighbors. It's that great unknown you mentioned, and the press. They have a way of killing the magic. I'm sure they have some idea by now, but when they learn the extent of Abby's story, they'll be all over us. This thing has way more mileage than news of Chelsea having babies. And just wait, after they have enough on Abby, they'll start savaging me for being an opportunist."

Hearing a hint of bitterness creep back into Hillary's tone, he said, "I'm not so sure about that. The mainstream press has a hands-off policy toward children. I can't speak for rightwing radio, but I'd like to think that guys like Limbaugh leave kids out of it."

"Darling," she said, laying her makeup out on the sink, "don't be naive. Nastiness is their bread and butter. If he went after Chelsea, you know he'll have a field day with us parenting a black child."

Bill frowned. "Matter of fact, I got a call from Watson, the Harlem Hospital administrator, telling me there'd be no leaks from his end."

Indignant, Hillary said, "Well, of course he can't talk about it. Why'd he even bother to reaffirm standard policy?"

"Apparently, a guy from the New York Post called, saying he'd just heard about their boarder babies and wanted to do a story. Request denied. That hospital is no stranger to the scurrilous press. I'm sure Watson was just reassuring me."

"Oh, God," Hillary groaned. "Don't tell me it's already starting. And I just thought of something else. We might have to deal with crackpots. Mark my words: someone will come crawling out of the woodwork, claiming to be Abby's long-lost mother."

CHAPTER 22

WHEN THE BOSS IS AWAY

Three weeks had passed since Ray escorted the chief and his friend Alex to Issa. Now, enjoying his Saturday night off, he was back, occupying the same stool as before. The weekend crowd was larger, and without the ex-president in tow, it took a while to get more than a friendly wave from André, who was working with a different bartender. When André came over, Ray ordered a beer then said, "I hope our presence the other night didn't attract too much undue attention. I'm afraid you got a glimpse of Bill Clinton's famous temper."

"Not a problem, and I understand where he was coming from. As I mentioned then, more than a few customers have complained about that mother and child. It was just really cool to have Clinton in here. Word spread, and now everyone's hoping he'll come in again."

"Good," Ray said, relaxing and feeling fairly certain that his boss's flair-up hadn't gotten blown out of proportion. "When we talked before, you hadn't finished telling me about Faith's business empire."

"Yeah, empire. Hadn't thought of it like that, though it's fitting. Faith's got her fingers in dozens of pies. Supposedly, she also conducts séances." Clearly content to talk about his boss, he said, "Some old timers around here call her a Vodoun Queen."

"Vodoun, as in voodoo?"

"It's a West African term; basically they're one and the same, but whether she's really into the occult, I couldn't say. At my Catholic mission school, the nuns didn't believe in that stuff, and I followed their every rule. The sisters took me and my sister in, when our parents died of AIDS."

Ray nodded solemnly, acknowledging André's early troubles, but something didn't jive with what he'd told him the first time. "Didn't you say this woman was a successful business person? Now she's into voodoo?"

"Look, I was raised Catholic, but you don't grow up in Africa without some exposure to tribal religions. I didn't know much then, but I knew enough to respect the old priestess in my village who claimed to be in touch with spirits of the afterlife. Though most of those old women couldn't read or write, and Faith has had more education, she has a similar aura about her."

"Excuse my ignorance," Ray apologized, bowing to the other man's knowledge of African tradition and culture.

"No offense taken," the bartender said evenly, "but you ought to know that many priestesses are like Faith: wise women with money and power over other women, especially young needy ones. Their ways are as old as Africa. But that's not what you asked. We're off the subject."

"Not really; tell me more."

"Faith counsels troubled young girls and women. Sometimes they're Africans, like herself."

"What does she do for these ladies?"

"Tides them over with small cash gifts, helps them find jobs, housing. And another thing: she's big on dishing out those herbs and plants she grows in her garden, back behind the building next door."

"Sounds like my grandmother." Ray laughed at the memory. "She used to make me drink her special tea. It did help my diarrhea, but I wonder why Alex's lady friend, Sarafina, would seek this woman out. Any ideas?"

"None at all." André waved off the question. "I steer clear of Faith's affairs. Unless," he reconsidered, "my eyeballing the chicks who hang around here is getting into her business. We get a lot of lookers. A new girl's been in a few times lately. If she's the one you asked about, she stood out big time."

"Mind breaking it down? In what way did she stand out?"

André gave Ray's inquiry some thought. "It's funny you ask, but an hour or so before you guys came in, I sorta asked myself that same question when I saw her sitting there. Besides being a fox, this one wasn't on the make. Often, chicks come in here to meet guys. They're coy, usually classy about it, but this lady I could tell was looking for something different."

"Did she ever hook up with this famous Faith?"

"I'm not sure, but you can ask her yourself. I believe that's her who just walked in."

Ray's head snapped around in time to see two women pause inside the door. The shorter, slightly plumper of the duo pointed to the middle of the room. Ray assumed that the tall lady wearing yellow, with long curly hair pulled back with a matching ribbon, was Sarafina. Watching as they threaded around tables, Ray willed himself to be cool. André, his elbows propped on the bar, grinned and winked. "Good luck, buddy."

As the bartender retreated, Ray recovered his composure. "Look, man. I'm just following up for the chief and his friend."

"Follow away." André laughed as he went to take orders from one of the waitresses.

Ray enjoyed an occasional drink when he was off duty, and right now his icy brew had never tasted better. Smacking his lips, he sipped and studied Sarafina, hoping she didn't notice. Without checking, he knew that every man in the joint was aware that she was unescorted. If he was going to make a move, he decided, he'd better do it fast. His legs felt like lead, but somehow they propelled him toward her table. Usually Ray's heavy Glock forced him to wear bulky jackets. Tonight, for a change, he'd dressed with care and was packing a leg holster and had on a formfitting shirt. If he had to say so himself, his mirror reflection hadn't looked bad. All that time in the gym served more than one purpose.

Ray knew how to read body language, and even at twenty feet away, he saw something in Sarafina's demeanor, an alertness, maybe, that told him she knew he wanted to talk to her. Sensing no obvious cold shoulder, he breathed easier. Now, here at the table, he swallowed excess saliva and cleared his throat like a blushing high-schooler.

"I hope you'll excuse the intrusion ladies, but ..."

Sarafina rescued Ray with the same smile in her voice that Bill had detected weeks before. "You were sent by the president, is that not so?" she asked.

Pleasantly taken aback, he answered, "Why, yes. I mean,

no, not exactly. But, how did you know? A few weeks ago, he, myself, and another gentleman were in here looking for you. But how did you know who I was?"

Looking off to some spot behind his shoulder, she replied, "It's of no matter ... Mr.... ?"

"Ray. Just call me Ray. The chief gave me the weekend off," he added unnecessarily.

"Well, you have found me. I am Sarafina. This lady is Keisha."

Keisha, still buoyant after another session with Faith, had tuned into the exchange of words when she heard "the president."

"You work for Clinton?" she asked with interest.

"Sometimes." Ray quickly moved on. "Pleased to meet you both. What can I get you ladies from the bar? But first," he said, bubbling with excitement, "may I have permission to join you?"

Sarafina confidently answered for both of them by patting the empty chair. "Please be seated." He followed her directions and sat on the edge of the chair. Then, without needing much time to decide on a drink, Sarafina said, "Earlier, I hear a gentleman request Manhattan. In honor of this stretch of earth, why don't I have Manhattan?"

"Right." Ray, thinking he might explode with happiness, was certain he'd never seen a finer specimen of woman. "A Manhattan it'll be." Popping up again, he almost forgot to take the other woman's order but caught himself in time. "And what about you, Keisha?"

Glancing at her watch, Keisha said, "Actually, I'll pass. My grandmother's babysitting, so I'd better run before she falls asleep." Standing, she waved a goodbye to Sarafina and said to Ray, "I'd be much obliged if you'd help me get a cab."

"No problem. Just wait inside the door until I flag one down."

Barely believing his good fortune, Ray thought he was walking on air and hurried outside. Lady Luck was with him all the way tonight. Not only was the other chick leaving, but a cab was just pulling up to discharge two passengers. He hustled over, pulled open the back door, than waved Keisha over. As she approached Ray, Keisha touched his arm in a motherly way.

"Thank you," she said, ducking into the taxi. "You look like a really nice fella. Before you go back inside, you might want to know that Sarafina thinks she's a ghost."

Back in his apartment, Ray could think of nothing else besides Sarafina, who was now loving him as though her survival depended on exciting every nerve ending in his body. He hadn't been with a woman in months, not since his last girlfriend who'd turned him off by saying he was good husband material.

But with Sarafina, even his toes had tingled at Issa, when she'd put her mouth next to his ear and whispered. "As the hour grows late, the gentleman at the bar desires to return to his home, and we mustn't further detain him." Now, two hours later, that same beautiful mouth was silently tormenting him. Burning with desire and aching to please her, he gently turned her over and slowly slipped inside her silky wetness. He hadn't intended to come so quickly, but after a dozen or so piston-like strokes, his need usurped all rational thought and he exploded inside her with a shuddering finish.

After catching his breath, he lay there a minute then rolled to his back and gathered Sarafina closer. Smoothing her mussed hair, he pushed a damp tendril behind one ear for a clearer view of her face. Willing her to face him, he rubbed her cheek. "Pretty lady, do you know what you just did to me?"

Earlier, at the restaurant, while she sipped three Manhattans with no apparent effect, he'd gotten under-the-radar drunk on five or six beers, although he'd stopped counting. They'd sat and talked until André, weary from the long night, kicked them out at closing. But after spending hours getting acquainted, Ray realized he'd done most of the talking. Sarafina remained a mystery. Words like "exotic" and "seductive" could also be stirred into the mix.

The woman was a blend of dazzling sex appeal, poise, and something he couldn't quite put his finger on. Maybe it was innocence, although she clearly knew how to turn a man on. Right off the bat, she'd opened the door for their night together by clarifying her relationship with the chief's friend.

"Alexander seem to been in and out of my life forever. He come and go like a shadow," she'd described him. "Now, though, it needs be that I become the one to seek what I must find," she'd inexplicably stated. Ray remembered tipsily clinging to her every word, but now that he was mostly sober, he still wasn't sure what her words meant.

"At first Alexander be troubled I no longer desire to be his woman, but he is no longer the one I need," she'd told Ray. "Now, since he meet another lady, he recover in a goodly way." She had laughed then and thrown her head back, exposing the tender length of her lovely throat, causing Ray to plant a kiss on the spot. "In truth," she'd concluded, confusing him further, "there still be connections between me and Alexander."

"All right," he'd said, feeling no need to press her. Why spoil a magical night? Nothing mattered except she was now with him.

Waking from a doze, he felt his penis stirring but was determined to take his time when they made love again. His old granddad trick never failed to slow him down. So he conjured up the wrinkled black face that had terrified him as a child and no doubt still would if the mean, old bastard was still alive. It worked every time, and he felt his member soften and shrink. With his erection at half mast, he also figured he'd better void the beer sloshing around his bladder.

Seeing him about to leave the bed, Sarafina reached out to touch him. As she did, the top sheet slipped, revealing her full breasts. "Is something amiss?"

Staring at the dark nipples aimed unselfconsciously at him, he started to get hard again. "Only that I can't get over you." Shaking his head, he hopped out of bed. "Don't go anywhere. I'll be right back. I just seriously need to make a pit stop."

"Pit stop?"

"Sorry, that's guy talk. I have to pee."

When he came out of the bathroom, he found her standing before his sliding glass door. Her figure was classic. Long legs, small waist, and full hips that her height minimized. As she opened the door to step out on the balcony, he grasped her gently round the waist. "Whoa, you might not want to do that. Hmmm, delicious," he said, nuzzling her neck and running his fingertips across her breasts. "Don't let the darkness fool you. This city is starting to come alive."

Impatient to see the view, she wriggled away, protesting. "But the world lies beyond your doorway."

"True." He sighed, letting her go. "The ocean is just a few miles away. More importantly," he pointed toward his south wall that had no windows, "the guy who shares my balcony is probably already up. He leaves for work at six thirty every morning. I'll get you a cover."

Ray leaned inside to grab a shirt from a basket of clean laundry on the chair next to the bed. Shaking it out, he slipped her arms in the sleeves and buttoned it up, resisting further touching. Then he led her out to the balcony. Silently, they looked down at the lights of the bridge, one of several linking this part of Upper Manhattan to the Bronx. This early in the morning, the bridge lights shimmered through a gauzy fog. Beneath its span, the river was a strip of black tarmac.

Sarafina started to speak at the same time as Ray; instead they both laughed. "You go first," he said. "What were you going to say?"

"That I ... I watch you sleep. You sleep peacefully, like a child. Have you no troubles?"

"Not when it comes to sleep," he answered immediately. "When I'm off duty, I sleep soundly; always have. As for troubles, if you're asking if I have issues, the answer is no. My concerns arise through the actions of others. It's partly my training. I'm so focused on other people's crises, I've don't have time for one of my own."

"Do you speak of your chief, as you call him?"

"That's right. We've been through a lot together. He's like family; at least that's how I feel. In fact, the old dog's about to add to his family. If he goes through with it, I told him I want to be more than a bodyguard. Something like an uncle, or maybe a godfather would be my preference."

"Your soul is filled with kindness. I feel it most recently when you prevent me from exposing myself. You respect, not possess. Please, now your turn. Finish the thought upon your tongue."

He felt suddenly shy in her presence. "Okay," he laughed. "So you watched me sleeping, and I watched you standing nude at the window. Guess who had the better view?" She looked over and smiled at him, and he felt her shiver. "The early morning air is cool. Can I entice you back to bed?" he asked, gently snuggling close to cradle her body. Caressing the smooth mounds of thigh and hip, he brought his hands to rest on her rounded backside.

"Sarafina," he whispered into her neck. "How many men have compared your body to that of Venus de Milo? No, wait." He realized the indelicacy of the question. "Allow me to rephrase that. Has anyone ever said you have the body of a Venus or Aphrodite?"

With her back to him, she said, "I don't know anything about this Venus and Aphrodite you speak of."

Embarrassed, he understood too late that her schooling may have been limited. With them hitting it off so well, he didn't want to run the risk of sounding judgmental by asking about education. Her accent was unusual, and sometimes he wondered if her odd syntax and rapid sing-song delivery was related to the Gullah language.

Years ago, as a boy of seven or eight, he and his mother visited cousins on St. Helena, one of the sea islands in South Carolina where Geechies lived. The old folks down there still spoke in Gullah, a mix of African and English dialect that reached back to the seventeenth century.

He'd never forgotten how his mother had lashed out at him after catching him mimic two old ladies. "Boy," she'd yelled, grabbing him by his shirt collar, "for as long as you live, don't ever let me catch you making fun of how these people talk; you've got a lot to learn about your heritage." Maybe, after a cup of coffee, Sarafina would tell him about her accent and where she came from. She probably had an interesting background.

Sarafina waved a hand across his face, scattering his image of South Carolina. "Ray," she repeated, "tell me of these Venus and Apricot ladies."

"Oh Sarafina, Sarafina," he said, laughing. "Where have you been hiding?" Anxious to touch her in new ways, he pulled her close then eased her back into bed. "Where do I start?" he asked, holding tight. "You're an angel sent by God; you're a ripe apricot, full of wonder and delight," he teased, "a mouthful of golden, delicious sweetness."

With her back spooned into him, he didn't see tears pooling in her eyes. "Go on," she urged softly, "say it right, about the true-named woman."

"That," he started in, "would be Aphrodite, a goddess known for her perfect figure and sensual beauty. People from ancient societies believed she had the power to control emotions of the heart, like love and sex. Many men loved her. Venus de Milo is a famous marble statue that depicts Aphrodite." When he finished speaking and Sarafina didn't comment, he asked, "Do you see why one might compare you to the perfect beauty? Do you think God has provided another Venus, with you?"

"I think," Sarafina said, slowly twisting toward him, "I think God providing what Mistress Mary once say He'd do—'a ray of hope for a better tomorrow.'"

A ray of hope. Hmmm, I like that, he thought, peering through the darkness, thinking those words might be prophetic. Idly wondering who Mistress Mary was and how she fit the equation, he reached over and switched on the light. "Uh, oh," he gulped, confused at the sight of tears. More ominously, he didn't like the faraway, heartsick look in her eyes; she seemed to stare right through him. Gathering her in his arms, he felt his heart racing and knew some part of this lovely woman was badly damaged.

"Sarafina, please don't cry," he pleaded, rocking her back and forth. "Whatever upset you is past. If you'll have me, I'm here and won't ever let anyone hurt you." As words— commitment words he'd never used before—tumbled forth, he knew he meant them.

"Talk to me, baby," he urged, turning her toward him, needing to hear what she felt, wondering if she cared. "Don't leave me hanging."

"Ray, tell me how Aphrodite got happiness in her heart?"

Sarafina's response wasn't the one Ray expected. He ceased rocking. Searching his memory for pieces of the myth, he said, "I can't recall, but she married the wrong god. It was a loveless marriage; that much I remember. Aphrodite's true love was a mortal named Adonis, who died. So I guess happiness was short-lived for her."

"I'm sad for her."

Charmed by her innocence, he couldn't help smiling and rubbing his nose against her cheek, still damp with tears. Seeking to lighten the mood, he said, "Sarafina, if you're going to fret, it shouldn't be over myths and make-believe. Look at it this way: without the Aphrodite story, we might not believe love has the transformative power to sustain us, even after death."

Later, when they made love again, it started slow and easy. He stroked her inner thighs, tongued their creamy softness, moved to the mossy fringe above, and loved her there. While he pleased her, she moaned with pleasure, and he wanted to believe this meant more to her than a tumble in bed. Still, she gave little away.

Now, kneeling above her, he was master of the universe, taking his time, teasing her opening until she reached and guided him in. Hoping to wait for her, he tried pulling back, but there were limits to his self-control. Within minutes, her velvety embrace received him.

For a long time afterwards, as they lay entwined, they dozed off and on. Here in the bedroom, early rays of sunshine promised a beautiful day, reflecting Ray's euphoria. Totally smitten, he thought about a thing called love at first sight and wondered if, after all, his mother was right and he needed a woman in his life.

CHAPTER 23

HARD HIT

Ray picked up the phone to call his mother. He hesitated then hit the off button. Maybe he needed to have his ducks lined up before getting his mom excited about a new lady in his life. He could just imagine their conversation. "Oh, Raymond," she'd squeal, "I've been praying and praying that you'd meet the right girl. And, praise God, my prayers have been answered!

"Tell me all about her. What's her name? Describe her. Wait, hold on a minute so I can get comfortable in your father's old recliner. You still there? Go ahead. Tell me everything, Where's she from? What do you know of her people?"

Nope, he thought. He must be crazy. It was way too soon to share this with his mother and get her excited. He'd see Sarafina tonight and get a few answers about her family, the very things his mother would want to know.

He'd insisted on escorting her home, but it had been a struggle, with her just as vehemently insisting no one could hurt her. The location turned out to be one of Faith's buildings.

Once inside his car, Sarafina had been like a little kid, fiddling with knobs, changing stations, but oddly, she hadn't known how to use his DVD player, which worked the same as those in most cars. When he stopped in front of the apartment house she indicated, she told him it was one of Faith's buildings. Then she'd asked him to stay in the car, and he'd watched uncomfortably until she disappeared behind a glass door. Tonight when they talked, he'd explain the importance of security.

Since being with Sarafina he'd become energized, walking around with a silly grin on his face. After returning to his apartment, he spent the afternoon dusting, vacuuming, and catching up on laundry.

Now, looking around his place with a fresh set of eyes, Ray realized it could use some improvement. His dingy white walls needed something; maybe he could start with a new paint job. His spartan furnishings were old and shabby. He might even consider remodeling his kitchen and bath the way his upstairs neighbors had. The building was getting old, nearly thirty years, but his unit was a respectable two-bedroom with a river view, and there was enough space for a second person, if necessary. Thinking again of Sarafina's soft skin and that face framed in a wreath of curly hair made him grin harder.

CHAPTER 24

A VOLATILE MIX

Exhilarated by the run from his place on 155th Street to the chief's house, Ray slowed to a walk so he could cool down. Officially he was still off duty, but he needed to talk with Clinton before the ex-president left town, and he wanted to do it in person. Also, he had to find out more about the upcoming assignment with Abby, who hadn't yet been assigned her own agent.

When Mattie opened the door for him, Abby was standing behind her wearing a pink, pint-sized apron smeared with chocolate.

"Good to see you Ray. Come on in." Mattie led him into the kitchen where she distastefully eyed his sweaty shorts and soaked-through T-shirt. "Unless you always puff like a chimney, I guess maybe you could use a chair. Hold on a minute; let me get the stool." Placing a replica of an old-fashioned wooden step stool in front of him, she ordered, "Sit down."

"Thanks, but I better not. If I sit too soon after running, my legs cramp. But, this cool air is a blessing." Ray stood under the air conditioner vent, letting it blow right on him.

"He's expecting you," the housekeeper said, lifting her eyes to the ceiling, "although he's still up there on the phone with Mrs. Clinton. Seems like that poor woman goes from one crisis to the next. Something must be happening in Washington, because he's flying down this afternoon."

Despite working for the Clintons, Ray knew Mattie didn't closely follow politics. The boss would attend a state dinner tonight, plus Hillary was preparing to address the nation in a few weeks and probably wanted Bill's opinion.

Even when she was apprised of happenings in Washington, Mattie dismissed most news about the Clintons as "a pack of lies." Opting not to explain what was happening in DC, Ray waited while she opened a couple of lower cabinets until she found what she was looking for, a can of lemonade. Another shelf produced the pitcher into which she dumped three heaping scoopfuls of powdery yellow mix and added ice water.

"Abby? The cat got your tongue over there?" Mattie observed the child from the corner of her eye. "Come on over here and say hello to Ray. He won't bite. A minute ago you were talking my ear off." Pouring two lemonades, she placed one before Ray and, to entice Abby closer, offered her the second glass. "While he's here, why not tell him about the outing?"

Ray downed the cold liquid but felt the heat of Abby's quizzical stare. "Ah, that hit the spot." Smacking his lips, he said, "Thank you," as Mattie poured a refill.

He then turned his attention to the little girl. "So what's up, cutie? Did I hear something about a boat ride?" Under Abby's scrutiny, he wiped his mouth self-consciously then walked to the sink to wash his face and hands.

"Hold it," Mattie barked, blocking his path, "not in my sink! Don't you see those chicken breasts and thighs defrosting on the counter?" Pointing to her left, she ordered, "Go wash those nasty hands down the hall; that's what the bathroom's for."

Ray backed away, muttering, "Sorry, ma'am," before slinking down the hall. Quickly checking the small mirror, he soaped up then gave his face a quick lather. Damn, he thought, as he carefully refolded the guest towel into thirds, being around Mattie is just like being around my mom.

"Sorry about my appearance. I'm a mess, but the run felt good." Sipping the rest of his lemonade, he said, "Abby, weren't you going to tell me about an outing of some sort?"

Her eyes were wide, and Ray saw the child was ready to share her news.

"It's a boat ride. But how come there's something different about you today?"

"Is there?" He winked, impressed by her intuitiveness. "I guess I'm all worked up over you inviting me to spend the day with you. It'll be cool," he said, meaning it. "Where are we going? On the Circle Line? Maybe something like that?"

"Uh, huh." All of Abby's reserve dissolved into a childish jump for joy. "We're riding on a boat," she squealed, hopping up and down. "It's the Trevor Day cruise. All the kids are going."

Ray noted that Abby had stopped calling her summer camp program, Ever Day. He plopped down on the step stool and patted the chair next to it. "Come sit by me and let's hear the details. I haven't been on a Hudson River cruise since I was about your age."

"We're going far." Her dark brown eyes grew wider as she crept closer. "We have to take a picnic lunch," she explained, warming to the topic. "The letter also said to bring a camera and a sweater."

"Lunch might create a problem," he teased. "I can handle the sweater and camera, but see, I'm not a very good cook."

"It's okay," she assured him, the shyness forgotten. "It's not till tomorrow, and me and Mattie just made brownies. In a little while, she's going to teach me how to bake chicken so we don't have to only eat brownies."

Ray looked over at Mattie with something akin to gratitude. What he saw was another strong black woman stepping in to care for someone else's child. In these past hectic weeks, Mattie had assured the chief that she would be available 24/7 to help the girl transition to her new life. Ray was far from an expert when it came to kids, but he saw from Abby's increased self-confidence and interaction with him that she was thriving.

"Well, Abby, if you're going to provide the food, I guess we've got a date."

Just then, Bill, wearing a business suit, entered the kitchen. "Hi, everybody," he greeted, while sniffing the air. "What's this I hear about food, and do I smell brownies baking?"

"Yeah. For the boat ride." Abby ran to peek in the oven door's glass panel. Checking over her shoulder, she reminded him, "You said it was okay for Mattie to teach me how to make brownies. Later we're going to cook chicken."

"Sweetheart," Bill said as he walked over and stooped down to Abby's eye level, "you don't have to ask my permission to cook with Mattie. This is your home now. In fact, you better learn how to rustle up grub, because I'm terrible at it."

While still squatting, Bill mimicked the child's action and checked the oven window. "If a menu's settled, then it sounds like everything's under control." Turning to Ray, he joked, "I guess you know the important facts of this assignment: boat ride, food, fun; that's about it. Still, I'm glad you insisted on dropping by." Bill lowered his voice and led the agent down the hall toward his study and away from the women. "On the phone you seemed excited about something. Still do," he added, laughing at the broad smile lighting Ray's face. "My airport detail isn't picking me up for another—" he checked his watch— "ten minutes. So what's up?"

As soon as the door closed behind them, Ray started talking. "Remember," he said, taking a deep breath, "how you're always asking if I'd ever consider settling down?"

"Yeahhh, buddy," Bill drawled, anticipating big news. "I've brought that up a number of times in the past year, and all I ever get from you is a laugh." Bill wasn't sure what his bodyguard would say, but he knew it was good. "Are you about to make some kind of announcement?"

"No." Ray laughed. "Nothing so momentous, although I really like this lady. We've been out a few times, and she's awesome," he said with a blush. "I might be in love." The agent rushed the words, relieved to say them aloud.

Ray could tell Bill was happy for him, so he hurried to get to the potentially messy part. "Everything's cool, but here's the thing I want to tell you. Right up front, she made it perfectly clear that she's no longer involved with the other guy. Also," he breathlessly rushed ahead, "I simply met her like any other woman, so I don't expect it to conflict with my official duties, but I thought I owed you an explanation before you see us together."

Intrigued, Bill's grin widened and he folded his arms, listening.

"See," Ray said, "it's Sarafina."

Suddenly a look of horror twisted Bill's face, and he blurted, "Oh, no, Ray, you can't do that." Backing away, he said, "She's ... she's ... a phantom. It's out of the question. Leave it alone. You don't want to do this. Sarafina's not the real thing."

"Beg your pardon, but what are you saying?"

Afraid of the question, Bill inched back a few more paces as though increased distance would provide a way out of this agony. From down the hall, snippets of conversation between Abby and Mattie reached him, and he envied their innocent tranquility.

Despite the muffled female voices, his office was deathly still, and Bill could hear his battery-powered clock's soft tick when the minute hand advanced another notch.

"All right. We'll do it your way." Ray broke their tense standoff. "You just told me the woman I'm seriously interested in is a phantom, a figment of my imagination. Maybe you meant phenom, whatever. Either way, I caught the part about, 'Don't do it ... Sarafina's not the real deal,' or something like that. Okay," Ray said, moving closer to Bill. "Now let me just ask you something, and I'm going to lay it on the line, because right now we're talking mano a mano."

Warily, Bill met the agent's eyes.

"Okay," Ray repeated. "Here's how I see it. Sarafina's no longer interested in this Hamill fellow. But, the lady has shown pretty keen interest in me. Follow?" Ray asked, but this time he didn't expect an answer. "See, guys don't say things like that to each other. Even if one was once president. When my best buddy married a conniving bitch, I held my tongue. It wasn't my business to tell him what to do. He knew what she was like, but he loved her anyway. Sarafina's not a bitch. She's sweet and innocent. So I need to ask if you object because maybe you're interested in Sarafina yourself."

"Oh, good Christ, no," Bill yelled, vigorously shaking his head and backing away. He had to think fast, and Ray was right; he should have kept quiet. But no matter how big a mess this was, he first had to dispel any impression that he was interested in Sarafina.

"Ray," he started, "so help me, God, you couldn't be more wrong about me being interested in that woman. I swear on a stack of Bibles and my mother's grave, that's the last thing I meant."

Throwing his hands up, the agent didn't look appeased. "Then what is going on? I don't get it. I just don't get it."

In misery, Bill watched Ray clench and unclench his fists as confusion turned to anger. Bill knew, in a less-disciplined man, such fury could lead to violence. Despite the pain they were both experiencing, a pain he'd caused, Bill couldn't think of an explanation that wouldn't make a bad situation worse.

Not receiving the mea culpa he hoped for, Ray strode across the floor. At the door, he stopped, turned, and said with emotion, "Sir, I swore to perform my duty and uphold the integrity of my country and the United States Secret Service. Unless you see fit to relieve me of my duties to you, I fully intend to honor those principles to the best of my ability."

Listening sadly to the agent's automaton recitation, Bill wanted to grab and comfort him. Instead, he said, "Ray, you don't have to justify anything. You're superb at what you do. Look, buddy, you're upset, but please believe me, I want only the best for you. I'm sorry, but it's complicated; the whole thing's just flaky."

"Chief," Ray uttered the familiar title, but to the ex-president's ears, it sounded jagged, edgy. "Tell Abby I'll see her tomorrow."

Bill looked on helplessly as his bodyguard walked through the door.

After leaving Clinton, Ray sprinted home at a faster clip than he had on the way over. But now, instead of feeling better, his left knee ached and he felt a new twinge in his recently healed shin splints. Ray knew he should prepare a couple of ice bags, but instead, he steadily paced back and forth on his already-worn carpet.

He tried pulling himself together but despaired over his boss's sorry choice of words. Just what was the world coming to, he wondered, when someone like Bill Clinton would so boldly bad-mouth a perfectly fine woman?

Ray knew he wouldn't let personal feelings come between him and an assignment. Over the years, despite guarding some real turds, he'd put his life on the line for them. Still, he was having a hard time letting go of his anger. "Damn," he muttered, partly out of frustration with his boss, but also because a new pain shot though his left knee signaling more than a minor ache.

He was limping toward the kitchen for ibuprofen and ice, when he suddenly remembered something. For the first time since he'd met Sarafina, Ray recalled what Keisha said the night he put her in a cab outside of Issa.

Before he closed the cab door, she'd leaned forward like she was doing him some kind of favor and confided, "You look like a really nice fella. You might want to know that Sarafina thinks she's a ghost." He'd attributed her stupid comment to a dumpy broad who was jealous of Sarafina's beauty. But, the chief? Why would he want to fuck with his head?

CHAPTER 25

BILL SAYS NO

Increasingly annoyed, Bill paced around his office. It was nearly an hour since Hillary's secretary had called and asked him to stand by, saying his wife needed to speak to him before he returned to New York. Years had passed since his presidency, but he had never asked Hillary to meet him in the office then made her wait an hour. He recalled the day everything went to hell in Mogadishu, when American soldiers were captured, tortured, and killed. Chelsea was starring in a school play that night, and the first thing he did was call both her and Hillary into the office and explain that he wouldn't be joining them for the evening.

He wouldn't even be in DC today, if it weren't for last night's state dinner for President Binto-Halia. He'd worked his tail off making small talk with the man's exceedingly dull wife, struggling with her accent, which, like the scent she wore, was thick enough to slice with a knife. As tedious as such dinners sometimes were, he realized his presence was essential when dignitaries visited the White House, even from small emerging states such as Binto-Halia's. It hadn't been an elaborate dinner, but the roast duck was top-notch, plus he'd enjoyed witnessing several insufferable Republican senators eat crow at the dining table of another President Clinton.

But now he should be on his way to New York, where he needed to repair the damage with Ray. "Damn," he swore under his breath. Why had he told him, especially like that? Ray would eventually learn the truth, or would he? Did it even matter that the poor bastard's heart was about to break because of a woman? Yeah, it mattered, because Ray's current flame was a ghost ... a frickin' spook, in every weird and ugly sense of the word.

More importantly, Bill knew that any fallout from this mess would land in his and Hillary's laps. If the media learned that one of the Clintons believed in ghosts, much less consorted with them, Congress might start another impeachment process, and who would blame them? Sometimes it was exhausting to think of all the chaos women had created in his life. And it didn't seem to matter whether they lived down the road or up above.

He looked outside his window and up at a sky full of fluffy white clouds. In conversations with Alex, he purposely avoided asking the founder what it felt like to be dead or to live in heaven, perhaps even on a cloud like the one slowly pushing past the White House. When he met his maker, Bill hoped to be pleasantly surprised by the accommodations. His bad boy days were long past, so he wasn't expecting any negative surprises when he arrived at St. Peter's gate.

The phone shrilly interrupted his reverie. "Bill," Hillary's voice came through the line. "I'm so sorry to keep you waiting.

Can you come right over?" she asked and hung up, not waiting for an answer. Having immediately detected the tremor in his wife's voice, he was no longer annoyed and hurried down the hall.

Nowadays, when he entered the Oval Office, the first thing to catch Bill's eye was an odd looking sofa that Hillary called a fainting couch. It was a piece of whimsy she'd unearthed while touring the warehouse that stored presidential furniture and memorabilia from prior administrations. The couch once belonged to Mrs. Lincoln, and Bill recalled Hillary's excitement when it arrived at the White House. "I'm totally in love with that old thing," she told him. "It's going in my office so no one will dare accuse me of not being feminine enough." This time, when Bill stepped in his old office, all he saw were the worry lines on his wife's face that hadn't been there last night when they turned in.

"For God's sake, Hillary, what's going on? Chelsea and everyone in the family is okay, right?"

"Yes, they're fine. Please, sit down." He parked on the edge of her desk, and she grabbed his hand, squeezing harder than she realized. "Bill, the secretary of state is stepping down. I need a replacement, and I wish it could be you."

Bill stood up. "What? What are you talking about? You just appointed him."

"I know, and there's more." Removing her glasses, she rubbed her eyes. "Around five this morning, Ed's wife and two daughters were in a head-on collision in Maryland, on I-95. You may remember, Rosemary won't fly. She was driving back after taking the girls to visit their grandmother in Colorado. Now one girl is dead; Rosemary and the other daughter are critical, although the doctors say Rosemary should recover. She suffered a broken pelvis and fractures in both legs. They're not so sure about Kaitlin, the youngest girl."

"Jesus. A man's worse nightmare. Did she fall asleep? Was it a drunken driver or someone texting? They've gotten as bad, if not worse than drunks."

"I have no idea, but whatever the cause, you can imagine the secretary is devastated and feels he can't leave his family now and continue traveling around the world. I've accepted his resignation. The press just got wind of this, and they're expecting me to make a statement this morning. I wish I could replace him with you. You could step right in, but things like that don't happen. President Hillary Clinton, former Secretary of State, taps her husband, former President Bill Clinton to be the new Secretary of State. Even to my ears it sounds ludicrous."

"Secretary of State is not a job I'd take right now," he said, resettling again on the front of Hillary's desk. "Just for fun, let's suppose that if under these same tragic circumstances, you were offering me the UN ambassadorship; then we might have a deal. At the UN, I would at least spend some time in New York."

"Bill, that's an odd thing to say; besides, the UN is not your thing; not enough action. But more to the point, you never expected me to curtail my ambitions in the '80s when we were young parents. It almost sounds like you're lobbying for a part-time schedule because we now have Abby. Am I reading you right?"

"If you'll remember, I've already been lying low because of your new job, so yeah, I guess my current focus is on sticking closer to home."

"It's not like we don't have plenty of resources to help with child care. This is the twenty-first century. I know Mattie loves her new role, but several of my cabinet members have full-time nannies. Maybe we should still hire one to help Mattie."

An image of a nanny popped into Bill's head, one in a cape with a Mary Poppins accent, carrying an umbrella and telling Mattie how to organize her kitchen. Or worse, advising her to stop serving Abby fried eggs and bacon, which to be truthful, was a meal he didn't exactly approve of either. Still, he almost laughed. "I'm sure that would go over well. Mattie's doing just fine without additional help, and frankly she's the kind of role model Abby and plenty of other children need.

"Remember, Abby will shortly be exposed to a fancy private school and our muckety-muck friends and their precocious kids who've had every advantage. Frankly, some of these helicopter parents could use a few of Mattie's lessons on how real children live."

"You're right, but don't blame our generation. Helicoptering is a new parenting style. We didn't spoil Chelsea, and I hope she won't be the type of a mom who indulges her kids' every wish." Hillary smiled at her husband and walked over to take his hand again. This time she didn't squeeze but surprised him by bringing it to her mouth and kissing his fingers. Then she reached up to smooth his hair.

"I pride myself on not making a lot of mistakes," she said, "but lately I've screwed up, big time."

When he didn't say anything, she looked into his eyes and laughed. "I'm about to make a confession here, aren't you curious?"

"I am, but I know you're going to tell me anyway."

"Really?" She seemed surprised.

"Yes, really. We've been married forever, remember. Whether we know it or not, we have wordless ways of communicating with each other."

"Do you think I'm that transparent around the public?"

"Hillary, look at me." He pulled her closer to him, bringing her attention back from wherever it had wandered. "I'm playing around. Relax, okay?"

"I know," she said, refocusing. "Keep reminding me, will you, that I need to chill. Where was I?"

"You screwed up."

"Right. I was about to say, I screwed up by failing to go to the mat for you on my original UN appointment. You might not have been confirmed, but let's suppose you were. You would have been a natural. Catherine Pickett, despite her distinguished record with the State Department, is a little lacking in personal charm. Seriously, if anyone ever asked her to make a toast, she'd probably say, 'I'm not your maid.'"

"If I wasn't such a nice guy, I'd say, 'I told you so.'"

"Well, you can say it in a minute, after I apologize for continually underestimating the depth of your commitment to Abby. I still don't understand that special bond between the two of you, but I feel its strength."

"By jove," he joked, "I think you've got it."

"I already said that I'm proud of you, but your unselfish actions will do so much to encourage other folks to become foster or adoptive parents."

Smiling broadly, he encircled his wife in a tighter embrace. When he let go, she stepped back and said, "I refuse to feel guilty for these few satisfying moments with you, but we've had a tragedy in our political family and a tough job just got a lot harder. I better get back to work, and you need to take care of things in New York."

"Okay, but let me know what I can do."

"Pray for Ed's family."

CHAPTER 26

CAN EVERYONE PLEASE CALM DOWN?

Ray had a few stops to make before picking up Abby, and with the long day ahead, he forced down a glass of orange juice despite a queasy stomach. After showering he carefully shaved, and then mindful of unpredictable temperatures on the river, he riffled through his closet before grabbing a light windbreaker that provided a roomy cover for his gun. Checking behind him one last time, he scooped his keys from the bowl, flipped off the lights, and pulled the door tightly shut behind him.

A half mile away, in the kitchen of Bill's townhouse, Mattie and Abby were finishing breakfast when the housekeeper asked, "You still have that dollar tied up in the hankie I gave you?" From her pocket, the child pulled out an old-fashioned white lace handkerchief. "Good," Mattie said approvingly, "no young lady should leave the house without emergency mad money."

"But I won't get mad at Ray. I like him. Last time I saw him, he taught me to play poker. We used colored toothpicks for money."

"What?" Mattie reared back, shocked. "See what I mean? Sometimes grown men just don't know how to act. You have no business playing that kind of card game."

Afraid she'd just gotten Ray in trouble, Abby asked, "May I be excused?"

"Come on, eat a little more. He'll be here soon."

"I'm full. You made too much," Abby said, eyeing a bowl of cooling oatmeal.

"You need more meat on your bones. You're too skinny."

"When I was at the hospital, Nurse Lorna said kids are supposed to be skinny. She said Americans are too fat."

"Did she also teach you to talk fresh like that?"

"No, ma'am." Abby dropped her eyes. "But I don't like oatmeal."

"Well, it's cold now, anyway." Mattie removed the bowl. "At least you ate your toast and bacon."

Outside, three doors from Clinton's house, Ray maneuvered the big SUV into a tight spot. Knowing the child would be eager to leave, he got out, said a few words to the agent parked in front of the house, then bounded up the steps, two at a time.

"Yippee. You're early." Abby had been watching at the window and opened the door for him. "I told Miss Mattie you wouldn't be late, because the boat would leave us."

"Spoken like a true sailor," he said, noticing she was dressed in a white middy blouse and denim bell bottoms; tiny pink whales were embroidered on the cuffs. A sweater, in the same pink, was tied at her waist.

"Honey, you're cute as can be in your sailor outfit. No wonder little girls are made of sugar and spice and everything nice."

"Huh? Who says that?"

"You know ... Mother Goose, Humpty Dumpty, those guys."

When her expression didn't budge, he explained, "They're nursery rhymes." He realized Abby's developmental stages weren't the same as his friends' kids who'd had classic stories read to them as babies. But, on the upside, a book of nursery rhymes might be the perfect gift for Abby. "Just wait," he said, "I'll bring you a whole book of them."

"Ray," Mattie interjected drolly, "get with the program. You should see what this one can already read; she's a smart little cookie. She's been tested, and she's reading on a fifth-grade level. Remember, she's seven years old, not three."

"I'm almost eight," Abby corrected her.

"Well, big girl," he said and gave her a thumbs up, "I guess I better put a little more thought into this. I'll come up with of something to match how grownup you look today."

"I know. I love these pants." Abby blushed and whirled, giving him the full view. "Mrs. Hillary fedded it to me from Washington. It came on a delivery truck, and the box had my name on it."

"FedEx-ed it?" Ray laughed, looking to Mattie, who confirmed the carrier by nodding and raising her eyebrows in amusement.

Mattie passed Ray a straw picnic basket loaded with chicken, deviled eggs, and brownies. Stating the obvious, she said, "The child's overly excited. Keep a close eye on her so she doesn't run herself right over the side of the boat."

"Hear that, young lady?" He scrunched low, making eye contact. "What Mattie just said is important. How about we make a deal: no running until we get to Bear Mountain Park."

"Deal!" she agreed, slapping her little hand into his, surprising him with her stinging high-five agreement.

"With an arm like that, pitching's definitely in your future. Ever play softball?" he quizzed her.

With a frown, she said, "No way. That's for boys."

Smiling at her expressive face, Ray realized how much she'd blossomed in just a short time. Every day now, she appeared happier and more outgoing.

To Mattie, he asked, "Will you still be here when we get back around eight tonight, or do I pull more babysitting hours?"

Her pocketbook in hand, the woman followed them outside, pulling the door closed and signaling the agent out front. "Of course I'll be here. Until her tutoring begins in three weeks, I'm here around the clock. Made myself comfortable in the spare room. But while you're entertaining the child, I need to check my mail, pay bills, and spend a few hours at my own apartment."

"You're a special lady," he said respectfully. Except for her devotion to Bill and now Abby, Ray knew little of the housekeeper's personal life. As an afterthought, he added, "I hope the chief knows what a gem you are."

"Oh, he knows," she replied with customary frankness. "I learned a long time ago, you got to set men straight, or they take you for granted."

"Well," he said, chuckling, "on that note, we better hit the road."

Tossing a lighthearted "Bye, Ms. Mattie!" over her shoulder, Abby skipped ahead, leaving the adults behind. Ray followed the girl down the steps but turned back to Mattie. "Don't rush your errands. Remember, both the on-duty guy and I have a key to the house in case we get back early."

Out at the curb, he saw the child make a beeline toward the front passenger door of his SUV. "Hold your horses, Abby, I brought along a special guest. Today your onboard seat assignment is rear, right window. Just let me stow our lunch away." Her hand in midair, Abby put on her brakes and looked at the closed passenger door. "You have to sit in back, but the door's heavy. I'll open it," he said, catching up.

Ray knew Abby couldn't see into the midnight-black window, but something inside drew her attention. "There's a lady in the car, isn't there?" she mumbled, glancing over at Ray. "Peas," she mouthed in wonder. "She smells like fresh garden peas. That's what I smelled on Mr. Bill; now I smell it on you."

"What's that, honey?" Ray looked at the sky as a passenger jet roared overhead. "Wait until the plane passes."

Tossing the basket in back, he watched disbelievingly as the slight girl, seemingly with superhuman strength, tugged the Navigator's armor-plated front door open. Peering inside the car, Abby's eyes and mouth flew open as she locked onto the passenger, then slowly, like an inchworm, crept closer.

"Mama," she whispered in reverence. "Auntie said you'd come back. It's me, Mama. I'm Abby."

With the big-eyed girl standing resolute and refusing to let go of Sarafina's hand, Ray gave up. "Okay," he said, not knowing how to handle a stubborn kid, although the rapture on Sarafina's face showed she clearly didn't mind the imposition.

Somewhat belatedly, he added, "Abby, I see you've met my friend, Sarafina, so I guess introductions aren't necessary.

"Honey," he prompted, when she still didn't respond, "It's a bit unusual, but I suppose you can squeeze in front with Sarafina, if she doesn't object." With neither of them paying him any attention and the woman beginning to pull the girl into her lap, Ray felt he needed to set some parameters. He stuck his head inside to talk to Sarafina.

"You two can sit together for a minute, but before I pull out, Abby has to crawl into the back and buckle into her own seat."

Ray shrugged. With a sinking feeling, he realized a full day of babysitting might prove harder than anticipated. Walking around to the driver's side, he climbed behind the wheel and waited a few beats, shaking his head at the unpredictability of females, even young ones. Chicks are really into hugging, he thought. Abby's long legs crowded the gearbox, while Sarafina ran both hands over her as if she were a lost love.

"What the hell?" He did a double take at the sight of large tears suddenly spilling from Sarafina's eyes.

"Forgive me, child," Ray heard Sarafina say. "I couldn't prevent what happened to us."

Startled at the intense scene unfolding, he thought, Oh no. This is too weird. Surely Sarafina can't be Abby's missing mother!

"Ladies, someone say something," he urged, as Sarafina, seemingly in a trance, now rhythmically rocked the child back and forth. "What's going on here?"

Turning slightly with a faraway look in her eyes, Sarafina said, "Many years before, my child Judith were cruelly stolen from me. Of late, I feel her spirit reach out to me through Mr.

Clinton. Now, here she be."

Feeling his stomach heave, Ray moaned, "Oh God." The length of his throat filled with the taste of sour citrus. Struggling out of his seat belt, he hit the asphalt in time to retch violently into the gutter. Gulping air, he steadied himself against the car, then reached in back and rummaged through the wicker basket for paper napkins. Gratefully he sopped his brow and then used the sodden wad to wipe his mouth and shirt.

Still trembling, he leaned on the SUV, lowered his head, and continued gulping fresh air. Shakily, he looked over at Sarafina, who'd gotten out of the car to come over to help him. Abby followed, but at the sight of puke, she made a face and backed away.

"Until this moment, I see no need to tell you of my child from before. Still, you mustn't remain like this." Dismayed, Sarafina scanned the block for a more suitable location. "Let us gather elsewhere."

"It's my stomach, not my ears, that isn't working too well," he answered without moving. "Say your piece, right here."

"Ray, this a story written in the hand of God." Sarafina beckoned to Abby, but the girl remained at a safe distance, staring at the adults. Turning again to Ray, Sarafina said, "Only with God will answers be found."

Abby, having maneuvered closer to Sarafina's side, said, "Mama, Ray, don't be sad. It's okay. Every night when I said my prayers, and sometimes in the daytime too, Auntie came to visit. She said my prayers about Mama would be answered, and now they have been. Mama, I live with Mr. Bill. Auntie said you would want me to."

Shoulders slumped and his jaw slack, Ray's sweaty brown

skin had assumed a grayish cast. "Auntie?" He looked up. "You mean Abby has other kin in New York? Who's this Auntie?"

"She's ... she's the ancient—" Sarafina began, but Abby interrupted.

"Auntie's my imaginary friend, silly."

Frowning, Sarafina blinked rapidly, shook her head, and appeared confused. Searching Abby's earnest face, her breath coming rapidly, she asked, "Imaginary? Child, why you say such a thing? Judith well knows Auntie's ancient roots."

The girl looked at both adults as if they were dunces. "Auntie lived under the radiator in my hospital room. She said you moved to the other side. Mama, where were you?"

His voice cracking, Ray asked, "Other side? What is that supposed to mean? What the hell kinda game have you been running down? First, that woman at Issa said something about you thinking you were a ghost; then the chief implied the same thing."

It was Abby's turn to look askance. "Ghost?" she asked, giggling. Then, nervously squinting at Ray and Sarafina, who both wore tortured expressions, Abby burst into tears.

"Mama, I thought you'd be happy," she sobbed, collapsing against Sarafina, who'd gone rigid. "Are you sad because I didn't remember my name was Judith?" she asked. "I'm sorry. I'm sorry. Please don't be mad."

Grasping for a chain around her neck, Abby spoke to the stricken woman, "Look. Now I'm Abby, see?" Fishing a tiny filigreed name pendant from under her middy blouse, she twisted its short chain so Sarafina could better read the letters. "A-B-B-Y," she spelled. Sounding out the letters seemed to reassure the girl. "It's real gold. The nurses gave it to me when

I left the hospital."

"Nurses, necklaces!" Ray held his head. "Could someone just tell me the truth?"

Sarafina started to speak but instead eased her tall frame next to Ray's by the running board. "Truth, Ray? What do I know of truth?" Then she looked around for Abby, who had suddenly dashed back toward the townhouse where a government car was discharging Bill. "For a moment," she said to Ray, "I thought truth had found me."

Stepping from the car, Bill did a quick sweep of the street and noticed Ray's SUV, just as the excited child barreled into him. "Well, hello there, little darling. Why aren't you in the car with Ray? You two should be on your way to Bear Mountain."

Instead of answering, Abby grabbed his hand and yanked. He frowned when he saw that she was crying.

"Come quick. Mama came back, but she doesn't remember me, and Ray is sick."

"Mama?" Bill froze and suddenly panicked, remembering Hillary's words about lunatics claiming to be Abby's long-lost mother. "Hold on, hold on, Abby. You say someone's claiming to be your mother and that Ray's hurt? Then we need to turn around and quickly walk back toward the man standing by the car I just left." Bill glanced over his shoulder, wondering why the damn driver just stood there. And where had the on-duty agent gone? Around back?

"No, no. Ray threw up," Abby said, pointing to Ray's SUV. "Mama's his friend," she added, "but they're sad."

Bill hesitated. "What? Does Ray need an ambulance?"

"Nooo," Abby wailed in frustration. "Just come."

Reluctantly letting her pull him along, Bill glanced back at the other agent, who stood alert, scanning the empty street, but didn't move. Following Abby, he prayed he was doing the right thing. *Whatever this is about, I needed to be here and not in DC*, was Bill's last thought before Abby led him to the driver's side of Ray's car.

What he saw staggered him. "Sweet Jesus," he muttered at the sight of Sarafina sitting next to his physically powerful bodyguard, who'd never before looked so vulnerable. Bill worked his mouth, but no sound came out.

"Chief, forgive me," Ray said, trying to get up from the car's sideboard where he was seated. When Sarafina gently touched his elbow, he shrugged away. "Sir, I'm afraid that what you see is as bad as it looks. I know you tried warning me she was a flake, and God knows, I should have listened. Sorry, sir. I didn't mean to bring trouble into your family. I am prepared to resign immediately."

Bill ignored Ray's offer to resign. He steadied himself and asked in a measured tone, "Sarafina, what's the meaning of this? What are you trying to do here?"

Raising her head, Sarafina directed her comment to Abby. "The child claims to remember me as her mother, but … it cannot be …"

In a barely controlled voice, Bill said, "At least you've got that right. It's not possible."

"A child of mine would not fail the test of kinship with Auntie, who makes us the same."

Bill noticed that Sarafina had assumed the same spooky, faraway voice that had so unnerved him when they first met for breakfast at the coffee house. "Auntie," she continued, "binds me to Judith."

"Auntie's my friend, and you're Mama," the little girl insisted.

Bill turned from one troubled face to another. "Auntie? What the hell does some auntie have to do with this?"

"She's my imaginary friend," Abby clarified. Then, sticking out her thumb as a measurement, she explained, "She's this big. I couldn't see her, but she lived under the radiator."

Bill hadn't observed Abby playing with her imaginary friend since that first visit to her hospital room when he heard her pretend-talking. Still, he thought he saw a way to defuse the present situation and to reassure Abby.

"Well, of course. I heard you talking to her one day at the hospital."

Nodding and edging closer to him, Abby said, "Auntie still lives there. She didn't move with me to your house."

Bill felt it important to let Abby know he believed at least part of her claim. "Sweetheart, that's how it goes sometimes. Cricket, my daughter's imaginary friend, once lived with us in Arkansas, but he also stayed behind when I took Chelsea with me to our new house. Sometimes good friends have to say goodbye."

Squirming and toeing the ground with her sandal, Abby said, "Mama doesn't remember me."

Though pleased that the story of Cricket had stemmed Abby's tears, Bill remained unsure of how to disabuse her of this mother fixation over a ghost, or what to say next to move the conversation in the right direction. Out of the corner of his eye, Bill saw the Mayfield Nursery minibus roll by, leading him to think it best to keep addressing his remarks to the child.

"Abby," he began, "you arrived at the hospital when you were three. Now you're almost eight, and five years is a long time. Memories grow faulty with time, so it's possible you're wrong about Sarafina."

"I'm not."

Although he saw no point in continuing this dialogue with a stubborn kid, this thing needed resolving. And where was Alex? Usually he showed up like a bad penny, at the worst time, but right now he might actually be of help. Glancing disdainfully at Sarafina, Bill willed her to use some of her divine connections with spirits, or whoever she claimed to call upon, to clean up this mess.

As though reading Bill's mind, Sarafina turned to Abby, who remained firmly planted between the two men. Then, apparently making a decision, the woman pointed to a space next to her on the running board and said, "Daughter, won't you come nearer?"

Bill let out a groan.

CHAPTER 27

GOODBYES

A few days after the fiasco in front of his house, Bill, though still shaken and unsure how to handle the situation with Abby and Sarafina, had gotten some unsolicited advice from Mattie while helping to put away groceries. "I'll tell you one thing about Abby," she offered, "that child's a deep one."

Interested in Mattie's interpretation of "deep," Bill asked, "In what way?"

"I mean she's wise beyond her years."

"Well, sure. Her hospital records described her as bright and intuitive, if that's what you're saying."

"I don't know about all that, but the other day she saw my pills sitting by the sink and asked what they were. I told her I had an ear infection, and out of the blue, she pipes up, 'Miss Mattie, garlic oil will make your earache go away.'"

"'Abby,' I told her, 'those kinds of old folk remedies disappeared with the horse and buggy. Where did you hear something like that?' She couldn't remember but insisted it was true."

"Probably heard it from one of the nurses," Bill suggested.

"Maybe, although those ladies are scientific-bent. They use antibiotics, not vegetable oil. But so what? Just as I humored her about the garlic, everyone ought to just keep letting her think this woman, Sarena, is her long lost mother."

"It's Sarafina, but I'm not sure if encouraging that fantasy is a good idea."

Ignoring him, Mattie continued her thought. "The child spent five years designing a mother in her imagination. Now, along comes this image who fits the bill. I say, just leave her alone with her fantasy."

Glancing over at his housekeeper, Bill realized that, as usual, Mattie might be on the right track. Since he couldn't think of a better way of disabusing Abby of her feeling about Sarafina, he cautiously said, "Mattie, you may be right."

"I believe I am," she answered and without pausing added, "and I'll tell you something else. That Serena is a strange woman, a real spook if you ask me." Bill caught the mayonnaise jar before it slipped out of his hand. "Whoever heard of someone saying she's located her child, then just dreamily turning around and announcing she'll be leaving? Be careful with that glass jar," she ordered. "Half the time Abby runs around here with no shoes on."

Now, glancing at Abby sprawled on the den floor with her huggy pillow while waiting for the final answer on Kids' Jeopardy, Bill's thoughts flashed to the thousands of homeless children he'd met in his world travels. Some were now safe in the orphanages that his foundation and other organizations helped establish, and that was comforting. Still, he wished there was a way for every child to grow up with a family.

In the short time they'd had Abby, she had grown an inch and had acquired, thanks to Mattie's daughter, a new hairdo with dozens of tiny French braids hanging down her back. She'd also been prescribed a pair of tortoise-rimmed specs. The glasses, for nearsightedness, had stopped Abby from squinting at people.

Setting aside the New York Times crossword, he asked, "How'd you do? Get any questions right?" Abby's left flip-flop bounced up and down as her foot followed the catchy beat of a jingly fast-food commercial.

"Jeopardy was kinda hard today."

"So was my crossword puzzle."

"But," she brightened, "I knew three questions in the 'City Centers' category, like that Beijing is the capital of China."

"Excellent. Where'd you learn that?"

"From World Capitals, the book Ray gave me."

"Next time he's here, be sure to tell him how it helped you. Ray put a lot of thought into your welcome-home presents."

After the commercial, they listened as an Alex Trebek wannabe revealed the final answer to be A.A. Milne as the author of Winnie the Pooh. "Darlin'," Bill said, "that's enough TV for a while. You've been watching all morning."

Taking a last glance at the tube, Abby reached up to turn it off, then scooped Bootsy up into her arms and exchanged kisses with the furry creature.

From the kitchen, Mattie's old transistor blared 1010 Radio News. Over static and chatter, Bill heard silverware rattling and knew he'd better get on with the topic he most dreaded, because Mattie would shortly be calling them for lunch.

Unable to think of sugarcoated words for what needed discussing, he finally said, "Abby, did Sarafina tell you that she leaves tomorrow?"

"Yes."

That's something, he thought, waiting for more. Seeing that Abby wasn't going to make this easy, he plowed ahead. "You know she's going away and not coming back, ever?"

Still focused on the cat, she answered, "Mama said it's good for me to be with you and Mama Hillary."

"What do you think about that? You know Hillary must take care of the country and that sometimes I get called away too, to help her."

"That's okay." She got up and walked to the sofa, climbed up on the end, and folded her long legs under her. Hugging a different pillow, she said, "When you're not around, Ray and Ms. Mattie can take care of me."

"That's right. They both care an awful lot about you."

"Ray loved Mama, didn't he?"

Bill moistened his lips. "Yep, he kinda did."

"Mr. Alex loved her too," she added.

Damn, Mattie's right, he thought. This kid has an uncanny sense about everything.

"Yes and no, on Alex. They knew each other in the past, but now they're only friends." Wanting to hurry through this, he said, "Just to make sure the air is clear between us, may I ask something else?"

"Sure. Go ahead, shoot."

Sure? Shoot? Bill almost laughed. Aloud, he said, "Did

Sarafina tell you why she can't stay and take care of you?"

Abby calmly met Bill's eyes. "Yes. She explained that my destiny is with you and Mama Hillary."

So far, so good, he thought. "Right, but do you understand what that means?"

"Yeah, sorta, at least the part about destiny being like something that happens in the future."

Anxiously nibbling his chapped bottom lip, he asked, "Did she talk about things you don't understand?"

"Yeah."

Fearful of the answer but just as afraid of not knowing, Bill asked, "Abby, what didn't you understand?"

"When she said my destiny is as bright as the heavens but hers is a diminishing star, or something like that."

Breathing easier, Bill searched for the right tone before speaking again. "I think that's another way of Sarafina telling you that she's happy you're staying with us. But now I have one last question. After meeting her, are you going to be satisfied with us?"

"Uh, huh. I like it here," she said shyly. "And Nurse Lillian told me a long time ago that mothers sometime make painful decisions, but they do what's best for their kids."

Bill relaxed, eased back in his chair, and marveled at Abby's capacity for both understanding and forgiveness. Mattie was right about her sometimes seeming older than age seven. "Honey, I'm proud of you for feeling that way. In a similar situation, some grownups I know wouldn't be so generous."

He debated saying more but remembered the social worker telling him to keep it simple and not prolong conversations about her past unless she asked for specifics. Instead, he said,

"Yep, Sarafina made a very good choice by wanting you to stay with us.

"Tell you what, though." He stood up and motioned toward the kitchen. "I think for now, we've pretty much got this thing called life under control. Let's say we go eat some of Mattie's chicken salad. After lunch, while I talk with Alex, I understand Mattie's taking you grocery shopping at Fairway."

"Is that the big grocery store?"

"Uh, huh, why?"

"Can I buy something too?"

"Well, sure, but you can just ask Mattie to add it to her list, pending her approval, of course."

"But I want to buy gifts for you and Ms. Mattie and Mama Hillary."

Bill paused to think if he should say 'Thank you,' or 'That isn't necessary,' or if he should just give Abby some money. Now that he was responsible for a young child's well-being, he'd stopped being careless about keeping cash in his wallet. Deciding to use some in this instance, he reached into his back pocket.

"Since we haven't discussed an allowance, I'll set you up with a little starting kitty of cash. Here's five dollars. Do you think that's enough?"

Nodding solemnly, Abby took the money and looked at it for a long time. "It's more than I've ever had."

Bill swallowed the lump in his throat. "Abby, come on. Let's eat."

❖

Alex arrived punctually at twelve thirty. Bill led him to the deck and poured two glasses of iced tea from a round Mickey Mouse pitcher. In the back of Bill's garden, the red bougainvillea, heavy with blooms, wound through a series of trellises and clung to the brick wall. Four months ago, on a chilly April evening, Bill was picturing that much-anticipated blaze of summer when Alex suddenly walked through the bricks and forever changed his life. Today, Alex knew how to properly announce himself: ring the bell, submit to an inspection, and get checked off the visitor's list.

"Well, my friend," Bill said, "I suppose you could say we've come full circle."

"Except for tomorrow's jubilee," Alex reminded him. With his brow furrowed, he asked, "Are you certain that when the ceremony commences, I'll be remembered in a favorable light?"

"Most definitely. Now that Harlem knows more about your contributions, you're a hero in this community."

"Sir, do you recall our first meeting?"

"Vividly. Why?"

"When I pronounced you to be among the best modern presidents, you retorted, 'To whom are you comparing me?'"

Bill smiled. "Well, yes. That was one of about a thousand questions I had. What of it?"

"Forgive my ignorance, but who are the other heroes of Harlem? To whom are you comparing me?"

"Oh, wow. You may be putting me on the spot, here, but let me think. Harlem has had many. A few twentieth-century civil rights figures would be Adam Clayton Powell, Jr., Thurgood Marshall, Malcolm X." An image of Malcolm X in his early years as a Black Muslim, when his platform consisted of flame-throwing separatist rhetoric, flashed though Bill's mind. "Of course," he added, "some of their styles differed considerably from yours. I believe you would have gotten along well with Supreme Court Justice Marshall. He was a distinguished jurist and, like you, has a long history of helping minorities and less-privileged Americans."

"Thank you for the comparison. It gladdens me to learn heroes still sit on the Supreme Court."

Bill nodded but didn't mention his concerns about the court's direction. "I should mention that some advances came from creative individuals. They heightened public awareness of injustice through art, poetry, music, film, and literature. One of my favorite poets is Langston Hughes. Ever hear of him?"

"I'm afraid not."

"Then hang on; I mean, just wait here a minute or two. I want to look for something." Bill stood and picked up both their iced tea glasses. Alex's was watery, the glass warm to the touch. "While I'm inside, do you want anything? Perhaps a fresh glass of tea with more ice, maybe a piece of fruit?"

"You're most kind, sir, but I must decline. Forgive me if I appear unsociable, but as my body prepares the spirit for its return, I can no longer imbibe earth's impressive array of potables or solids.

To the naked eye, Alex still appeared to be an ordinary man, albeit a small and unmistakably eccentric one. Searching for consoling words, Bill realized there were none, so he nodded, went inside, and put Alex's glass on the counter. From the fruit bowl, he plucked a peach, sniffed, then gently squeezed. Too hard, he decided and put it back in favor of an apple and a partially green banana. He pressed his glass against the ice dispenser, filled it halfway, and added more tea.

Bill knew he could stand to put on a few pounds, and he still felt hungry despite his lunch. He'd thought about hiring a cook, but the ill will likely generated with two cooks in "Mattie's kitchen" was not worth it. Anyway, his schedule was too erratic. It was a small comfort to know that if or when he was back in the White House full-time, and it was looking more like when than if, Chef Nancy Klingenberg would prepare anything he desired.

Back in his study, Bill munched on his apple and woke up the computer. He quickly located an online copy of "A Dream Deferred," pushed Print, and grabbed the sheet off the printer.

Out on the deck, Alex was bending over the railing, staring at the small bed of vinca, lantana, and plume celosia. In instances like this, Bill sometimes wanted to snap a picture for posterity. But who knew what might appear on the lens if he photographed a ghost? Mainly, he didn't want to leave any physical evidence of Alex.

"Those are some of my annuals. Do any of today's flowers look familiar?"

"Perhaps something like this. They're quite lovely." Alex pointed to the pale pink lantana. "It would be good for my home's provenance if my gardens were to be recreated."

"In time I'm sure they will, Alex. While we're discussing beauty, I'd like you to read this poem." Bill handed over the sheet of paper. "In his brevity, Langston Hughes speaks volumes about inequality; the injustices that men like you and him addressed. It will give you some context for tomorrow's speech.

"Alex, I'll miss you. Not the headaches you've given me, but

I'll miss our extraordinary discussions, including your, shall I call them, suggestions. I've faced some unpleasant aspects about myself. Initially, I was resentful of your highhandedness, how you lectured me on my shortcomings. My priorities are shifting. There are no guarantees, but in the future, I hope not to make it all about me."

His emotion showing, Bill seemed to find something interesting on the cuff of Alex's tan slacks, which he noticed for the first time were showing signs of wear. Along with being frayed and too heavy for the hot weather that had settled over the city, the pants could have used a trip to the cleaners. Bill never detected body odor on Alex, and he wondered for the first time if he bathed, or even needed to. Such a pity that so many questions, most more pertinent than hygiene habits, would remain unanswered about Alex.

When Bill raised his head, his tone was lighter. "I'll go one step further and bet my bottom dollar," he winked at his companion, "that not a day will go by, when you won't still be with me—in spirit, that is," he said with unnecessary irony.

"Kind sir, I humbly accept your words as the ultimate compliment."

Bill leaned back and folded his arms. "With me spending less time in Washington, I hadn't realized how separate Hillary and I had become, but Abby has brought us closer. Our family living arrangement will likely change at the first of the year; until then Abby will be homeschooled. Meanwhile, barring a national emergency, Hillary and I are planning a getaway next weekend at Camp David."

"At a military installation?"

"No. It's a wooded retreat in Maryland for use by the sitting president. History books are filled with stories about Camp David. During World War II, President Roosevelt and Churchill planned the Normandy invasion down there."

"Is Camp David only used to resolve conflict, or is it also a lover's retreat?"

Throwing his head back, Bill enjoyed a good laugh. "I suppose that depends on Hillary. Often, she works late into the night, but we're hopeful of the latter. Which reminds me, how did things work out with you and your friend Liz?"

"Alas, sir, not well. I'm afraid my lack of punctuality caused the lady to doubt the sincerity of my motives."

One thing Bill appreciated about the founder was his baronial manner of expression. "You're such an optimist. I'm surprised you gave up on her so fast, but it's probably for the best, since she didn't know about your, um, permanent address or that you'd soon be returning to it."

"No, and naturally my earth status was a difficult subject to broach, although at one point, I thought I saw an opening. I regret our liaison was short-lived, but might I add, it was quite an educational one."

Yeah, I'll bet, Bill thought. After encouraging Alex to get out and make friends and meet some women, the last thing he wanted to do was joke about his experiences.

"Overall," Alex continued, "there is much to be pleased about this visit, especially concerning your future, which frankly has preoccupied my thoughts more than tomorrow's festivities. Thus, I hope tomorrow won't be anticlimactic. Your momentous decision to parent the child cannot be superseded by speeches and remembrances."

"Thank you, but don't minimize the importance of your

day. Your name is becoming a household word around here. Granted, some people are asking, 'Who's this old white dude, Alexander Hamilton, that everyone's talking about?' That's okay. That's how kids learn. Adults too. And I'll tell you something else. Because of all that's happened, I'm contemplating writing a novel about a ghost, a little girl, and a man. Ex-presidents are prolific writers. What do you think of my book idea?"

"I'd say there's a ring of truth to it."

"Indeed. One of our late great writers, Mark Twain, penned the words, 'Truth is stranger than fiction.' You haven't by chance met Twain, um, in heaven, have you?"

"Unfortunately, I've not had the pleasure. You must understand that there are as many, if not more, souls in heaven than here on earth, thus it's not possible for us to all be acquainted."

"Of course. However, I confess to not having thought of heaven and earth in terms of ratios. As for my book, I'm still jotting down ideas, but I'm getting psyched. That means I'm excited about it."

"Why do you want to write this?"

"First, I'm interested in trying my hand at fiction. A novelist might be one of the few honorable endeavors where one can simply make things up. Second, readers enjoy ghost stories. Now that I know a good bit of about ghosts, I should be able to write a helluva story."

"In my day, the American novel, though in its infancy, showed promise in exploring the human condition. I'm pleased to be an impetus for your artistry."

"I've yet to run this idea by my editor, but he's bound to find it more appealing than my current project."

"My dear fellow," Alex interjected abruptly, "Have I mentioned that Abby is a delightful child? I also noticed how her physical features—the pointy chin, small ears, widespread eyes—remind me of those of my darling first born girl, Angelica, who was blessed with musical ability. At an early age, she excelled on the piano.

"Alex, what did you just say?"

"About little Angelica being musical?"

"No, just before that. What did you say before that? Something about a physical description."

"I was describing Angelica who, unlike Eliza, her younger sister, favored me more than her dear mother."

Bill pinched the bridge of his nose, then massaged his temples to alleviate a sudden throbbing behind his eyes. With all this drama around Sarafina's long-dead daughter, he now wondered if Alex knew who the child's father was. Had it been one of the men in the house where Alex met her? Perhaps the master of that household? Or could it have been Alex? Bill tried to recall what Alex had told him about when and what type of relationship he first had with Sarafina.

"Sir," Alex spoke close to Bill's ear. "Are you quite all right? I've repeatedly called your name and you didn't appear to hear me."

"Oh, sorry. I guess I'm a bit off after all that's happened lately. But my musical instrument is the saxophone," he said nonsensically." Then, to assuage Alex's troubled expression, he quickly added, "You were speaking of musical instruments of your day, weren't you? The piano is still quite popular, but the saxophone wasn't invented until the nineteenth century."

Alex's long ago love affairs were none of Bill's business, so he changed the subject. "Look," he said, as the sound of St. Luke's Church bells softly chimed three o'clock, "I'd like to ask you a few things about Sarafina before my grocery shoppers return. For instance, did she ever hint that she'd come down here to stir up trouble about things that happened long ago?"

"Certainly not. Yet, of late, I believe her melancholy edged into delusional thoughts. When I revealed your good news about Abby joining your family, I'm afraid it unleashed Sarafina's demons about her own child's disappearance. Though she professed to share your joy, I might add, she again claimed to feel the presence of someone walking over her grave."

Bill made a distasteful face. "Back in Arkansas, I heard that old superstition repeated dozens of times, with almost as many explanations for what it means. I hope you don't take this the wrong way, but honestly, Sarafina creeps me out, way more than how I first freaked when I saw you.

"Still, in all fairness, after she initially linked on to this fixation of being Abby's mother, she handled things about as well as can be expected. She even acts like she's trying to pacify Abby by playing along."

Alex frowned. "Despite her first preposterous assertion about the grave, there was something else."

Warily, Bill asked, "What?"

"That evening, when Sarafina spoke of the grave, she had a premonition that her dead child was trying to communicate with her."

"Obviously, the trauma surrounding her daughter's loss deeply impaired Sarafina's reasoning. Since you told me about that overseer savagely beating the woman in St. Croix, I keep thinking about cruelties inflicted on slaves." Bill shuddered.

"The callousness of separating a mother and child had to be one of the worst."

"Indeed. The internal scarring of Negroes was as harsh as the physical punishment." "But it is odd, wouldn't you agree, that Sarafina never found solace once she got to heaven? One would think so, yet that night when she was at her low point, she apprised me of an ancient African belief that was still commonly adhered to by Negroes during our lifetime."

"Alex, many old slave beliefs and superstitions survive today. But what in particular did Sarafina say?"

"She said when a mother doesn't properly see her dead child into the ground, its spirit remains restless."

"Hmmm, that's funny."

"Sir, whatever you may think of Sarafina, she was most sincere when she spoke of this matter."

"Yes, of course. I don't mean to minimize her pain and loss. It's just kind of coincidental that the nurses described Abby in much the same way. They called her a restless spirit."

CHAPTER 28

THE FOUNDER HAS HIS DAY

Stepping lively so as not to miss the start of Alex's celebration, Bill, with Ray accompanying him, followed the precinct captain, two agents, and several cops who hustled them along the winding sidewalk of St. Nicholas Terrace.

"Except for all these fans trying to get a piece of you, I'm loving this festive atmosphere," Ray said as his boss managed, without missing a beat, to shake several hands.

"Ditto. It's a helluva party and just getting started." Bill, at his best in a crowd, waved to a little boy behind the barricade whose hand he couldn't quite reach.

Ray noted the slogan, "Alexander Hamilton Rocks" that emblazoned the backs of several youngsters' T-shirts. "Whoever designed those shirts sure came up with the right catchphrase to get the little kids involved."

"Yep, it's never too early."

When they reached the bottom step, a NY1 reporter, his cameraman in tow, called out asking for a statement from Bill.

"Sorry, fellas, some other time. Today's focus isn't on me." After passing the reporter, Bill turned to his bodyguard. "By the way, did you learn anything new about Brad Davis, that guy who lives around here and can be a pain in the ass?"

"I'm not sure yet. My brother didn't know anything, but I talked with Davis myself and asked if he was covering you, or planning to."

"Is he"?

"Said no, if you can believe anything he says. But, without much prompting, he volunteered a tidbit on your pal, Alex. Claims he saw him with Elizabeth Wellington, his former boss's daughter. Davis used to work for Gordon Wellington, the big gun at one of the cable stations. I checked into Elizabeth's life, which, by the way, is a story and a half. But, there's no evidence Alex ever hooked up with her. You know anything about it?"

Not sure if he should answer yes or no, Bill finally said, "He mentioned meeting a woman. Probably someone else."

"For such an unassuming guy, he sure gets around."

Bill ignored the comment. "Did Davis reveal anything else?"

"Just that she's a ballsy chick; defied her family, pulled out of her wedding at the last minute, and left a train wreck behind her. Maybe Alex should watch his step."

Trying to hide a grin, Bill said, "I'll pass that on."

"By the way, Chief, in the last two days, we've talked about everyone except Sarafina. It's okay to mention the name. I'm over her. It never should have happened, and I'm honored you didn't fire my ass. Business and pleasure don't mix. I was walking a thin line, taking advantage of my special relationship with you. I hope you'll accept my apology, sir."

"If memory serves, I accepted about six apologies ago."

Ray gave a weak laugh. "So you are keeping track."

"Hardly, but we might both relax, since Sarafina is leaving today."

"So I heard," Ray responded just as they reached the roped-off security area. "Chief, stand here by our man, Tony Squire, who's up from DC for the day. I need a minute with Captain Rodriguez to make sure his guys are in place during the speech. Four more of our guys are dispersed around here too." Bill stood where he was told, next to a redheaded Secret Service agent with shoulders the size of King Kong's, wearing the prerequisite wire in his ear, aviator sunglasses, and a size 46, extra-long suit.

Before Ray ducked inside the security booth, Bill tapped his arm. "Look, I wish you wouldn't bother with all this. You know how I feel about spectacles when I'm not with Hillary."

"Sorry, sir, but we didn't have any choice today. This occasion is a joint venture with NYC Park's Department and the National Park Service, which is a federal jurisdiction. You know how it goes."

Bill started to say, "No, I don't know how it goes." Instead, he exhaled in exasperation and leaned against the booth. A glance around the park made him feel less picked-on, since the area was heavy with security officers who were searching backpacks at each entrance. Bill couldn't help smiling at the sight of a baby-faced cop standing next to the big, redheaded federal agent and sizing him up.

He scanned the crowd again, trying to see if Alex was by the children's tent where Bill told him to wait. Unable to see through a thicket of red, white, and blue balloons tied all over the area, Bill reached for a discarded folding chair that was leaning against the booth. Seeing the older man grab the chair, the young cop hurried to ask, "Sir, can I help you with something?"

"Here, hold his dang thing steady, so I don't break my fool neck." Doing as ordered, the astonished young man watched Bill unfold the rickety wooden chair, climb up and pan the crowd. Bill glared and waved off the federal agent who looked like he was about to pull him down. He spotted Alex, wearing the same tan linen suit. He'd also donned the straw fedora Bill found and insisted he wear to help avoid a potentially awkward comment from an alert passerby who might notice that Alex was a dead ringer for Hamilton.

Having satisfied his questions about park security, Ray rejoined Bill in time to see him gingerly stepping down off his perch. "I know," Ray sighed, addressing the patrolman whose face was beet red, "the chief does these things all the time."

Still observing the crowded meadow, Bill spoke. "I asked Alex to meet me by the children's tent. When we get over there, I want a few minutes with him before we take our seats."

As they neared the tent, Bill hoped he'd always remember the little man's expectant look as he anonymously surveyed people of all colors and hues who'd gathered to pay him homage. Alex didn't notice Bill's approach until he said, "My friend, it's a good turnout, wouldn't you agree?"

Both the question and Bill's arrival produced a look of pride on the guest-of-honor's face. "Truly, sir, not since we defeated the English, when all eighteen thousand New York City citizens, including a few thousand Negroes, turned out for the victory parade, have I seen such a festive crowd."

"I doubt we'll generate that many folks this afternoon, but

it's still a banner day. The precinct captain estimates this crowd at about six or seven thousand. Not bad for a long-dead guy," Bill joked, "who was all but forgotten on these streets, until a few thoughtful folks brought you out of obscurity." Once he had adjusted to the new "normal" and had gotten over the creepiness factor, Bill no longer flinched when inadvertently making dead jokes or referring to Alex's paranormal status.

Still, he redirected the conversation. "As always, you're looking slick in your Tom Wolff-style suit."

Alex, who was following the fluid movements of a statuesque young woman, didn't hear Bill or ask about whom he was referring. The girl glided by, wearing a pair of platform shoes that added four or five inches to the six feet she already carried. If her sculpted cheekbones and African princess looks weren't enough of a crowd pleaser, her short-shorts and tube top completed the picture.

Alex turned to Bill, who likewise pulled his eyes away as the girl passed with several dignitaries trailing in her wake. One of them was Sessions Murrow, today's speaker.

"The program is about to start, but I'm wondering if you've seen Sarafina?"

"Only briefly," Alex replied. "She graciously conferred good wishes for my honor today, and I reminded her that our departures, which draw near, might occur at different times."

Despite the buzz of children's voices, adult chatter, someone's yapping dog, and the incessant drone of city sounds, Bill checked to make sure Ray remained out of earshot. "Why would you two leave separately? After the turmoil she caused, I thought she had cozied back up to you."

"Turmoil, indeed, but her unfortunate decision to uphold

Abby's wish to identify with a mother figure has no bearing on the fact that our earthly journey might expire at different moments."

"Expire? What do you mean? Don't you control when you take off?"

"Alas, sir, I do not. You might remember that this sojourn was arranged pending today's celebration."

Wondering if Alex was being melodramatic, Bill scanned his face. The human-looking sadness staring out from those tiny black pupils made his heart flutter. "See that large rock over there?" Bill indicated a flat glacial outcrop jutting from the grass. "How about you sit there during the program? It'll give you a bird's eye view of the speaker, okay? I'll be right behind them, in the first row. I wish like heck that you could sit in a place of honor, but you know that's not possible. Now I better get to my seat. Afterwards, meet me there by the rock. We can go back to my house, have a final drink on the deck, okay?"

Smiling ruefully, Alex said, "I'd like nothing better, sir, but perhaps we'd best consider yesterday's visit our last formal goodbye. As the day wears on, I confess to feeling a reduction of corporality."

Bill saw Ray raise his hand, signaling that he was about to approach. When he did, he leaned over to whisper, "Chief, they're waiting for you to be seated."

Impulsively grabbing Alex, Bill held him in a bear hug. When he let go, he winked. "This is your show. Enjoy it. Just meet me at the rock when this is over." Watching that Alex settled into a spot where he would find him, Bill then hurried toward the mellifluous baritone of Manhattan Borough President Sessions Murrow.

"Ladies and gentleman," Murrow boomed, "today we gather in front of this magnificently restored and relocated mansion." He paused so the audience could feast their eyes, not on him, but on the backdrop of a dramatically altered Hamilton Grange, the centerpiece of the day's festivities. With its elegant front and side balconies reattached for the first time in a hundred years, the house appeared doubled in size from a few years ago. "We are here to honor its owner, Alexander Hamilton," Morrow said, "a founding father, great American, war hero, and friend to African American people."

The dapper Murrow wore an Armani pinstripe suit, but his shiny black face was awash in perspiration. Bill was sweating too, but he looked up gratefully at a partly cloudy sky that was doing its best to help them though this humid August afternoon.

Bill listened to the borough president recite Hamilton's many accomplishments. Among the crowd, under the dappled shade of giant maple trees where he'd have preferred to be, Bill recognized several neighbors, including BJ from the coffee shop. Abby, under the watchful eye of Mattie and an agent, was playing in the children's outdoor area. Adults doing babysitting duty listened on loudspeakers.

"In this man," Murrow continued, pointing to Giuseppe Ceracchi's marble bust of Hamilton, on loan for this celebration, "America had one of its first pragmatic businessmen. He laid the groundwork for a nation that would become an economic powerhouse. And folks," he pounded the podium for effect, "as a politician and businessman myself, I'm here to say we could use his common sense in government today.

"Now, some people around this great land—I call them Johnny-come-latelies—might be wondering why all this hoopla is taking place in Harlem. Well, let me tell you why. It's simple: the black folks of Harlem, more than any other group, thought it well past time for someone to thank this guy, not only for what he did to help America, but for what he did for African Americans."

"Until recently," he continued, "not enough Americans knew or cared about Hamilton." The speaker let listeners soak that in before saying, "Schools right here in Harlem omitted him from the curriculum. Today he might garner a few lines, but for years, publishers left him out of history books; at least he wasn't in mine. How about you, ma'am?" he asked a well-dressed older woman in the front row. She appeared to be in her eighties and was likely one of the neighborhood elders who'd fought for years to have this mansion restored. "Was Alexander Hamilton mentioned when you went through school?" The woman's head moved side to side.

"No," Murrow shouted, "they were too busy crowing over a handful of other founders. But we must give credit where it's due. Those early Americans were smart men of vision, but some of those visionaries only paid lip service to the principles of freedom they wrote into the Constitution.

"Please," he raised his hand at the sound of clapping, "hold your applause. "But Hamilton," Sessions continued, "he honored the principles of freedom by using his resounding oratorical skills, by lobbying, brokering deals, and being the lead author of the Federalist Papers. And," Murrow paused for effect, "though he did not get his wish, Hamilton worked to halt the institution of slavery. He tried his damnedest to stop the evil from festering and metastasizing into a cancer that lasted another one hundred fifty years, a cancer whose remnants still gnaw at the fabric of American society today."

Applause and irrepressible shouts of "Amen!" and "Yes, that's right!" erupted from the racially diverse audience that had risen to its feet.

"Hamilton fought the good fight," Sessions crooned. "Furthermore, what many of you don't know," he shouted, "is that Alexander Hamilton not only endeared himself to persecuted blacks, but also to American Indians, our brothers in oppression, as well as to destitute women and needy children of all colors."

He's right about that, Bill concurred, and for the moment he tuned Murrow out to reflect on how God worked His mysteries, never more so than in these last months. The celebration today brought gratification to the community who'd grown to appreciate "the forgotten founding father," as many locals had taken to calling Hamilton. For Bill, the day also crowned a summer that had turned his life around, and at the moment, he felt God's presence more than usual.

When State Senator Fred Jenkins, who was sitting next to him, stood up and started clapping loudly, Bill awoke from his reverie. Struggling out of his seat, he joined the rousing round of applause and celebratory handshakes.

"This was a wonderful day, Mr. President," said a distinguished, stocky gentleman with a handlebar mustache, who came over to shake Bill's hand. "Just as it was mighty fine of you to take in that needy child without caring that she was of the dark race."

"Thank you, sir," Bill responded. "Thank you for those kind words."

"It's in keeping with the message we heard today about this

founder, Hamilton, who knew we were all God's children."

"Indeed he did. I'm honored by the comparison."

"Folks in Harlem have a long memory, and we know you always did right by our people, and your wife is continuing the tradition. I wish you and the president much happiness with the latest addition to your family."

"Much obliged, sir. We'll do our best."

Quickly grasping a few more outstretched hands, Bill glanced anxiously at the departing crowd. "Excuse me," he finally muttered after another person held him up. "I need to catch a buddy of mine before he leaves town."

Finally in the clear, Bill glanced over at the rock. It was now late afternoon, and the sun glittered crazily off shiny purple veins running through the black schist rock where Alex waited. Momentarily blinded, Bill shifted slightly and shaded his eyes to block the sun. When he looked again, Alex was gone.

ACKNOWLEDGEMENTS

Thanks to my TBC friends Phyllis Bernstein, Judy Deutsch, Kathi Crane, Mary LaBarge, Peggy Crowe, CeCe Leucking, and also to Ellen Usher and Erin Williams for your generosity of time and insightful comments. Thank you Jim Cummins, my longtime friend, Harlem homie and award-winning photojournalist of legendary rock, R&B and jazz greats; you rock!

My thanks to Dr. Patrick Majors for that day you engaged me in a conversation about personality types; and to Ron Cherow for giving life to Alexander Hamilton and sparking my interest in "the forgotten founder;" thanks also to another fine American writer, Rick Skwiot, who first introduced me to the idea of writing fiction and continues to be there when I need advice. To my two young friends, Sarah Leander and Zoe Maffitt, I thank you for trying valiantly to keep me on task with my least favorite chore. For the guys in my life: Mike, Brennan and Colin and to Masha, I love you. Mike, thank you for being a history geek and coming up with a crazy idea.

ABOUT THE AUTHOR

Terry Baker Mulligan is the author of *Sugar Hill: Where The Sun Rose Over Harlem*, which won the first place 2012 Independent Publishers (IPPY) Gold Medal for Adult Multicultural Nonfiction. In 2013, *Sugar Hill* won First Place Benjamin Franklin Awards for Autobiography/Memoir and Multicultural Writing. She grew up in Harlem across from the Grange, Alexander Hamilton's home, and now lives in St, Louis, MO.